DHANANTER

THE SANATANI CRUSADER

AMRESH VASHISHT

Made with ♥ on the Notion Press Platform
www.notionpress.com

I dedicate this work to the timeless sages, the silent waters of the Saraswati, and the seekers of truth who continue to walk the sacred path of Dharma.

— Amresh Vashisht

Contents

Preface   *vii*

Acknowledgements   *ix*

Prologue   *xi*

Author's Note   *xiii*

1. Chapter 1   1
2. Chapter 2   7
3. Chapter 3   13
4. Chapter 4   20
5. Chapter 5   28
6. Chapter 6   34
7. Chapter 7   41
8. Chapter 8   45
9. Chapter 9   52
10. Chapter 10   55
11. Chapter 11   63
12. Chapter 12   70
13. Chapter 13   74
14. Chapter 14   79
15. Chapter 15   85
16. Chapter 16   92
17. Chapter 17   102
18. Chapter 18   107
19. Chapter 19   111
20. Chapter 20   115
21. Chapter 21   118
22. Chapter 22   125

Contents

23. Chapter 23 132

24. Chapter 24 136

25. Chapter 25 142

26. Chapter 26 149

27. Chapter 27 157

28. Chapter 28 162

29. Chapter 29 171

30. Chapter 30 177

31. Chapter 31 185

32. Chapter 32 191

33. Chapter 33 196

34. Chapter 34 203

35. CHARACTERS 210

Preface

Writing Dhananter - The Sanatani Crusader has been a journey through time, history, and spirituality. As I delved into the ancient wisdom of Sanatana Dharma, the legends of the Saraswati River, and the timeless hymns of the Vedas, I was captivated by the profound connection between the ancient past and our modern world. This book is my humble attempt to bring that connection to life, merging history, mythology, and fiction into a narrative that I hope will inspire and enlighten readers.

This story is not just a tale of adventure but a tribute to the eternal flame of Dharma that has guided humanity through the ages. It is a celebration of our ancient heritage, our timeless wisdom, and the enduring quest for truth. Through Dhanater's (Sanatani) journey, I hope readers will rediscover the forgotten glory of the Saraswati River and the spiritual essence of our civilization.

— Amresh Vashisht

Acknowledgements

My deepest gratitude goes to my family, whose unwavering support made this book possible.

I extend my heartfelt appreciation to the scholars, historians, and spiritual guides who have enriched my understanding of Vedic wisdom and ancient history. This book is also a tribute to the seekers who preserve our timeless heritage.

Finally, I thank my readers—may this book inspire you to seek the eternal flame of Dharma.

Prologue

In the age when the rivers sang and the mountains whispered to the stars, the sages gathered by the sacred banks of the Saraswati. Amidst the hymns of the Vedas and the glow of the yajna fire, they chose a soul—Dhananter, a seeker of truth. Clad in the sacred aura of wisdom, he was blessed with a mission that would transcend time.

"Sanatani you shall be—timeless and tireless," declared the Saptarishis. "You will guard the wisdom of Sanatana Dharma, preserve the sacred hymns, and restore the Saraswati when the world forgets its essence."

And so began the journey of Dhananter, the Sanatani crusader.

Author's Note

Dhananter - The Sanatani Crusader is a work of historical fiction, blending mythology, ancient history, and spiritual philosophy into a grand narrative. While the story is inspired by the Saraswati River's ancient glory and the Vedic sages' wisdom, it is ultimately a fictional tale meant to inspire and enlighten.

I have taken creative liberties with historical events and mythological legends to create a narrative that is both captivating and spiritually enriching. I invite readers to explore this story with an open mind, appreciating the timeless wisdom of our ancient civilization.

— Amresh Vashisht

CHAPTER ONE

<u>THE UNYIELDING PUZZLE</u>

The cold, dimly lit room in the heart of the agency's headquarters was a stark contrast to the bustling metropolis outside. The air was thick with tension and the faint smell of antiseptic, mixed with the metallic scent of blood, hung in the air. The walls were lined with an array of sinister tools and instruments; each one meticulously cleaned and neatly arranged—a testament to the brutal interrogations that had taken place here.

In the center of the room, under the harsh glare of a single overhead lamp, sat the chief of the secret agency, General Abdul Sattar. His stern face was partially obscured by shadows, but the intensity in his eyes pierced through the darkness. The sparse room, with its concrete walls and minimal furnishings, reflected the gravity of the situation. A large map of the region was pinned to the wall behind him, marked with strategic locations and red circles highlighting areas of interest.

General Sattar, known for his unwavering dedication and strategic brilliance, leaned forward, his fingers steeple under his chin. The silence in the room was palpable, broken only by the faint hum of the lamp above. On the table before him lay a dossier, its cover stamped with the words "Top Secret" in bold red letters. Inside were documents detailing the latest intelligence reports, photographs, and encrypted messages?

He took a deep breath, his mind racing with the complexities of the mission at hand. The stakes were higher than ever before, and the fate of countless lives depended on the decisions he would make in the coming hours. As he waited for his team to assemble, his thoughts turned to the shadowy threats looming on the horizon and the delicate balance of power that needed to be maintained.

The door creaked open, and his top operatives filed in, each one a specialist in their field. They took their seats around the table, their expressions mirroring the seriousness of the task ahead. General Sattar cleared his throat, ready to brief them on the critical operation that would determine the course of their mission and, ultimately, the security of their nation.

His grizzled face was etched with lines of frustration and exhaustion, his eyes dark and hollow from countless sleepless nights. The sleeves of his crisp, military uniform were rolled up, revealing muscular forearms and scarred knuckles—evidence of his hands-on approach to interrogation.

Before him, slumped in a metal chair, was the spy. Once a figure of youthful vigor and defiant spirit, he was now a broken shell of a man. His body was emaciated, ribs protruding under bruised and battered skin. His fingers were mangled, nails cruelly extracted, and his once-clear eyes were now vacant, staring blankly ahead, the light in them extinguished.

General Sattar stood up, his chair scraping loudly against the concrete floor, and turned to face his senior subordinates who had gathered at his command. They stood at attention, their faces a mix of respect and concern as they awaited his words.

"Gentlemen," Abdul Sattar began his voice gravelly and laden with resignation, "I have done everything within my power to extract information from this man." He gestured towards the spy, his hand trembling slightly. "I have used every technique, every method of persuasion, every form of physical and psychological torture at our disposal. And yet, he has yielded nothing. Not a single word of value."

The officers exchanged uneasy glances. Colonel Salim Mirza, a tall man with a stern demeanor, stepped forward. "General, perhaps there is some other way. Some other method we have not yet considered."

Abdul Sattar shook his head slowly. "No, Colonel. We have exhausted all avenues. This man is either exceptionally well-trained, or he knows nothing of significance. I am inclined to believe the former. Regardless, our efforts have been in vain."

In the dimly lit interrogation room, General Sattar stood towering over the spy, scrutinizing the frail figure before him. "Why is he losing weight?" he questioned Mirza. , His voice laced with frustration. "He has lost three kilograms in the last ten days. This should not happen."

Colonel Mirza, standing at attention beside the General, cleared his throat. "Sir, it's the vegetarian food. The spy has specific dietary requirements—no onion, no garlic. It's becoming increasingly problematic. He's demanded a separate set of utensils for the preparation of his meals."

General Sattar frowned. "And what did you do to address this?"

"We attempted to change his eating habits," Colonel Mirza continued, "by not serving his requested food for five days. Strangely, he never mentioned the food once during those days. But after the fifth day, we resumed providing his regular meals to prevent further health decline."

General Sattar sighed heavily. "Ensure his demands are met. We need him healthy enough to extract the information we need. Make whatever arrangements necessary, but keep him under strict watch."

Colonel Mirza nodded, understanding the gravity of the situation. The spy's resilience was unnerving, and accommodating his unique dietary needs had become an unexpected challenge in their efforts to break him.

He took a deep breath, the weight of his decision evident in his posture. "It is time to admit our failure and escalate this matter. The Prime Minister must be informed. This is no longer within our jurisdiction."

There was a murmur of surprise and unease among the officers. Sattar raised his hand to silence them. "This is not a decision I make lightly. But we cannot continue to expend resources and manpower on a dead end. The Prime Minister needs to be aware of the situation and decide on the next course of action."

Brigadier Abid Ali tried to ask something but withdrew at the last moment. General Sattar sensed his hesitation and turned towards him. "Abid, if you have something to say, speak up."Abid straightway asked, "Sir, what is the opinion of the National Security Advisor who visited the prisoner two months back?"

Sattar smiled and addressed the gathering. "The NSA is in shock after meeting him. The prisoner told him about a sun mark on his body and said it has been in his family for thousands of years. He claimed the mark was made during a yajna at Mohenjo-Daro by accident when ghee spread around the fire. His ancestor, one of a four-member team providing ghee to the flames, received the mark when Vashisht Rishi was singing hymns in praise of Agni. The ancestor considered it Agni's blessing and was blessed to carry the mark until the age of the Sun."

The room was silent, eyes wide with astonishment. Sattar continued, "General Jaffar, the present NSA, verified the story. He found that every member of his family, from his great-grandfather to grandson, carries the mark at the same place on their bodies. General Jaffar withdrew from the investigation, concluding that the prisoner might be one of the eight Chiranjivis of Hindu mythologies, who never die. He is least interesting in keeping the spy in captivity. Whenever we sought clarifications on such issues, he responded only with folded hands, refusing to speak."

Turning back to his subordinates, Sattar issued his final command. "Prepare the communication. I will speak with the Prime Minister myself. We will arrange for the transfer of the prisoner and all related documents. This is now a matter of state security."

Sattar's next words carried the weight of their mission: "A nation at war wants nothing less than complete information of her enemy. It is hard for the mind to conceive exactly what 'complete information' means, for it includes every fact which may contain the lightest indication of the enemy's strength, her use of that strength, and her intention. The nation which sets out to obtain complete information of her enemy must pry into every neglected corner, fish every innocent pool, and collect a mass of matter concerning the industrial, social, and military organization of the enemy which, when correlated, appraises her strength and her weakness. Nothing less than full information will satisfy the mathematical maker of war."

We have always been precociously fond of international statistics, especially of India. India is our all-time enemy, and every piece of information of India is a gold mine for us. Thus, the present tense is equally applicable—full information of India and her allies so as to attack their vulnerable points. We are the secret agents and 24-karat hidden warriors of our country. To fetch the information we do employ on Indian soil, planned and executed bribery, sedition, arson, the destruction of property, and even murder, not to mention lesser violations of Indian law; how we sought to subvert to the advantage of the Central Powers the aims of the Government of India. We never failed to obtain desired results on Indian soil. But we are helpless before one man only who is in our captivity since long and we have failed to generate any clue how to deal with him. On the other hand, he has informed us about our ancestors thousands of years ago. He looks towards us as his own brother though he is Hindu and we are Muslim. He neither recognizes Hindu nor Muslim or any other religion. He talked about Sanatan.

General Abdul Sattar stood at the head of the conference table, his grizzled face etched with lines of frustration. Colonel Salim Mirza, who had personally interrogated the spy and failed, spoke up. "Sir, can we have more months to deal with him? Breaking this failure news may result against our professional career and reputation. I admit that he is not an ordinary human being. He told me that my ancestors were part of a boat team supplying grains at Mohenjo-Daro. He mentioned me related to Khevats clan who were there to drive the boats on the waters of Indus. I confirm that my family belongs to that Khevats clan." Mirza took a halt, and then continued, "Still, I feel we should solve this mystery on our own."

Another junior officer pointed out his affirmation, calling for a pause on the idea to surrender before the political force, fearing it could lead to much repulsion. The room buzzed with agreement, a collective murmur of uneasy support for Mirza plea.

General Abdul Sattar raised his hand, silencing the room. "I understand your concerns, but this matter has already escalated beyond our control. I have already communicated all the matters with the Army Chief, and he has given a firm opinion to communicate with the Prime Minister by bye passing his office. He just gave his nod if we can ignore him in this matter. He is not averse to this idea. Moreover, it's certain that the man under our captivity is not an Indian secret agency RAW asset. The present deputy chief of RAW, who is our asset, out rightly rejected our claim of having any such person. The American agency CIA has also given up and, fearing it as an Indian RAW asset, they isolated themselves from any move or any knowledge of this captivity."

The room fell silent, the weight of Abdul Sattar's words sinking in. After a moment, he continued, "Now, everyone, we will visit the man under investigation one last time. After that, we will come to a unanimous decision to place all of this before the Prime Minister."

The officers nodded in reluctant agreement. Abdul Sattar's decision was final, and the gravity of the situation demanded swift and decisive action. The door opened, and they filed out, a procession of determined men heading towards an uncertain future.

As they walked down the dimly lit corridor towards the interrogation room, Abdul Sattar felt a heavy sense of foreboding. This decision, once made, would change the course of their efforts and perhaps the fate of their nation. But it was a necessary step, one that had to be taken, no matter the cost. The heavy door closed behind him with a resounding thud, marking the end of one chapter and the uncertain beginning of another.

CHAPTER TWO

<u>INTERROGATION OF THE IMMORTAL: THE UNRAVELLING OF SECRETS</u>

The sun hung low over the horizon, casting long shadows across the dusty courtyard of the military compound where Spy was being held. The Spy sat on a wooden stool, hands bound behind him, his eyes scanning the room as two guards stood watch by the door. The air was heavy with tension, the silence broken only by the distant call to prayer echoing through the bustling streets of Islamabad.

Adjacent to this interrogation room was a separate, dimly lit room partitioned by a thick glass wall. This observation room, equipped with state-of-the-art surveillance technology, was where General Sattar and his senior officers now sat. The glass wall provided an unobstructed view of the interrogation room, allowing them to monitor every detail without being seen.

General Sattar's gaze shifted to Col. Mirza, a seasoned operative with a reputation for extracting information from even the most tight-lipped adversaries. "Col. Mirza," Sattar commanded his voice steady but firm, "I need you to visit the spy and interrogate him in your own way. We need answers, and we need them now."

Col. Mirza nodded, a resolute expression on his face, and made his way towards the interrogation room. The tension in the observation room was thick as the team watched his every move. Through the glass wall, they could see the spy, a disheveled figure handcuffed to a metal chair, his face a mask of defiance and no fear.

As Mirza left the room, the atmosphere shifted. He approached the spy with deliberate steps, his presence commanding and authoritative. The overhead lamp cast long shadows, adding to the drama of the scene.

In the observation room, a team of experts, including behavioral analysts and body language specialists, scrutinized the spy's every twitch and flicker of expression via the CCTV feed. Their eyes darted between the monitors and the glass wall, capturing and interpreting the subtle nuances of the spy's reactions.

"Do you think they'll break him?" one guard whispered to the other, glancing nervously at Spy.

The other guard shrugged. "He's a tough one, but everyone has a breaking point."

The door creaked open, and a high-ranking officer, Colonel Mirza, entered the room. He was a tall man with a stern face, his uniform immaculately pressed. He approached Spy, his eyes cold and calculating. Mirza began his interrogation with a measured calmness, his voice low but insistent. He began his voice devoid of emotion. "By which name should I call you Spy? You have been caught red-handed. It's time for you to tell us everything."

A man under custody took a deep breath, the weight of his predicament pressing down on him. "I suppose there's no point in denying it," he said, his voice steady. "I'll tell you what you want to know."

Colonel Mirza nodded, signaling for the guards to leave the room. He pulled up a chair and sat down opposite Spy, ready to listen.

The Colonel's expression remained unchanged, but there was a flicker of interest in his eyes. "Go on."

"My mission is never about causing harm," he said, his voice softer now. "It was about a civilization and accomplishment of a mission given to me thousands of years ago by the Saptarishees. The mission will go on till it accomplishment. No one should have a doubt about it. It is immortal and shall happen one day.

Colonel Mirza studied Spy for a long moment. "Your story is compelling, but how can I trust you? You are, after all, a spy."

Spy met his gaze, unwavering. "Because I have nothing left to lose. And sometimes, the truth is all we have."

One analyst, Dr. Shama Ansari, leaned forward, her eyes narrowing as she observed the spy's micro-expressions. "Look at his eye movements," she murmured to her colleague. "He's hiding something. There's a cooked tale when he glances to the left—classic sign of deception."

Another expert, a former interrogator named Major Arbaz, added, "Watch his hands. The tension in his fingers is increasing. Mirza's getting under his skin."

General Sattar remained silent, his eyes fixed on the scene unfolding before him. Every moment was crucial, every reaction from the spy a potential lead. The room was charged with anticipation, each officer acutely aware that the information they sought could be the key to preventing a looming disaster.

As Col. Mirza's interrogation intensified, the spy began to crack, his defiance slowly giving way to the pressure. The entire team in the observation room leaned in, their collective focus razor-sharp. The battle of wills in the interrogation room was more than just a quest for information—it was a race against time, with the fate of their mission hanging in the balance.

The exhausted Colonel stood up, his chair scraping against the concrete floor. "We'll see about that," he said, turning to leave. "For now, you'll stay here. But remember, we're not done yet."

As the door closed behind him, Spy was left alone with his thoughts. He knew the road ahead would be tough, but he was determined to survive. The sun had set by the time the guards returned, casting the room in darkness. Spy looked up at the night sky through the small window, finding a strange sense of solace in the stars. He knew his journey was far from over, but he was ready to face whatever came next.

Everyone disbursed silently as Mirza didn't utter a single word after coming out from the interrogation room. He stood helpless before his seniors and tried to eat up his words for one more attempt. He realized the truth that nothing can be drawn from him.

Next day, General Abdul Sattar walked over to the spy, placing a firm hand on his shoulder. "You have endured more than any man should. If there is anything left within you that can help your cause, now is the time to speak."

The spy's head lolled to the side, his lips parting slightly, but no sound came out. Sattar sighed deeply, the finality of the moment settling over him like a shroud.

Turning towards Dr. Shama Ansari, Sattar gave her a free hand to make a last-ditch effort. Shama suggested a drug she had obtained from a CIA team during their visit. Dr. called her assistant to bring a double dose of LSD. She was confident that the team would have at least seven hours to question the spy while he remained semi-conscious. Dr. Shama, relying on her experience with the drug regularly used by CIA operatives, injected the entire liquid into the spy's veins.

For the next ten minutes, everyone was at ease, preparing themselves to question the spy. After ten minutes, a voice broke the silence, shocking everyone. The spy addressed General Sattar, "You told me if there is anything left within you that can help your cause, now is the time to speak. I want to clarify once again, that time will never come. I have shared your past and your belongings as your ancestors helped me in timeless efforts of praying to the nature Gods for the well-being of humanity."

"I don't understand what this man is saying!" shouted Dr. Shama, clearly frustrated. The spy awoke from his narcotic stupor, his sudden return to consciousness silencing the team, who believed they had ample time to deal with him. Dr. Shama, sitting closest to the spy, was alarmed and, in her attempt to distance herself, fell off her chair in surprise. The others in the room stiffened. Dr. Shama's rational mind argued that this was impossible: it hadn't been ten minutes. How did he regain consciousness? In his extensive experience, no one had ever woken up from such a state so abruptly, without any sign of physical disturbance.

General Sattar was equally stunned and disoriented. His knowledge of medicines told him that the spy should not have regained consciousness in less than seven hours after the injection, given the dose. This defied all the norms ever studied and practiced. Everyone, including Dr. Shama, was horrified and clueless about what was happening. The spy looked at them without trying to free himself from the shackles. When he spoke, his tone was calm and peaceful. "Why have I been brought here? What do you people want?"

Dr. Shama didn't respond to the spy's inquiry. She looked over to General Sattar across the room. The spy also turned towards him. "We have kept in our captivity because there are some answers we need. What do we want? Nothing but the information you possess," said General Sattar in a bossy tone.

"How much do you know about me?" the spy continued.

"Well, not much for now. Just that you are not an ordinary human being. Are you one among the eight chiranjivis like Ashwatthama, Parshuram, or the great warrior God Hanuman, or are you using other fake names?" The spy shut his eyes tightly, a wave of pain and sorrow crossing his face.

At this point, Colonel Mirza, losing his cool, said in an authoritative tone, "We can kill you easily, but our bosses have rejected it bluntly, which is why you are surviving. Moreover, your body's healing properties have proved that in all circumstances, you recover fully with the first ray of the sun of the next day."

Dr. Shama moved closer to the spy to inject him again, but General Sattar intervened and told her to leave the spy and to assemble in the meeting room.

In the meeting room, everyone appeared worried about their fate. After a brief discussion, General Sattar ordered them to prepare for the Prime Minister's meeting. The officers snapped to attention and moved quickly to carry out his orders. He instructed them to keep away from the media.

General Abdul Sattar watched them go, his mind a tumult of thoughts and regrets. As he turned to leave the interrogation room, he cast one last glance at the spy, a flicker of respect in his eyes for the man who had withstood so much. There was a murmur of agreement, a subtle nodding of heads. The spy's endurance had earned a grudging respect, even among his tormentors, while leaving the office, staff told him about the date and time fixed for the meeting.

CHAPTER THREE

<u>THE PMO PAKISTAN</u>

General Sattar stood in front of the mirror, adjusting the medals on his immaculate uniform. Each medal glinted under the soft light, a testament to his long and storied career. Today was different. Today, he had a meeting with the Prime Minister.

The clock read 8:45 AM, and the meeting was scheduled for 11:00 AM. He needed to be there by 9:30 AM, but as always, he planned to be early. By 9:15 AM, General Sattar was already seated in the waiting room of the Prime Minister's opulent bungalow, a five-hectare estate with a lush green lawn that stretched as far as the eye could see. Through the window, he observed the Prime Minister's family enjoying the morning sun, a picture of tranquility that contrasted sharply with the weight of the issue he was about to discuss.

As General Sattar settled into the comfort of the opulent waiting room, his anticipation began to build. The familiar environment of the Prime Minister's estate, typically a symbol of security and authority, now seemed to amplify his underlying anxiety about the forthcoming meeting. Every glance through the window at the serene setting outside, every rustle of the leaves in the gentle morning breeze, seemed to mock his inner turmoil.

At 9:45 AM, the door opened, General Habib, a colleague of Sattar's from numerous military campaigns and strategic meetings and presently military attaché to the Prime Minister. The sight of a familiar face in such a high-stakes situation should have been comforting, but it only served to heighten General Sattar's nerves.

"Sattar, good to see you here," General Habib said, extending his hand with a firm grip that had always characterized his no-nonsense approach to military life.

"Habib," Sattar responded, his voice steady but his heart racing. He couldn't help but notice the slight tremor in his own hand as he returned the handshake. The two generals took seats across from each other, their chairs angled towards the window, offering a view of the picturesque landscape. Colonel HQ attached to General Habib excused himself, mentioning he would check on the readiness for meet with the Prime Minister.

With his departure, an awkward silence fell over the room. General Sattar felt the weight of the upcoming discussion pressing down on him. He glanced at Habib, hoping to find a reassuring ally, but Habib seemed preoccupied, his gaze fixed on a distant point outside the window.

"So, Sattar," Habib finally broke the silence, his voice low and serious. "This isn't a routine briefing, is it?" His eyes locked onto Sattar's, searching for unspoken truths.

"No, it's not," Sattar admitted, letting out a slow breath. "We're dealing with something... unusual. Something, which could very well change our understanding of security and human capability."

General Habib raised an eyebrow, his interest piqued. "Sounds more like science fiction than our usual fare," he remarked dryly. Sattar nodded, feeling a brief moment of camaraderie in the shared skepticism. "I wish it were fiction, Habib. But what we've encountered is very real. And it has implications that reach far beyond our military protocols."

As they delved deeper into the details of the mysterious case, Sattar found himself grappling with a mix of emotions—fear, uncertainty, but also a growing resolve. He needed Habib's strategic mind and, perhaps more importantly, his unyielding support in the conversation that would soon unfold with the Prime Minister.

By the time Colonel HQ returned to escort them to the Prime Minister's office, Sattar felt a renewed sense of purpose. The nervous energy that had been churning within him was now channeled into a focused determination. He straightened his uniform once more, the medals catching the light as he moved, each one a reminder of battles faced and overcome.

As they walked through the corridors, the sound of their polished shoes echoing off the marble floors, Sattar felt the weight of history with every step. This meeting could very well be another pivotal moment in his career, a new kind of battle for which no medal could be awarded but the stakes were higher than ever.

At precisely 11:00 AM, two soldiers appeared in gallery and saluted General Sattar, who returned the gesture crisply before following them into the Prime Minister's office. The room was an architectural marvel with six walls, long curtains, and walls adorned with framed art. A golden sofa set occupied the center, with crystal items delicately placed on a polished wooden table. The Prime Minister, seated behind a large mahogany desk, rose to greet him.

"General Sattar," the Prime Minister said warmly, extending his hand. "Please, have a seat."

The formalities were brief. The Prime Minister's demeanor shifted as they moved to the crux of the matter. "General, I'm aware of the situation, but I need you to brief me personally."

General Sattar took a deep breath, recalling the strange events of the past eight months. "Eight months ago, the Sindh police apprehended a man near Mohenjo-Daro, a UNESCO World Heritage site of significant historical importance. The initial investigation was brutal, but no information could be extracted. The man, though he looked like any one of us, was not a Muslim. Despite severe torture, he never uttered a word about his origins or intentions."

He paused, collecting his thoughts. "What was peculiar, Prime Minister was his remarkable healing ability. Every injury inflicted upon him, no matter how severe, healed overnight. The police were baffled, so they contacted us. We bought him here to Islamabad, subjected him to the same measures, and met with the same results. He spoke of ancient histories and family lineages with uncanny accuracy but revealed nothing of substance."

The Prime Minister listened intently, his expression grave. "And you believe he might be one of the Chiranjivis, the immortal beings from Hindu mythology?"

"The NSA suggested as much," General Sattar replied. "His conduct, his resilience, it's beyond any known human capability. Despite depriving him of food for five days, he remained unaffected. Our top agents, even those in collaboration with the CIA, are at a loss."

The Prime Minister leaned back in his chair, contemplating. "Has he mentioned anything specific about Mohenjo-Daro?"

"Not directly. He frequently references it, along with names of prominent Rishis, often under the influence of what we suspect is LSD. Yet, none of these connections have led us to any concrete conclusions."

The Prime Minister sighed. "And what do you propose we do now?"

"We need to escalate this matter," General Sattar said. "This is beyond the scope of military or intelligence agencies. We need diplomatic intervention, perhaps a direct discussion with the Indian Prime Minister."

A long silence followed as the Prime Minister pondered the situation. Finally, he spoke. "I need to meet this man myself. Ensure the media knows nothing of this. We'll arrange an official visit to your agency under the guise of its 50th anniversary."

"Understood, Sir," General Sattar said, saluting before exiting the room.

The next day, the newspapers carried a small column: "Prime Minister to visit Secret Agency Headquarters on the occasion of its 50th anniversary." The public remained unaware of the extraordinary reason behind the visit.

General Sattar, having secured the Prime Minister's agreement to visit the secret agency headquarters, felt a mix of relief and anxiety. He knew that the next step would be crucial. He needed to prepare the mysterious spy for the meeting, ensuring that everything went smoothly.

He walked down the dimly lit corridors of the agency, his footsteps echoing off the polished floors. His mind raced as he considered the complexities of the situation. The spy had been an enigma from the beginning, and now, more than ever, it was imperative to understand him and gain his cooperation.

Entering the heavily guarded detention area, General Sattar took a moment to collect him before stepping into the spy's cell. The room was stark, furnished only with the bare essentials—a cot, a table, and a single chair. The spy sat calmly, his eyes closed as if in meditation. The sight of him, so serene despite the circumstances, sent a shiver down Sattar's spine.

"Please, have a seat, General," the spy said without opening his eyes, his voice calm and eerily soothing.

Sattar took the seat opposite the spy, his authoritative demeanor momentarily slipping as he struggled to find the right words. For a few moments, he simply observed the man before him—this seemingly ordinary individual who had defied every attempt to break him, to uncover his secrets.

"Listen," Sattar began, his voice uncharacteristically trembling. "We've reached a point where our conventional methods have failed. The Prime Minister himself is coming to see you. This is unprecedented."

The spy opened his eyes slowly, looking directly at the General with an inscrutable expression. "And what do you expect from me, General?"

Sattar felt a lump in his throat. This was a man who had endured the unendurable, whose very existence challenged everything Sattar believed in. He took a deep breath and continued, his tone shifting from commanding to pleading.

"I need you to cooperate with us," he said, his voice barely above a whisper. "When the Prime Minister arrives, I need you to act decently, to help us understand what you know. This is beyond military or intelligence protocols; it's about understanding something far greater. Please, I'm asking you to work with us."

The spy's eyes softened, but he remained silent, studying Sattar's face. The General, feeling the weight of the moment, did something he had never done in his career—he folded his hands in a gesture of supplication.

"Please," Sattar repeated, his voice breaking slightly. "This is crucial for all of us. Help us make sense of this situation. We are ready to listen, to understand your story, but we need your cooperation."

The spy looked at Sattar's folded hands and then back into his eyes. There was a moment of silence that felt like an eternity. Finally, the spy nodded slowly.

"I will cooperate," he said softly. "But understand, General, that what you seek is not simple. The answers are not easily found nor easily understood. But I will meet your Prime Minister and speak with him."

Relief washed over General Sattar, and he let out a breath he hadn't realized he was holding. "Thank you," he said, his voice filled with gratitude. "Thank you."

He stood up, feeling a renewed sense of hope. As he left the cell, he turned back to the spy one last time. "Remember, no hints to anyone here. This must remain confidential until we understand what we're dealing with."

The spy gave a slight nod, and General Sattar exited the room, his mind already racing with the preparations needed for the Prime Minister's visit. This was a step into the unknown, but it was a step that had to be taken. The importance of this visit could not be overstated—it was a pivotal moment that would influence the agency's operations and, potentially, the nation's future security.

Over the next few days, the agency buzzed with activity. Security was tightened to unprecedented levels, with additional personnel deployed and state-of-the-art surveillance equipment installed at key points. The compound was transformed into a fortress, with checkpoints established at every entrance and exit, and a thorough vetting process for everyone who entered.

General Sattar oversaw every detail, ensuring that nothing was left to chance. He convened meetings with his senior officers, laying out detailed plans for every aspect of the visit. From the moment the Prime Minister's convoy would enter the gates to the precise timing of each scheduled event, everything was scrutinized and rehearsed. No stone was left unturned in their quest to ensure absolute security and seamless execution.

CHAPTER FOUR

TIMELESS GUARDIANS: THE SECRET OF THE ETERNAL SPY

The day of the Prime Minister's visit arrived swiftly, and with it, a palpable tension hung in the air. The agency's headquarters were immaculate, the result of tireless work by the staff to present an image of efficiency and control. Uniformed guards stood at attention, their eyes sharp and alert, while plainclothes agents mingled discreetly, ready to respond to any threat.

The early morning breeze brought a refreshing touch to the otherwise clear, blue sky. However, it was evident that the sun's heat would soon intensify as the day progressed.

The tranquility of the cantonment was abruptly interrupted by the distinctive sound of the Prime Minister's chopper. The rhythmic thumping of the helicopter blades broke through the silence, drawing attention and signaling the significant presence about to arrive.

The area, which had been peaceful moments ago, now braced for the arrival of the nation's leader, the Prime Minister, who was coming to see the Spy.

As the Prime Minister's helicopter prepared to land, the day was unfolding in a typical summer fashion. The sun blazed brightly, casting intense rays over the landscape. In the cantonment, the atmosphere remained serene and still, with a sense of routine calmness enveloping the area.

General Sattar stood at the main entrance, flanked by his top officers, awaiting the arrival of the Prime Minister. The convoy approached, a fleet of black SUVs moving in unison, their windows tinted and impenetrable. As the vehicles came to a halt, the doors opened, and a contingent of security personnel emerged, scanning the surroundings with practiced precision.

The Prime Minister arrived with minimal fanfare, his visit cloaked in secrecy. He was escorted to the secured area where the spy was held. General Sattar walked alongside him, briefing him on the latest developments and the anticipated interaction.

As they approached the cell, General Sattar felt his heart pound in his chest. The door opened, and the spy stood waiting, his expression calm and composed. The Prime Minister stepped forward, and the two men regarded each other in silence for a moment.

"Prime Minister," the spy said with a respectful nod. "Thank you for your curtsey to meet with me. The Prime Minister extended his hand. The spy folded his hands in honour and then extended his hand.

After a handshake, they moved to the small table in the center of the room, the General standing nearby, ready to mediate if necessary. The air was thick with anticipation as the Prime Minister began to speak, opening a dialogue that would hopefully unravel the mysteries surrounding the enigmatic captive.

This conversation was not just about uncovering secrets; it was about bridging worlds, understanding the extraordinary, and finding a path forward in a situation that defied all logic and precedent.

In the secure meeting room, the Prime Minister positioned himself near the enigmatic spy with a demeanor that conveyed deep respect and curiosity. He leaned forward slightly, an indication of his genuine interest, and began to speak in a tone that was both humble and earnest.

"An able spy is one who can assume an unsuspicious disguise, is fearless when caught, and never betrays his secrets," the Prime

Minister started, his voice calm and reflective. "Disguised as a monk or a mendicant, the master spy is a figure of great wisdom."

He paused, allowing his words to resonate in the quiet of the room. The spy listened intently, his expression unreadable yet attentive, as the Prime Minister continued to weave his narrative, drawing parallels that were both philosophical and poignant.

"We have learned," the Prime Minister went on, "that you as a saint spent your life quietly and simply observing the human condition." His tone suggested a deep reverence for the life led by someone so dedicated to understanding the depths of human experience. Prime Minister further added that

"You may be at the end of your life and as we are asking you to speak out and share the wisdom," he added, suggesting a turning point in the life of someone who had once been content to remain in the background. This narrative seemed to mirror the journey of the spy before him, who had also remained an enigma despite the intense scrutiny he faced.

The Prime Minister's next words were an invitation, a call to action for the spy to engage on a deeper level. "I hope your insights will spark your intuition and reveal the laws discovered within yourself," he said, emphasizing personal revelation over external validation.

"Do not see this scripture as something external," the Prime Minister advised, implying that the truths the spy held were not merely to be conveyed but to be discovered anew through introspection. "Meditation and reflection will reveal that its knowledge lies vibrantly alive within you."

With these words, the Prime Minister not only acknowledged the spy's profound resilience and depth but also expressed a hope that through self-reflection and meditation, the spy would find it within himself to share his unique insights, potentially bridging gaps in understanding or illuminating shared paths forward.

This approach by the Prime Minister was strategic, treating the spy not as a mere detainee but as a source of wisdom, potentially turning a tense interrogation into a transformative exchange. It was an effort to unlock the spy's secrets not through coercion but through mutual respect and the recognition of his deep, internal knowledge.

"The team interrogating you claimed that you are one of the chiranjivis of Hindu religion. There are eight chiranjivis, as I am told, but they could not identify them all. They believe you are one because you speak of events and people from thousands of years ago. How can anyone talk about happenings from so long ago unless they have lived through them? Your presence here puzzles us. Please, tell us more about yourself so we can reach a conclusion."

The spy joined the conversation, "Mr. Prime Minister, thank you for joining me and for your kind words about sainthood. I am neither a Chiranjeevi nor a spy. Be assured of that. I cannot speak about myself, and no force can compel me to. I am committed to Rishi Agastya not to reveal anything about myself to anyone. I am on a specific mission, and still am. My revelation can only occur if I am given a saropa and headgear by the Saptarishees. Only then will I reveal my identity."

"However, to satisfy your curiosity, let me enrich your journey along the Eternal Path, the Sanatana Dharma. Supreme God is praised not by one faith alone, but as 'God Primordial,' 'the Incomparable One,' 'the Gracious One,' or 'the Compassionate One.' In other words, everyone's God. Sanatana Dharma, now called Hinduism, is the world's most ancient religion, encompassing a broad spectrum of philosophies from pluralistic theism to absolute monism. It is a family of myriad faiths with four primary denominations: Saivism, Vaishnavism, Shaktism, and Smartism. These diverse beliefs share a vast heritage of culture and philosophy—karma, dharma, reincarnation, all-pervasive Divinity, temple worship, sacraments, manifold Deities, the guru-shishya tradition, and reliance on the Vedas as scriptural authority."

"Once in a while, a soul perfects their path and becomes a light to the world. In Sanatana Dharma, seven rishis emerged as such lights, now immortalized in the stars."

"Are you one of the seven rishis?" the Prime Minister asked, deeply curious.

"No, I am not," the spy replied, shaking his head. "I am different from the rishis or chiranjivis. I was given unique powers by the Saptarishees for my mission. Unlike you, whose birth and death are in the hands of the Almighty, the Saptarishees granted me the ability to control my own birth and death. I have died and been reborn many times over the last thousands of years."

"It is impossible not to be moved by your compassion and wisdom," the Prime Minister thought deeply. "Is that why we have failed to kill you? Are you able to decide for your own death? I have no reason to mistrust your words, but we have government protocols to follow. You mentioned a saropa and headgear. What is it, and how can we obtain it?"

The spy smiled ruefully, "The saropa and headgear authorizes me, has been missing since I returned from one of a mission visit to Mohenjo-Daro thousands of years back, where I was sent by Rishi Agastya to submit the Vedas at Mohanjo Daro. Before I embarked on my journey to Mohenjo-Daro, Rishi Agastya entrusted me with a solemn vow: 'Upon your return, you shall first seek the darshan of the sacred saropa and headgear. Until that moment, you must reveal nothing about yourself, your life, or your mission. Remember, you were created for a singular purpose, and until that purpose is fulfilled, rest is not yours to claim. 'When I returned, Rishi Agastya had already left for the universal world, keeping my saropa and head with some locker. My saropa and headgear is depicted on an idol found at Mohenjo-Daro, now in the museum there. The idol that the world talked about the priest king is me. I visit Mohenjo-Daro every 25 years, as dictated by my mission. I must visit at least ten times in one life cycle, meaning my minimum age per life is 250 years. After that, I can take a new body and continue my mission for another 250 years. However I may have long years of my choice in my life"

The Prime Minister again greeted, settling into a chair. "I've heard a lot about you and your intriguing abilities. I'm here to understand more about your extraordinary claims."

The Spy responded with a smile. "I'm honored by your visit. What would you like to know more?"

"You mentioned being a minimum of 250 years old. That's quite a claim. Can you explain how that's possible?" the Prime Minister inquired, his curiosity piqued.

"Prime Minister, I said 'a minimum of 250 years' in one cycle. But there's no limit to how many cycles I can live through," the Spy replied calmly. "A minimum of 250 years in one cycle ? That's unbelievable. How can a human lifespan stretch that long?" the Prime Minister asked, astonished.

The Spy's eyes twinkled as he quoted a Sanskrit shloka:

"आयुषः क्षणकिा यस्य जीवने सुख-दुःखयोः। समं भजन्ति कालने सा जीवतिस्य निःश्रेयसा।"

"I apologize, but my Sanskrit is not very strong. Could you please explain that to me?" the Prime Minister requested, looking puzzled.

The Spy smiled. "It means: 'For one whose life is momentary, joy and sorrow come equally with the passage of time. That is the secret to the ultimate goal of life.' As time progresses smoothly and swiftly, man's life appears to shrink. The longer we live, the more we perceive the fleeting nature of time."

Reflecting on this, the Prime Minister said, "So you're saying that our perception of life's length is tied to our experiences of time?"

"Precisely. My existence transcends the typical human experience. Each cycle renews and continues, without a definite end," the Spy affirmed.

Interrupting, the Prime Minister asked, "You always mention Mohenjo-Daro. What is your connection to this ancient locality on the bank of the Indus in Sindh?"

"I was created for Mohenjo-Daro and will not die until my mission is accomplished." "It's fascinating, isn't it?" Spy began his voice steady despite the circumstances. "The city of Mohenjo-Daro was one of the largest infra of the ancient Saraswati Sindhu (Indus Valley) Civilization, under my command, it became more than just a city, it became a symbol of what human ingenuity and organization could achieve."

PM eyes narrowed, but he remained silent, allowing Spy to continue.

"Mohenjo-Daro, meaning 'Mound of the Dead,' was unlike any other city of its time. The infrastructure, the planning, the sheer scale of it—unprecedented. It was a city built to last, a testament to the advanced engineering and societal organization of the Indus people."

"Were we Hindus too?" the Prime Minister asked softly.

"Your ancestors provided cow milk and managed the cow shelter for the 30,000 inhabitants of Mohenjo-Daro. You belong to Sahiwal, which is why you carry the legacy of Sahiwal cows. Rishi Atri blessed your ancestors to lead wherever they lived. That is why you are meeting me as the Prime Minister today. Your ancestors were directly involved in managing affairs at Mohenjo-Daro."

"Everyone was Sanatani at that time," The spy pointed out, referring to the ancient Vedic religion that was prevalent in the region. "The spiritual and cultural practices were deeply embedded in their daily lives. That was a society that valued harmony, order, and a connection to the divine.""No one is Hindu, but you are certainly a Sanatani and it's hardly a matter that you have changed your praying pattern. Time is the root of all creation; uncreated, of pleasure and pain. Time creates existence, destroys it, and renews it. Time watches while all sleep. Time is unvanquished," replied the spy.

The Prime Minister stood, visibly impressed. "Thank you for your time and your insights. This conversation has been enlightening."

"It was my pleasure, Prime Minister. Safe travels," the Spy replied with a respectful nod.

"Until next time," the Prime Minister said with a smile, nodded in affirmation and left the room, deeply contemplating the spy's words. departing with much to ponder about the nature of life and time.

Entering the meeting room, the Prime Minister was utterly confused. Never before in his lifetime had he felt so weak and indecisive. In an authoritative tone, he asked, "What do you suggest now, General?"

The General, having already anticipated the issue, was well aware of the likely outcome of such a meeting. Spying on billions to safeguard his country's interests had given him a unique perspective. He suggested, "We should contact the Indian Prime Minister on this issue and involve other dignitaries to seek a diplomatic resolution."

"Fine, General. Leave your current post as Chief of Secret Services and join the Pakistan Embassy in Delhi as Military Attaché. Your papers will be cleared by their government, and you will be able to meet the Indian Prime Minister. I will arrange it through the hotline and a meeting between our National Security Advisors."

The next day, a news headline appeared: "NSAs of Both Countries to Meet Next Friday over Indus Waters Treaty."

CHAPTER FIVE

<u>THE SPY WHO BRIDGED TWO NATIONS</u>

General Jaffar, the NSA of Pakistan, arrived at the office of the NSA of India, a visit shrouded in speculation despite its official premise: the Indus Water Treaty. Signed on September 19, 1960, and brokered by the World Bank, the treaty delineated the rights and obligations of both countries concerning the Indus River system. This treaty had often provided a platform for offline diplomacy, a necessity given the persistent tensions between the two nations. Remarkably, the meetings under this treaty had never been postponed or canceled.

An undersecretary received Mr. Jaffar at the South Block. Accompanying him was General Sattar, the newly appointed military attaché to the Pakistan Embassy in Delhi. Together, they followed the undersecretary to the office of the Indian NSA, Abhimanyu Singh. Upon their arrival, Abhimanyu stood promptly, came around his desk, and embraced Jaffar warmly.

"Mr. Jaffar, it's good to see you," Abhimanyu said, pointing towards General Sattar. "This is the gentleman for whom we expedited the paperwork."

Abhimanyu shook General Sattar's hand firmly before guiding them to the sofa. While sitting, Abhimanyu passed a printed paper for the declaration at the end of the meeting. He laughed, "Our media is questioning the NSA meet over the water treaty. So, for all purposes, we talked about the free flow of waters obstructed by stone shelling. We agreed on a joint inspection next month."

General Jaffar and Sattar read the declaration in one breath and turned to Abhimanyu. Today, General Sattar was to brief top officers of Indian side on the enigma that was Spy, unraveling a story that seemed more legend than reality. Jaffar initiated the dialogue, turning towards General Sattar, "Please brief Abhimanyu on the whole episode."

General Sattar stood, the weight of the mysterious spy's tale bearing heavily upon him. The spy had been a subject of intense scrutiny and curiosity since his capture. General Sattar began his voice steady but edged with the gravity of the situation. "I need to recount the journey and captivity of the spy. His story is unlike any we've encountered before."

The officers settled into their seats, the room falling silent. Abhimanyu, the Indian NSA leaned forward, his eyes reflecting a mix of skepticism and intrigue.

"The Spy claimed to be a Sanatani," General Sattar started. "He spoke of ancient traditions and philosophies, his words steeped in a wisdom that seemed timeless. From the moment we captured him, it was clear he was no ordinary man. His calm demeanor, even in captivity, suggested a deep inner strength, perhaps even supernatural abilities."

"Supernatural?" Abhimanyu interjected, raising an eyebrow.

"Yes," Sattar nodded. "He spoke of controlling his own birth and death, of living through multiple life cycles. He maintained that his current age was at least 250 years, which he described as merely a minimum in one cycle of existence. He claimed that there is no limit to the number of cycles he could endure."

The room was thick with disbelief. Officers exchanged glances, some muttering under their breath.

"But that's not all," Sattar continued. "We've observed some unusual occurrences. Despite our best efforts to break him, he remains unfazed. We've tried to alter his dietary habits, withholding his specific vegetarian meals devoid of onion and garlic. For five days, he went without food, yet he never mentioned it, never complained. When we resumed his regular meals, he continued as if nothing had happened."

Abhimanyu leaned back, rubbing his chin thoughtfully.

Abhimanyu sighed, shaking his head. "His story sounds fanciful, almost mythical. But our Prime Ministers are now aware of him. We need a structured approach to deal with this."

General Jaffar nodded. "Indeed. Until we ascertain his true nationality and origins, we will refer to him as 'Silver.' He is a joint asset now, a person of interest not just for us but for higher authorities as well."

The room buzzed with a low hum of agreement. The officers understood the gravity of the situation. Silver was not just a captive; he was a mystery wrapped in ancient wisdom, a potential key to secrets beyond their understanding.

"Silver's journey is shrouded in mystery," Sattar continued. "His claims of magical powers, his ability to control life and death, these are not things we can take lightly. We need to approach this with a blend of caution and open-mindedness. Our goal is to understand him, to see if his knowledge can be of use to us, but also to ensure he remains under our control."

Abhimanyu leaned forward again, his eyes piercing. "We need to establish a protocol for interacting with him. Psychological evaluations, perhaps even bringing in experts in ancient philosophies and languages. His background is as much a puzzle as his abilities. We must be thorough."

General Sattar nodded in agreement. "We'll bring in the necessary experts. And we'll keep a close watch on him. His diet, his habits, his interactions—all will be monitored closely. Any sign of deception, any attempt to manipulate us, will be met with immediate action."

The meeting continued, the officers delving into the logistics of handling Silver. The challenges were many, but the potential rewards of understanding such a unique individual were immense. They would proceed with caution, yet with a keen sense of purpose.

As the meeting drew to a close, General Sattar's thoughts lingered on Silver. His calm demeanor, his cryptic statements about life cycles and ancient traditions, had left an indelible mark. The journey ahead would be complex, filled with uncertainty. But one thing was clear: Silver was not just a spy; he was a mystery that needed unraveling, a puzzle that held the promise of knowledge beyond their wildest dreams.

Abhimanyu, still perplexed, asked General Sattar, "Why did you mention supernatural powers? What do you mean by that?"

General Sattar leaned back in his chair, his face serious. "During our interrogations, we pushed him to his limits, almost to the point of death. Yet, the very next day, with the first ray of the sun, he was fully recovered. No matter how severe the injuries, they vanished by morning. Even the harshest wounds, which would take days or weeks to heal for a normal person, were completely gone overnight. That's why I said he had supernatural powers."

Abhimanyu's eyes widened in disbelief. "Are you saying he heals instantly with the sunrise?"

General Sattar nodded. "Precisely, it's unlike anything we've ever seen. His body rejuvenates completely with the first light of day, as if the sun itself is his healer."

Abhimanyu sat back, absorbing this astonishing revelation. "This changes everything. We need to understand the source of his power. There must be a reason behind this extraordinary ability."

Jaffar agreed. "Indeed, Abhimanyu. We must uncover the truth behind his powers and find out who he truly is. His abilities could either be a great asset or a formidable threat, depending on whose side he is on."

The two men sat in silence for a moment, contemplating the mystery before them, realizing that their journey had only just begun.

Everyone nodded in agreement. Abhimanyu turned to General Sattar, "Can you brief our Prime Minister personally? This situation is unprecedented."

Sattar agreed. Abhimanyu stood, spoke into the phone at his desk, and returned as tea was served. They discussed tea plantations in Pakistan, with Jaffar mentioning their high-quality production for local consumption.

Abhimanyu's phone buzzed with an urgent reminder. He glanced at the screen and noted the reminder for their 2:30 PM meeting with the Prime Minister's Office (PMO). "It's time," he said, signaling to General Sattar and the Pakistani officers. They left the briefing room and walked briskly through the corridors of the South Block, where Abhimanyu directed assistants and aides, ensuring everything was in order for the important meeting.

As they approached the PMO office, the gravity of the situation weighed heavily on their minds. The South Block, with its colonial architecture and imposing presence, felt like a maze of power and secrecy. Assistants scurried about, finalizing last-minute details as Abhimanyu led the group to the conference room.

At precisely 2:30 PM, the Indian Prime Minister entered the room, exuding authority and calm. His presence filled the room, and all eyes turned towards him. After formal introductions, they took their seats on the comfortable, gold-cushioned chairs, the atmosphere thick with anticipation.

The Prime Minister, having been thoroughly briefed, turned to General Sattar and asked, "I understand there are reports of Silver possessing magical powers. Can you elaborate on this?"

General Sattar exchanged a helpless look with his fellow officers before responding, "Yes, sir. During our interrogations, we pushed him to the brink of death. Yet, with the first ray of the sun, he fully recovered, no matter how severe the injuries. It was as if the sun itself was healing him."

The Prime Minister's eyes narrowed in thought. "When we open our eyes, we see the earth and the sun that reveals it. The sun, known as the 'Savita,' is the generator of this world. If Silver draws his strength from the sun, he is no ordinary human. I appreciate your Prime Minister's openness. We will leave no stone unturned to resolve this spiritual puzzle."

He turned to Jaffar, emphasizing the need for discretion. "This meeting remains unofficial and unquoted. Abhimanyu, you've faced many challenges, but this is unique."

The room fell silent as the gravity of the situation sank in. The Prime Minister's words echoed the thoughts of everyone present. They were dealing with something beyond their comprehension, a mystery that intertwined science, spirituality, and perhaps even destiny.

Everyone stood up, the formality of the meeting giving way to a sense of mutual understanding and urgency. As they exited the room, Abhimanyu leaned towards General Sattar and said, "Stay in touch. We'll need to work closely on this."

Outside, the sun was beginning its descent, casting long shadows across the South Block. The group dispersed, each member lost in their thoughts, contemplating the enigma that was Silver. The significance of the meeting was not lost on anyone; it was the beginning of a journey that could reshape their understanding of reality itself.

The next day, newspapers across the country carried the headline: "NSAs Talk in Cordial Tone – Committed to Strengthening the Treaty. Next Meet on the Table." The public remained unaware of the extraordinary revelations discussed behind closed doors, but for those involved, the journey to uncovering the truth about Silver had just begun.

CHAPTER SIX

<u>THE SILVER ENIGMA</u>

Abhimanyu entered the Prime Minister's Office (PMO) in a hurry, his mind racing. Today was the crucial meeting to discuss the progress on the Silver matter. Coordinating with the Intelligence Bureau (IB), he had gathered extensive information on various spiritual heads. Despite their efforts, success remained elusive. Before presenting the details to the Prime Minister, Abhimanyu needed to meticulously review every detail. No corner could be left unattended, knowing the Prime Minister's keen grasp of subjects and decisive nature.

In a secluded corner of his office, Abhimanyu spread out the documents and digital files provided by the IB. The task was to connect the dots: Rishi Vashisht, Rishi Agastya, Mohenjo-Daro, and the mysterious Sanatani who was said to control life and death. Despite top Acharya expressing skepticism about such a person's existence and General Sattar dismissing the possibility of a Chiranjeevi avatar, Abhimanyu pressed on.

Before heading to the Prime Minister, Abhimanyu had to discuss an important proposal with the NSA (National Security Advisor) of Pakistan. The plan was to install CCTV in Silver room with a link to the Indian agency, and reciprocally, they would share links from a dedicated spiritual war room. As he pondered over a virtual meet with the supreme spiritual heads, the hotline rang.

Abhimanyu picked up the phone. Jaffar, the Pakistani NSA, was on the line. "Our Prime Minister has consented to the CCTV installation and agreed to view PM meeting with your spiritual heads," Jaffar informed. They discussed the installation time, and Jaffar assured him it would be done promptly.

Abhimanyu called his assistant, instructing him to set up the virtual link in five minutes. He was relieved that everything was moving swiftly and in the right direction. Today, they would meet the top ten religious heads of Sanatana Dharma with the Prime Minister, and potentially, everyone would see and speak with Silver.

The seers gathered with the Prime Minister for a brief discussion before moving to the Spiritual War Room, guided by Abhimanyu. The Prime Minister decided to stay aloof and not join the virtual meeting directly. Cameras and audio systems were activated. The seers saw a man lying on a bed with his eyes closed. His face radiated a serene brightness, akin to the sun but cool and calm.

Dandi Maharaj, a respected seer, initiated the conversation by asking about Dharma. He started by quoting Jaimini: "The best definition of dharma appears to have been given by Jaimini in the words 'codanalaksano'rtho dharma,' that is to say 'dharma consists in beneficial directions.' These directions, however, are manifold; they direct us how to conduct ourselves in matters both religious and spiritual." This strategy worked; Silver opened his eyes, blinked thrice, and looked at the TV screen showing the seers. Unfazed by their presence, he made a respectful pranam. The seers responded with "Ayushman Bhava." Silver's eyes seemed to search for someone specific, but he didn't find them.

Dandi Maharaj continued, asking about Dharma. Silver replied with an in-depth explanation, referencing the Rigveda: "The term 'dharma' has been used in various senses in the Rigveda. The word 'dharma' is used sixty times without a particle, about eighteen times with a particle 'vi' and about fifty-six times with the particles 'sva' and 'satya.' When the word is used in masculine gender, it carries the meaning of upholder or supporter or sustainer. In some cases, the word dharma is used in neuter sense or in a sense of either masculine or neuter."

Silver elaborated on how Dharma has evolved in meaning, encompassing moral, religious, and cosmic principles. "In other cases, the word is used in the sense of religious ordinances or rites such as 'agnihotra' for the welfare of the gods and men. In the Atharvaveda, the word dharma is used in the sense of merit acquired by performing religious rites. In the Aitreya Brahmana, the word is used in the sense of 'the whole body of religious duties.' In the Taittiriya Aranyaka, the word dharma is used in the sense of living or vital force, the foundation of the cosmic order which pervades everything."

Silver continued, his voice steady and clear, holding the attention of every seer in the room. "In the Taittiriya Upanisad, the term seems to be used in the sense of right, duty, discipline, etc., which should be followed by one in his day-to-day life. This idea of dharma is highlighted in this Upanisad during the convocation ceremony while the preceptor advises his disciples to obey and follow moral and religious duties in their daily life. In the Chandogya Upanisad, the word dharma is used in the sense of duties belonging to different stages of life. In the first sense of the concerned passage, the word indicates the duties of a householder, such as study and charity. In the second sense, it indicates the duties of a hermit, such as austerities, and in the third sense, it indicates the duties of a celibate staying in the house of the preceptor. In the Brhadaranyaka Upanisad, the word dharma and satya are used as equivalents. Terming dharma as satya in the concerned passage, it is upheld that it is righteousness or dharma which rules even a ksatriya. Through the power of dharma or righteousness, even the weak rule over the stronger."

The unthinkable response from Silver to the top Sanatana spiritual heads left everyone in a state of awe. Silver spoke with a depth and clarity that seemed to transcend human comprehension. He delved into ancient scriptures; unraveling complex philosophies with ease, and his insights into the mysteries of the universe were nothing short of astounding. The spiritual heads, revered for their vast knowledge, found themselves fixed in rapt attention, unable to interject or question.

In their offices, both Prime Ministers witness of Silver's discourse. They were equally shocked by the profound depth of his knowledge. The Indian Prime Minister, in particular, felt a strange sense of unease as he looked at the face of Silver being transmitted to him. There was something hauntingly familiar about Silver's face, a resemblance that stirred something deep within him.

As he stared at him, the Prime Minister's heart began to race. There was something about Silver's eyes that struck a chord, a sense of recognition that he couldn't shake. "Who is he?" he wondered. "And who am I? Why do I feel such a strong connection to this man?" The Prime Minister's thoughts swirled with confusion and curiosity, as if some deep, hidden part of his soul was trying to surface.

Unable to contain his curiosity any longer, the Prime Minister turned to Abhimanyu. "Arrange a face-to-face virtual interaction with Silver over this facility," he commanded his desire to see Silver in real-time growing stronger by the second. There was urgency in his voice, a need to confront the mysterious connection he felt.

Abhimanyu, sensing the gravity of the situation, immediately picked up the phone and called Jaffar. "We need to set up a virtual face-to-face meeting after this meet between Silver and our Prime Minister," he said, his tone conveying the importance of the request. Jaffar, recognizing the urgency, nodded in affirmation and assured Abhimanyu that he would make the necessary arrangements.

Paschima Math's spiritual head asked Silver about his Dharma and the reason for his repeated births. Silver scanned the room again, not finding the person he sought. "I cannot share anything about myself," he said, "but my dharma has passed through several transitions of meaning, ultimately signifying the privileges, duties, and obligations of man, his standard of conduct as a person in a particular stage of life. My dharma is characteristic property, scientifically; duty morally and legally with its proper implications, psycho-physically and spiritually; and righteousness and law generally, but duty above all." His explanation again left the seers in awe.

The Dakshin Seer, a venerable figure with a serene presence, greeted Silver with a gesture of respect. He then asked, "What brings you here, and what are you seeking?"

Silver's expression changed subtly, his eyes reflecting a deep, ancient knowledge. He replied, "I seek knowledge and the truth about Augusta Ashram in Vatadipura now in Kaladgi District." The mention of the Ashram sent a ripple through the assembly. Everyone present knew its spiritual significance and the legacy of Rishi Agastya, whose presence there had enriched its sanctity.

Silver continued his voice steady with a timeless resonance, "I was a regular visitor to Augusta Ashram during Rishi Agastya's time on Earth. The sacred place holds memories of countless spiritual journeys and profound teachings."

The seers were stunned, their faces betraying a mix of astonishment and reverence. One of them, an elder with a long white beard, asked, "How can we confirm this extraordinary claim? What clues can you provide that would help us identify such a remarkable personality?"

Silver smiled gently, his eyes gleaming with ancient wisdom. "The answers lie at Augusta Peeth at Agastyarkoodam and at badami known as South Kashi. There, you will find the clues that will unveil my true identity. It is time now to fulfill the purpose of my existence. The mission that I have waited for thousands of years to complete is nearing its end."

Silver's voice grew softer, more contemplative. "I am looking for someone, and hopefully, everything is now coming full circle. The time is ripe for the fulfillment of the ancient prophecies. The mysteries that have eluded us for millennia are on the verge of revelation."

With that, Silver chanted a Sanskrit shloka, his voice resonating with an ancient power that seemed to transcend time and space. The room fell into a hushed silence as the sound of his chanting filled the air, invoking a deep sense of reverence and spiritual awakening:

"सत्यमेवजयतेतत्रधर्मः शक्तरिपुणेवर्ततोअयोनजिं वंदे त्वां संजीवनीम् अंशवन्मुखं॥"

"Truth alone triumphs there, where Dharma manifests in the form of power. I salute you, the eternal, who is the life force and the embodiment of all that is."

As the sloka ended, an overwhelming sense of peace and understanding washed over everyone present. The seers, deeply moved, found themselves connected to the ancient wisdom that Silver had awakened within them. They sat in silence, reflecting on the significance of his words and the resonance of the Sanskrit verses.

Silver's eyes scanned the room, meeting the gaze of each seer, their faces now illuminated with the glow of profound insight. "The journey we are about to undertake is not just mine; it is ours. We are bound by the same purpose, the same cosmic thread that connects all of us across the eons. The Augusta Ashram, the Peeth, and all that lies within are the keys to unlocking the final chapter of this timeless saga."

He paused, letting the weight of his words sink in. "The necessary belongings have recently been returned to Augusta Peeth. It is time to move on. In all these thousands of years, I have never been in captivity. Today, I find myself bound, and this situation is nothing short of extraordinary. The return of my personal belongings to Augusta Peeth from Kashi marks the beginning of an unusual spiritual regime. You, the seers, are known to me, as we were once there for a cause greater than ourselves."

As the meeting drew to a close, Abhimanyu stood up, his presence commanding yet serene. "The time has come. Let us proceed to Augusta Peeth, where the secrets of the ages will be revealed. Together, we shall walk the path laid out by the ancients, fulfilling the prophecy that has waited this very moment."

They resolved to charter a special plane to visit Augusta Peeth. The seers, moved to tears, never imagined encountering someone so profoundly connected to their spiritual heritage.

The next day's newspaper headline read: "Prominent Seers across India to Visit Augusta Peeth for Religious Discourse."

CHAPTER SEVEN

THE TAPESTRY OF DESTINY

Within moments, the preparations were underway. Technicians worked swiftly to set up the secure video link, ensuring that the communication would be seamless and uninterrupted. The anticipation in the room was palpable as the screen flickered to life, and Silver's image appeared.

The Indian Prime Minister leaned forward, his eyes locking onto Silver's through the screen. For a moment, time seemed to stand still. The Prime Minister's heartbeat echoed in his ears as he scrutinized Silver's face, searching for answers to the questions that had been haunting him.

Silver looked at the Indian Prime Minister, whose curiosity and internal turmoil had led him to this moment. "You, too, are part of this grand tapestry," Silver said, his voice resonating with a deep, knowing tone. "Your connection to me is not by chance. It is the hand of destiny that has woven our paths together."

The Prime Minister, now deeply engrossed in the unfolding mystery, nodded slowly, a sense of clarity dawning upon him. He understood that this was more than just a meeting; it was a convergence of destinies, a moment when the past and present melded into a singular, profound reality.

Silver, on the other end, regarded the Prime Minister with calm, knowing expression. His eyes, filled with wisdom and serenity, seemed to pierce through the screen, connecting with the Prime Minister in a way that transcended the physical distance between them.

"Who are you?" the Prime Minister finally asked his voice barely above a whisper.

Silver smiled gently. "I am a traveler on this journey of life," he replied. "And so are you. We are all connected, bound by the same threads of existence. The only difference between you and me is that I remain in the same body and spirit, while you have taken numerous births. Without you, it was not possible for me to arrange such a massive event at Mohenjo-Daro. You are not aware that your destiny was well defined for this time. We are meeting after a span of thousands of years."

The Prime Minister's mind whirled with Silver's revelations. "I have to remind you of the mission of our life," Silver continued. "Things are moving in the right direction, and you have a much bigger role to play now than you did thousands of years ago. You are Parmanand. I could not have dreamed of achieving anything without the perfect assistance from my younger brother, seeing you now give me the strength to finish our mission. In a few days, everything will become clear to you. This is a reunion. The seers who visited me today also met me thousands of years ago. Today, they find themselves in a new era; unable to connect the dots, but I will connect each and every one. The Saptarishees are orchestrating everything from the solar system, and now we must wait for the right moment to begin and reach our destination. Parmanand, you are not aware of your significant contribution to the Sanatana world. The most impactful suggestion you made, which we implemented, has been greatly appreciated by all the Brahmarishi, especially Jagat Guru Vashisht. Your idea to have a ceremonial bath right under the room of the Purohit of the Yagya, Vashisht, for the Rishis who were offering their prayers through the Sukta of the Rig-Veda was remarkable. The world today is confused about that bath, often terming it a community bath, but its true significance lies in its logical and sacred location. That bath has illuminated the place, and it stands as a testament to your labor. The bath at Mohenjo-Daro is dedicated to your efforts. No one else knows this, but I was the witness and remain the witness to your hard work for the Yajna."

The Prime Minister felt a shiver run down his spine. There was something about Silver's words that resonated deeply within him, as if they were unlocking a part of his own soul that he had long left. The sense of recognition grew stronger, and with it, a sense of peace. "I am Parmanand from thousands of years," he murmured to himself, the name feeling both foreign and intimately familiar.

As the virtual meeting continued, the Prime Minister's initial unease gave way to a profound sense of connection and understanding. The questions that had plagued him began to dissolve, replaced by a deep sense of purpose and clarity. He realized that this encounter with Silver was not just a coincidence, but a turning point in his own journey.

"The time has come," Silver declared, his eyes shining with conviction. "We must fulfill the prophecies and complete the mission that was set into motion thousands of years ago. Together, we will awaken the dormant powers within us and guide humanity toward a new era of enlightenment."

The Prime Minister, now fully aware of his role as Parmananda, felt a surge of determination and clarity. "These scrolls contain the knowledge and prophecies passed down through the ages," Silver explained. "They speak of our mission, of the roles we are destined to play in the grand tapestry of existence. Moreover these scrolls in philosophy, refers to the term 'Ātman' which ultimately refers to an individual's contemplative consciousness. Since Ātman pertains to the same subject, it is inherently subjective. However, the sense of selfhood or ownership, while related to subjectivity, should not be confused with it."

As the Prime Minister studied the scrolls, he began to understand the magnitude of their purpose. The scrolls detailed the convergence of destinies, the alignment of stars, and the return of ancient powers that would reshape the world.

As he committed himself for a work, he felt the guiding presence of the Saptarishees, the celestial sages who watched over him from the sormandal. Their influence was subtle yet profound, guiding his steps and illuminating his path. The culmination of his efforts came on a night when the stars aligned in a perfect symphony of light.

The meeting ended, but the impact of Silver's words and presence lingered long after the screen went dark. The Prime Minister sat back in his chair, his mind racing with new insights and revelations. He knew that this was just the beginning of a new chapter, one that would lead him to explore deeper truths about himself and the world around him.

Abhimanyu, standing by his side, could sense the change in the Prime Minister. "Are you alright, Sir?" he asked, his voice filled with concern.

The Prime Minister nodded slowly. "Yes, Abhimanyu," he replied. "I am more than alright. I feel like I've been given a glimpse into something extraordinary. And I intend to follow this path, wherever it may lead."

Abhimanyu smiled, relieved to see the Prime Minister so invigorated. "We will support you every step of the way, Sir."

And with that, a new journey began, one that would take them into uncharted territories of knowledge, spirituality, and self-discovery. The encounter with Silver had set into motion a series of events that would change their lives forever, revealing the interconnectedness of all things and the true power of the human spirit.

As the days passed, the preparations for the journey to Augusta Peeth intensified. The seers, the Prime Ministers, and Abhimanyu, now united in purpose, prepared to embark on a journey that would unravel the mysteries of the universe, bridging the realms of the known and the unknown. The echoes of Silver's shlokas lingered in the air, a timeless invocation guiding them toward the dawn of a new spiritual era.

CHAPTER EIGHT

<u>THE LEGACY OF RISHI AGASTYA</u>

As the seers prepared for their journey, Abhimanyu reflected on the day's events. The meeting had exceeded his expectations, opening new avenues for understanding the enigmatic Silver. The spiritual war room buzzed with a renewed sense of purpose. The journey to Augusta Peeth promised revelations that could bridge ancient wisdom with the modern quest for truth. Abhimanyu knew that this was only the beginning of a profound exploration that would reshape their understanding of Dharma and spiritual heritage.

As the seers boarded the chartered plane the next day, anticipation hung in the air. As the chartered plane descended towards Thiruvananthapuram , the anticipation among the seers was palpable. The flight to peeth felt like a pilgrimage, each moment filled with the weight of history and the promise of discovery. The journey to Augusta Peeth was not just a physical voyage but a spiritual pilgrimage, one that promised to unravel the profound legacy of Rishi Agastya. Upon landing, they were greeted with reverence and guided to the Augusta Peeth. The ashram, nestled amidst serene landscapes, exuded a timeless aura. Nestled amidst the serene landscapes, the ashram exuded a timeless aura, its sacred precincts whispering tales of ancient wisdom.

The seers, accompanied by Abhimanyu, approached the sacred precincts with a sense of awe. The air was thick with the scent of incense and the whispers of ancient chants. At the heart of the ashram stood a statue of Rishi Agastya, his presence almost palpable. The seers gathered in a circle, their hearts united in silent prayer.

The group settled in the central courtyard, a place steeped in history. The head seer began to recount the life and legacy of Rishi Agastya, whose influence spanned across the subcontinent and beyond.

Agastya's origins were shrouded in divine mystery. Pulastya, one of the revered Saptarishee of the Rig Veda, was his father. Agastya's miraculous birth followed a yajna performed by the gods Varuna and Mitra. Overwhelmed by the extraordinary beauty of the celestial apsara Urvashi, they ejaculated, and their semen fell into a mud pitcher. This pitcher became the womb in which Agastya grew, giving him the name 'Kumbhayoni'—born from a jar. In some mythologies, he was born alongside his twin, Sage Vashistha.

Agastya's life took a pivotal turn when he decided to marry to relieve his ancestors from their pitiful state. During a visit to Swarglok, he found his ancestors hanging upside down from a tree. They informed him that their condition was due to his unmarried and childless status, which prevented anyone from offering them oblations. Determined to change this, Agastya sought a suitable bride and found Lopamudra, the princess of Vidarbha.

Lopamudra was not only beautiful but also wise and noble. She agreed to marry Agastya without hesitation, leaving behind her palace comforts to live a life of austerity. Despite Agastya's engrossment in his austerities, Lopamudra remained a devoted wife. However, she eventually composed a hymn to remind him of his duties towards her and their future family. Moved by her plea, Agastya changed his ways, and soon, a son named Dhirdyasu was born, lifting his ancestors to the heavenly skies. The hymn of the RigVeda, attributed to Lopamudra, is remarkable for its candid exploration of personal and marital dynamics, reflecting Lopamudra's intelligence and independence. Lopamudra, a highly intelligent and renowned scholar, directly addresses her husband, Sage Agasthya, criticizing his neglect of marital duties. This bold expression highlights her desire for a balanced relationship where her needs are acknowledged and fulfilled.

Lopamudra is often mentioned in the context of being created by Sage Agasthya, embodying an age-old trope of desirable women being created by men. However, Lopamudra transcends this stereotype by asserting her desires and challenging her husband's negligence. This independence and self-assurance set her apart, making her a notable figure in Vedic literature.

Lopamudra's hymn reflects her self-confidence and demands for a marriage consummated with the same respect and dignity she experienced in her father's palace. She insists on proper attire and setting, symbolizing her refusal to settle for less than she believes she deserves. When Agastya mentions his scholarly limitations, she encourages him to use his knowledge to earn a livelihood, showcasing her practical wisdom and assertiveness.

On a deeper level, the hymn can be seen as a metaphor for spiritual pursuit. Lopamudra, representing hidden Divine Knowledge (Lopa meaning hidden and Mudra meaning gem or knowledge), calls upon Agastya, a symbol of stability, to pursue and attain the fruits of spiritual practice (sadhana). This interpretation suggests that true fulfillment comes from the pursuit and dissemination of knowledge.

Agastya's contributions to Vedic literature are profound. He is credited with several hymns in the Rigveda, where he ran a Vedic school, as evidenced by hymn attributed to his wife Lopamudra and his students. His hymns are known for their verbal play, similes, puzzles, and puns, embedding spiritual messages within striking imagery.

Another notable theme is the tension between monastic pursuit and household responsibilities. In a famous discussion between Agastya and Lopamudra, she presents her arguments about life, time, and the possibility of balancing spiritual and familial duties. Agastya, seduced by her compelling arguments, underscores that happiness and liberation can be achieved in various ways.

Agastya's influence extended beyond the Vedas into the Itihasa and Puranas. He is revered as one of the Saptarishee, the seven most revered sages in Vedic texts. His pioneering role in developing Tamil grammar, Tampraparniyan medicine, and spirituality at Shaiva centers in proto-era Sri Lanka and South India is well documented. Agastya is also a key figure in Shaktism and Vaishnavism, and his legacy is etched in the ancient sculptures and reliefs of South Asia and Southeast Asia's Hindu temples.

In Indian Vedic literature, Agastya is associated with Canopus, the brightest star in the southern constellation of Carina. This star, known as the 'cleanser of waters,' is said to coincide with the calming of the Indian Ocean's waters. Agastya is thus seen as a cosmic cleanser, his influence reaching both the earthly and celestial realms.

Agastya seat in Kashi seems to be replaced by his abode in Badami. His second stratum begins with his residence at Malakuta, three miles east of Badami (The ancient Vatapipura) otherwise known as Dakshin Kashi in the Kaladgi District. The third stratum gathers around him at Pothryil known also as Malaya in Kerala, one of the southernmost promontories of the western Ghats in the Pandyas Country founded first Tamil Academy. Nasik was also associated with the Rishi and this place is 800 miles from Nasik. He is also associated with Tirunelveili near Kanya Kumari and Thanjavur .

Before revealing the facts, the head seer shared a specific incident from the recent past. "We also have our Peeth at Kashi, near the mighty river Ganga. This Peeth is very old and the ashes of Rishi Augusta were sent to Kashi. The spiritual head of this Peeth, who carried the ashes, also transported many things from here to Kashi. Over time, the Peeth became submerged in the sands, and its then-infrastructure became the basement of that Kashi Peeth."

"No one was aware of this until recently. As the Kashi Vishwanath Corridor was constructed, many old buildings in the nearby areas were demolished. During this process, the basement of the Peeth emerged. The present incumbent in charge rang us, his voice trembling. He mentioned finding a wooden box. We sent a special team to handle these belongings carefully." The box had not been opened since the time of Rishi Agastya when he left the earth for his universal Yatra.

The seer continued, "We recently brought the box to this Peeth. We were clueless about its contents. No one had dared to open that wooden box, fearing it as misfortune because it contained the oldest objects of the Peeth. When the local IB team visited us, inquiring about any belongings from Rishi Augustya's time, we decided to open the box. We expected to find ashes inside. However, to our surprise, we found a saropa and a headgear. Thereafter we found a reference of the Saropa and headgear in one of the book indexes.

"The IB team was also looking for these items, which confirms that the person aware of these goods and claiming them to be his belongings truly exists since Rishivar's time."

With those words, the seers felt a surge of anticipation. The spiritual discourse at Augusta Peeth promised not just answers, but a deeper understanding of their own faith and the eternal truths that transcended time. Abhimanyu knew that they were on the brink of a revelation that would echo through generations, a testament to the enduring power of Dharma and the mystical legacy of Silver. The truth of Silver was beginning to unfold, and with it, the secrets of the past would soon be revealed.

A sense of profound reverence surfaced, the journey to Augusta Peeth marking a pivotal moment in their spiritual odyssey. The answers they sought were within reach, and the unfolding saga of Silver promised to illuminate their path with the light of ancient wisdom and timeless truth.

The head seer emphasized that understanding Agastya's legacy was crucial to grasping the enigma of Silver. The seers briefed their objective to visit the Peeth and inquired if any person connected with the Peeth still lived from the Augusta period and mentioned a Saropa and Augusta connection. The eyes of the Peeth head widened, and his expressions showed exceptional surprise. The Saropa, Maharishi Agastya, was keeping a Saropa and headgear in one of his wooden boxes. He always talked about it as a trustee of the Saropa and headgear. Both belongings were not of Agastya

Rishi, but he was a custodian of them. The Peeth head shared these goods with the visiting seers. Everyone was quite surprised that they were passing through Sanatana history, though they had been preaching Sanatana for so long.

"Can we see those belongings you have talked about?" Abhimanyu asked.

"I can't share them with anyone as they have been stored as Rishi Agastya's belongings for so long. However, the Peeth has never thought anyone would claim them, as their objective and storage have been buried for thousands of years," the head seer explained. Abhimanyu tried to change the ongoing reteamed of the head seer. I can't show but as you are present here with the top Sanatani spiritual heads of Bharatavarsa, I don't object to showing them in honor of your unprecedented visit to the Peeth." Everyone was glad to witness the oldest Sanatani goods, which seemed to be related to a person who claims to be a Sanatani.

Silver, the mysterious Sanatani, had often referred to Agastya and his teachings. The connection between Silver and Agastya hinted at a deeper, timeless wisdom that transcended eras and linked ancient spiritual truths with contemporary quests for enlightenment.

As the seers meditated in the sacred precincts, a sense of tranquility enveloped them. The presence of Rishi Agastya's legacy seemed to infuse them with renewed purpose and insight. The head seer addressed them once more, "Agastya's teachings are a testament to the eternal journey of Dharma. His life and works bridge the ancient and the modern, the celestial and the terrestrial. To understand Silver, we must delve into the depths of Agastya's wisdom."

Abhimanyu turned towards Dandi Maharaj and requested him to seek the head seer's permission to show the items only to Silver through virtual connection. He mentioned that Zaffar had told him that if he could get his Saropa and headgear, then Silver would talk about everything regarding his birth, mission, and continuing with the life cycle. It was Agastya Rishi who kept his belongings and sent him on a mission to Mohenjo-Daro, promising to give back his belongings and free him from his deemed silence over the issues.

Dandi Maharaj thought for a moment and then turned towards the head seer of the Peeth to show the belongings to Silver, who claimed such belongings. It was only to get a lead for further identification of Silver. The seer head found no reason to reject the proposal, and Dandi Maharaj now instructed Abhimanyu to make the necessary arrangements.

The wooden box was taken to the room and opened. Everyone stayed away from the box, their hands folded in reverence as it was kept open. Inside, they found a Saropa and a headgear placed on it. Everything that had been speculative settled down. Now, Abhimanyu confirmed it himself and instructed the counterpart in Pakistan to switch on the link to show the belongings to Silver.

Jaffar hurriedly entered the room and, while sitting close to Silver, pointed towards a big screen. Silver's expressions changed. He was crying and shivering. "You found it, Jaffar. These are my belongings, and I shall talk about the Sanatana history of thousands of years as soon as I receive them. Relieve me; I have to go and reach my belongings. I am on a mission and will surely achieve my destination before ending my life permanently. Now with these belongings, I could attain my Moksha." The CCTV was switched off by Jaffar, and Abhimanyu directed his assistant to cut off the broadcast.

The seers departed Augusta Peeth with a profound sense of reverence, their hearts and minds enriched by the timeless teachings of Rishi Agastya. The journey had illuminated their path, bringing them closer to unraveling the mystery of Silver and understanding the profound legacy of one of India's greatest sages.

As they boarded the plane back, the seers reflected on the day's revelations. The next steps in their journey were clear. They would continue to seek wisdom from the past to guide their present endeavors, ensuring that the legacy of sages like Agastya would light their way in the quest for spiritual enlightenment and truth.

CHAPTER NINE

THE INDIAN PMO

The seers returned from Augusta Peeth with a profound sense of reverence and urgency. The ancient wisdom they had encountered had illuminated their path, but the mystery of Silver remained unsolved. As they gathered in the Prime Minister's office, the atmosphere was charged with anticipation. The Prime Minister, a man of sharp intellect and decisive action, welcomed them warmly.

"Welcome, esteemed seers. I trust your journey to Augusta Peeth was enlightening?" the Prime Minister began, his eyes scanning the room.

Dandi Maharaj, the eldest and most respected among them, nodded. "Indeed, it was. We have much to discuss and decisions to make."

The Prime Minister gestured for them to take their seats. Abhimanyu stood by his side, ready to assist. "Let's begin," the Prime Minister said. "We must formulate our next course of action regarding Silver."

One by one, the seers offered their suggestions. Some proposed traveling to Pakistan with the sacred belongings to facilitate Silver's return. Others suggested a diplomatic exchange to bring Silver to India. As the discussions grew heated, Dandi Maharaj raised his hand for silence.

"These belongings of Rishi Agastya, left by one of the Saptarishees, cannot leave the boundaries of Augusta Peeth. They are not to be touched or opened by anyone other than Silver himself," Dandi Maharaj declared. "We cannot defy the sanctity of these relics."

The room fell silent. The seers nodded in agreement, understanding the gravity of the situation.

The Prime Minister leaned forward, his face thoughtful. "We must respect the sanctity of these items. Silver's desire to have his belongings should not lead us to compromise their sacredness. I assure you, we will do everything in our power to bring Silver here to India and to Augusta Peeth."

He turned to Abhimanyu. "Make the necessary arrangements."

Abhimanyu nodded and immediately set to work, fixing a hotline between the Indian Prime Minister and his Pakistani counterpart. The Indian Prime Minister, known for his diplomatic finesse, prepared to plead his case.

The hotline buzzed, and the Pakistani Prime Minister's voice came through. "Greetings," he said. "How can I assist you today?"

The Indian Prime Minister spoke softly but with conviction. "We request that Silver be allowed to come to India, specifically to Augusta Peeth, to retrieve his belongings and reveal the history that binds our nations."

There was a pause before the Pakistani Prime Minister replied. "We understand the importance of this matter. However, we have a condition. Our NSA Jaffar and General Sattar must accompany Silver at all times during his stay in India. For all purposes, Silver will remain in our custody until we decide his fate. He can visit India for the limited purpose of revealing the history."

The Indian Prime Minister considered this carefully. "Agreed," he said. "The history of our nations is intertwined, and we welcome your cooperation."

The seers and Abhimanyu listened intently as the Indian Prime Minister continued. "We will ensure the safety and respect of your officials. Let us work together to uncover this shared history."

The Pakistani Prime Minister responded with equal solemnity. "Very well. We will make the necessary arrangements for Silver's visit. Let this be a step towards understanding our common heritage."

As the call ended, the Prime Minister turned to the seers. "We have their cooperation. Silver will come to India, under the conditions set by Pakistan. Abhimanyu, prepare for his arrival and ensure everything is in place at Augusta Peeth."

Abhimanyu bowed slightly. "I will see to it immediately."

Dandi Maharaj spoke up once more. "This is a significant step. We must prepare ourselves spiritually and mentally for what lies ahead. Silver's revelations could change our understanding of our heritage."

The Prime Minister nodded. "Indeed. Let us move forward with hope and respect for the ancient wisdom that guides us."

The seers departed the office, their hearts filled with anticipation. The journey had been long, but they were on the brink of a revelation that could bridge the past and present, and illuminate the path to the future. As they prepared for Silver's arrival, they knew that the legacy of Rishi Agastya and the wisdom of the ancients would guide them every step of the way.

CHAPTER TEN

<u>RESURGENCE AT THE RUINS: RETURN TO MOHENJO-DARO</u>

Abhimanyu, the Indian NSA, prepared meticulously for his visit to Pakistan. The arrangements for Silver's journey from Pakistan to India were delicate and required precision. The proposal had been set: Silver would first visit Mohenjo-Daro for his ritual and then proceed to Augusta Peeth in India. This plan had the full backing of both nations' leadership, reflecting a rare moment of cooperation.

The flight to Islamabad was uneventful, but Abhimanyu's mind was racing with the tasks ahead. Upon arrival, he was greeted by Pakistani officials who escorted him to a secure location where he would meet Silver. The air was filled with a mix of anticipation and solemnity, each step forward feeling like a step into a deeper historical and spiritual understanding.

Silver was brought into the room, his demeanor calm and composed. He radiated an aura of ancient wisdom, his presence commanding respect.

Abhimanyu began. "I am from your Bharat; we have made the necessary arrangements for your visit to Mohenjo-Daro. After your rituals, we will proceed to Augusta Peeth."

Silver nodded, his eyes reflecting the depths of history he carried within him. "Thank you, Abhimanyu. I have been to Mohenjo-Daro countless times, and each visit is a part of a ritual that connects me to my past. After this, I will finally retrieve my belongings from Augusta Peeth."

Abhimanyu briefed Silver on the itinerary. "We will depart for Mohenjo-Daro shortly. Once your rituals are complete, a special aircraft from India will take us from Karachi to India."

The logistics were swiftly handled. Both the Indian and Pakistani governments were committed to ensuring the smooth execution of this unprecedented mission. The next three days were a blur of preparations, security checks, and diplomatic exchanges.

A special aircraft flew from Islamabad to Karachi, carrying Abhimanyu, Silver, and a contingent of officials. The flight was short, but the weight of the journey was immense. Silver, now a free man, was serene, his focus unwavering.

As they landed in Karachi, Silver was immediately transported to Mohenjo-Daro. The ancient site, a testament to a bygone civilization, stood in stark contrast to the modernity around it. Silver's face softened as he approached the ruins.

He stepped out of the car, bent down, and touched the soil of Mohenjo-Daro with his hands. He then applied the dust to his forehead in a gesture of reverence. The officials watched in silence, respecting the sanctity of the moment.

Silver moved towards a damaged structure near the famous Great Bath of Mohenjo-Daro. He performed a series of rituals, mimicking the act of taking a bath in the now-dry bath before entering what was known as the Principal's Chamber. This chamber, though in ruins, held a significance that transcended its physical state. Silver spent twenty minutes in silent prayer and ritual before returning to the car.

With the rituals at Mohenjo-Daro complete, the journey led by Silver, guiding the group with precise directions. Despite the uncertainty of their destination, all the vehicles followed Silver's lead. After a lengthy drive, they finally arrived at the bank of the Indus-Sindhu-Sindhu River. There, Silver pointed towards a boat at a river bank.

As they boarded the boat, they noticed the fishermen with oars in hand, their sweat-soaked attire evoking images of the ancient inhabitants of the Indus-Sindhu-Sindhu Valley. The atmosphere was filled with a sense of history and culture.

From their vantage point on the boat, they could admire the majestic Lansdowne Bridge with its graceful arches on one side. On the other side, the island shrine of Zinda Pir Khwaja Khizr stood, adding to the mystical ambiance of the journey.

The place they arrived at was Sadh Belo, a name that always felt like an ancient incantation, a wave on water, a ripple caressing the smooth surface of the Indus-Sindhu-Sindhu. Sadh Belo is located in Sukkur, where Silver once lived and frequently visited, as everyone with him noticed. Sukkur is in Sindh, a region named after the Sanskrit word for "river" or "ocean," fitting for an area nurtured by the Indus-Sindhu-Sindhu River throughout history and located by the coast. The river's course has changed several times and throughout history, it has taken on many identities.

After paying his offerings to the various deities and old Samadhi of the Rishi, Silver moved with a quiet reverence, touching and offering flowers he had collected midway. Each flower seemed to carry a whisper of the journey, a tribute to the history and spirituality of the place. The procession that followed him was completely silent. The only sounds were the gentle rustling of leaves, the soft lapping of the Indus-Sindhu-Sindhu River against the boat, and the occasional call of a distant bird.

No one spoke; words felt unnecessary in the presence of such profound tranquility. Each person was absorbed in their thoughts, reflecting on the ancient and sacred atmosphere of Sadh Belo. They moved in unison, their footsteps echoing a shared sense of purpose and respect for the rituals Silver performed. The air was thick with the scent of incense and the faint aroma of the flowers, creating a serene and contemplative ambiance.

In the moment of collective silence, the air was thick with reverence and an almost palpable connection to the ancient past. Each individual felt the weight of history, culture, and spirituality pressing down on them, as if the very air around them was infused with the whispers of the ancients. They weren't just following Silver physically; their hearts and minds were in sync with his purpose, united in a silent tribute to the enduring traditions of the Indus-Sindhu-Sindhu Valley. The atmosphere was charged with a sense of impending revelation, as if the waters themselves held secrets waiting to be unveiled.

Silver, ever vigilant, directed their boat towards a secluded riverside. His gaze was intense, scanning the surroundings as if searching for a hidden presence. The boat glided silently through the water, reaching a point where they were almost invisible from the banks, enveloped by the river's embrace. Suddenly, the stillness was broken as several boats surfaced from the depths, emerging like ancient spirits called forth by some unseen force. These were not ordinary boats; they were intricately carved, resembling floating houses more than vessels, their exteriors adorned with ivory and mirror designs that caught the light, making them shimmer like ghostly apparitions.

A loud, resonant voice echoed across the water, catching everyone by surprise. The voice, deep and voluminous, seemed to shift from one boat to another, carried by the rhythm of a drumbeat that reverberated through the air. It was a call, a summons that demanded attention and respect. Abhimanyu, overwhelmed by the intensity of the moment, felt a question rise within him: "Who are these people?" He turned, his curiosity piqued, towards the NSA of Pakistan. But even the top intelligence leaders, seasoned and unflappable, found themselves at a loss, their expressions blank with uncertainty.

As the drumbeat grew louder, the people on Silver's boat men, women, and children—began to lie down, facing the direction of the mysterious boats. It was a gesture of submission, of reverence, as if they were in the presence of something divine. The drums continued to pound, their rhythm synchronizing with the heartbeat of the river, growing more intense as the boat drew nearer to the ancient vessels.

A chorus of voices erupted from the carved boats, crying out in unison, "Welcome, Baba! Welcome, Baba! We hail you! You are welcome! We have waited for you for so long!" The sound was overwhelming, a wave of emotion that washed over everyone present. Silver, the enigmatic figure they hailed as Baba, moved from boat to boat, his presence commanding and assured. He was no longer just a leader; he was a living symbol, a beacon of hope for a people long forgotten by the world.

The boats belonged to the Mohanas, an ancient community of Sindhi people, descendants of the Indus-Sindhu-Sindhu Valley civilization. For thousands of years, they had lived on these traditional wooden houseboats, carved with the symbols of their heritage, floating on the waters of Lake Manchar and along Pakistan's southern coast. The Mohanas were fishermen, their lives intertwined with the lake's bounty, and they had kept alive the ancient practices of their ancestors, using trained birds to catch fish, living in harmony with nature as they had for millennia.

But there was more to their story. The Mohanas were the last remnants of the people left behind in Mohenjo-Daro after the Rishis had departed. Earthquakes and other calamities had forced them to abandon their homes on land and take to the waters, where they had remained ever since, bound by a sacred vow. They had waited for the revival of the Saraswati River, believing that only when its waters flowed once more would they be free to return to the land. Over the centuries, they had converted to Islam, but they had never forgotten their origins, their connection to the ancient river, and the promise that had kept them on the water for so long.

Silver, addressing them in a commanding tone, assured the Mohanas that the time had come for their liberation. "The time of waiting is over," he declared. "The waters of Saraswati will flow again, and with them, your vow will be fulfilled. You will be free to leave these boats and return to the land of your ancestors."

The Mohanas erupted in applause, their joy and relief palpable. But as Silver spoke, the intelligence leaders those who had been watching from the shadows felt a sense of helplessness. This was beyond their realm of expertise, beyond the reach of their power. They were witnessing something ancient, something sacred, and they knew that they could do nothing but watch as Silver led the

Mohanas towards their long-awaited freedom.

Then the car swiftly moved back to Karachi Airport. A special plane waited to fly them to Bangalore. The transition from the ancient ruins of Mohenjo-Daro to the modern aircraft was a stark reminder of the journey through time they were undertaking.

The flight to Bangalore was filled with a quiet anticipation. Abhimanyu and Silver sat in reflective silence, each preparing for the next phase of their mission. The Indian PMO and their Pakistani counterparts were in constant communication, ensuring that every detail was meticulously planned.

Upon landing in Bangalore, they were greeted with the utmost respect and efficiency. Security was tight, and the reverence for the mission was palpable. From Bangalore, they would travel to Augusta Peeth, the final destination in this journey of revelations.

The convoy moved from Bangalore to Augusta Peeth, where the seers awaited with bated breath. The Prime Minister had personally ensured that every preparation was perfect. As they approached the ashram, the sense of historical significance grew stronger.

Silver, stepping onto the sacred grounds of Augusta Peeth, seemed to carry the weight of millennia with him. The head seer welcomed him with a respectful nod, acknowledging the gravity of the moment.

"Welcome back," the head seer said. "The belongings you seek are ready for you."

Silver nodded. "Thank you. This moment has been long in coming."

As they proceeded to the inner sanctum, the air was thick with anticipation. The sacred wooden box, untouched for thousands of years, lay before them. Abhimanyu and the seers stood back, allowing Silver the space and reverence he needed.

Silver approached the box, his hands trembling slightly as he touched its ancient, weathered surface. The air around him seemed to thrum with an unspoken anticipation. With a deep breath, he slowly opened the box, revealing the Saropa and headgear resting inside. These sacred artifacts, imbued with the wisdom and power of countless generations, connected him to his ancient past. As he lifted the items, tears streamed down his face, each drop a tribute to his ancestors and their enduring legacy.

The moment Silver's fingers brushed the Saropa and headgear; a radiant light began to emanate from them. Everyone around him instinctively took a step back, their eyes wide with astonishment. The light, warm and pulsating, enveloped Silver, merging seamlessly with his body. It was as if the energy of the artifacts was being transmitted directly into his very being. His entire form began to glow with a soft, pink hue, and an otherworldly aura surrounded him.

Silver's initial tremors gave way to a profound sense of strength and tranquility. He stood tall, his smile radiant, as an unexplained glow illuminated his face. The transformation was undeniable; the once-trembling man now exuded an aura of power and serenity. The crowd watched in awe, their hearts swelling with a mixture of surprise and reverence. They were witnessing the emergence of a true Sanatani, a living embodiment of their ancient spiritual heritage.

"I have been waiting for this moment for thousands of years," Silver whispered. "Now, I can finally complete my journey."

The seers and Abhimanyu watched in awe as Silver donned the headgear and draped the Saropa around him. The transformation was almost palpable, a merging of the ancient and the present.

The Prime Minister, observing the scene online, felt a deep sense of fulfillment. He massaged privately to Abhimanyu. "This is a momentous occasion. Ensure that every step is taken with the utmost care and respcct."

Abhimanyu responded, his heart full. "Yes, Sir. We will honor this moment and the legacy it represents."

As Silver prepared to reveal the long-hidden history, the anticipation grew. The journey from Mohenjo-Daro to Augusta Peeth had not just been a physical journey but a spiritual pilgrimage, connecting the threads of time and history. The revelations that were about to unfold would bridge the past and present, illuminating the path to the future.

CHAPTER ELEVEN

ECHOES OF ETERNITY: THE SAGA OF SANATAN

Silver took a chair in the middle of the room, his presence commanding immediate attention from the gathered scholars and enthusiasts. He cleared his throat and began,

"I have promised General Jaffar to reveal the history of thousands of years of Sanātana Dharma known to me."

Silver's eyes scanned the room, ensuring that his audience was fully engaged before he continued.

"This history spans what is known as the Ādi Kāl, a period that cannot be measured in conventional years.
Before delving into the issues one by one, I would like to provide an overview of the central theme of this entire discourse. The questions are many, but foremost are the circumstances in which the Saptarishis gathered to address the issue related to their survival along the banks of the mighty River Saraswati."

That day the sun rose over the ancient land of Sapta Sindhu-Indus, casting a golden hue over the once-mighty River Saraswati. As I stood on the banks, I could not help but feel the weight of the river's legacy. Born in the Himalayas, Saraswati had long been the lifeblood of the settlements that thrived along its banks. The diverse mix of people from various regions had lived in harmony with its flowing waters for generations, and I was one of them.

As the morning light danced on the surface of the river, the inhabitants gathered on the banks, offering prayers to Saraswati, the

Mother of Seven Rivers. We believed that she carried the waters of all the rivers to the sea, nurturing the land and its people. The sound of hymns filled the air, reverberating off the ancient stones that lined the riverbed — a ritual we had performed countless times.

But as the years passed, I watched with a heavy heart while a shadow fell over our once vibrant community. The waters of Saraswati began to dwindle, leaving behind a dry, cracked riverbed that bore little resemblance to its former glory. The river, once worshipped as a goddess, now lay silent and still, a mere memory of its past.

Despite the dwindling waters, the people of Sapta Sindhu-Indus, including myself, continued to revere Saraswati. We believed that her spirit still lingered in the land, watching over us and guiding our way. The sacred sites along the riverbanks remained places of pilgrimage, drawing devotees from far and wide. Our faith was unshaken by the changing tides of time.

As the day wore on, I observed a group of young children playing near the edge of the dried-up riverbed, their laughter echoing through the barren landscape. One of the elders, a wise woman named Mira, watched them with a mixture of sadness and hope in her eyes.

"The river may have dried up, but its spirit lives on in each of us,"

she whispered to the wind. Her words resonated deeply within me, a reminder that as long as we remembered Saraswati and honored her legacy, our way of life would endure.

And so the people of Sapta Sindhu-Indus, including myself, carried on, our faith unshaken by the changing tides of time. For us, the River Saraswati would always be central to our existence — a symbol of resilience and reverence in the face of adversity.

The gathering of the Saptarishis at Kalibangan was a momentous occasion, steeped in both reverence and concern for the dying River Saraswati. As the eight revered rishis sat in deep contemplation, the weight of their decision to migrate from the banks of the sacred river hung heavy in the air. Kashyapa Rishi, known for his wisdom and foresight, broke the somber silence with a resolute voice:

"This land has been our ancestral home since time immemorial. To abandon it without making an effort to revive the nadītamā Saraswati would be a grave sin that our future generations will not forgive. We must act to restore the river to its former glory."

Inspired by Kashyapa Rishi's words, the Saptarishis unanimously agreed to conduct a grand yajña to invoke the blessings of nature and its divine elements — Water, Sun, and Agni. The yajña would be a spectacle of power and devotion, a testament to our unwavering faith in the sacredness of the River Saraswati. I could feel the weight of this decision, knowing that the revival of the Saraswati was not just a physical endeavor but a spiritual renaissance requiring meticulous planning and divine guidance.

As the Saptarishis formed a solemn circle, their minds focused on the monumental task ahead, Bharadvāja Rishi spoke with authority:

"We must choose the key functionary with the utmost care. This individual will hold the life-cycle in his hands until the completion of his assigned task. He must be responsible for identifying a pristine location for the ceremony, a place where the energies of nature and the divine converge in perfect harmony.

He will extend invitations to Brahmins of all gotras and sub-gotras, calling upon them to join us in prayers for the revival of the Saraswati. Additionally, he will oversee the establishment of a supply center to support around thirty-thousand inhabitants for a year, ensure go-dhan for the people, and build a township specifically for this purpose.

It is my opinion that our chosen functionary should be a bachelor, one who can devote himself wholly to this sacred mission. Given the extraordinary powers we will bestow upon him, his first task should be to identify the places and layouts for the required infrastructure."

The other rishis nodded thoughtfully. Selecting such a person was no small feat. He would need to be not only logistically adept but also spiritually attuned, capable of leading with both vision and humility. When Rishi Vishvāmitra proposed my name, emphasizing my knowledge in Ayurveda and my dedication to our cause, I was both honored and humbled.

I, Dhananter, a Saraswat Brahmin youth of Vashisht-gotra from the village Wadhi, was summoned by Rishi Vashisht. I joined the meeting with a mix of excitement and humility, seeking blessings from all the rishis. As they raised their hands in āśīrvād, I felt the weight of their expectations.

Rishi Vashisht summarized the discussion and informed me of my probable selection as the Key Functionary, provided I consented. Overjoyed, I wholeheartedly agreed, with only one request: to have an assistant like Parmanand who could travel with me and assist in all my duties. None of the Saptarishis objected, and I was granted permission to engage Parmanand as I saw fit.

However, the Saptarishis' powers would be granted to me only if my master plan for the yajña and site identifications were accepted. Maghā Pūrṇimā was fixed for our next meeting, and the responsibility of all preparations now lay squarely on my shoulders.

Counsel of the Sages

Parmanand and I delved deeper into our preparations, seeking guidance from each of the Saptarishis:

Rishi Agastya spoke of the importance of balance and harmony in nature.

"The river flows when the elements are in harmony. Our yajña must restore this balance."

Rishi Atri emphasized purity in thoughts and actions.

"The purity of our intentions will guide the river back to its rightful course."

Rishi Bharadvāja shared insights on ancient rituals.

"The sacred chants and offerings must be precise and heartfelt, for the gods respond to sincere devotion."

Rishi Gautama instructed me on herbs that could purify and rejuvenate waters.

"Nature holds the key; use these with reverence and care."

Rishi Jamadagni warned of the perseverance required.

"The path will be arduous, but with steadfast determination, we will succeed."

Rishi Kashyapa reminded us of the unity of all life.

"The river's revival is for every creature that depends on it."

Finally, Rishi Vashisht and Rishi Vishvāmitra, often at opposite philosophical ends, spoke in rare unity:

"Our combined wisdom and efforts will ensure the success of this sacred task."

With their blessings, Parmanand and I began our preparations in earnest. The path ahead was arduous, but with the collective wisdom of the Saptarishis and unwavering support from Parmanand, I felt empowered to fulfill this divine mission. The revival of the Saraswati River was not merely a task but a calling I was honored to undertake.

We started our journey from Kalibangan at dawn, the sun rising behind us and casting long shadows across the dusty streets. Days turned into weeks, and weeks into months as we crossed vast plains and dense forests. At times wanderers shared their campfires and stories with us, but much of our pilgrimage was spent in solitude, feeling the cosmos align with our mission.

We often starved for days, our bodies growing frail. The sun scorched us by day, and cold nights chilled us to the bone. Injuries were constant companions, yet by divine grace our wounds healed quickly, as though the gods themselves watched over us. Disease and natural disasters struck without warning, but we endured.

Our trek took us through numerous villages and towns, each with its own culture and traditions. We witnessed grand celebrations, humble rituals, and the simple joys of daily life, enriching our understanding of the land's vibrant tapestry. The extremes of climate further tested us, but we persevered.

At last, we reached a serene, secluded spot surrounded by lush greenery and blessed with a gentle river. The air was thick with tranquility and sacredness. We knew we had found the rightful place for the yajña. Exhausted yet exhilarated, we began preparing the site with gratitude and reverence.

Arriving at Kukkutarma, I began to understand the mission's true essence: not just performing a yajña, but bringing healing and harmony to the world. We selected an island near Sakkur in the Sindhu-Indus and named it Sādhu Velā as our command headquarters.

As we walked northward along the Sindhu-Indus, we spoke with local leaders, explaining our mission's significance. Many pledged their support. With each step we gathered more resources and allies, weaving a network along the river.

One evening by the river's tranquil bend I told Parmanand,

"We have come so far, yet the true challenge is to maintain the harmony we seek to restore."

He replied,

"Our strength lies in unity. Every person we meet and every alliance we form is a thread in the tapestry of success."

We met scholars who shared ancient knowledge, healers with rare herbs, and artisans who crafted implements for the yajña. Each contribution, however small, was vital to the grand design.

Near the northern reaches of the Sindhu-Indus we encountered sages devoted to sacred texts. Recognizing our mission's import, they offered profound insights and joined our quest. Their guidance on precise rituals and incantations refined our plans.

Our search led us decisively to Kukkutarma — a city where the river formed a distinctive chicken-neck curve. Renowned as the diffusion center of domesticated black chickens and adjacent to Sakkur, where the Saraswati meets the Sindhu-Indus, it was ideal for our purpose.

The sacred rituals were mapped with utmost care. The confluence of Saraswati and Sindhu-Indus symbolized merging divine energies. Nearby Sahiwal-Harappa, known as Brahminābād ("Foot of Hari"), was chosen as the supply center for its historical and spiritual resonance and logistical convenience.

As I stood on the banks of the Sindhu-Indus, watching the sun set beyond the horizon, a deep sense of fulfillment washed over me. Our journey had been long and arduous, yet profoundly transformative. We faced unimaginable hardships and emerged stronger, our faith and resolve unshaken. Now we stood ready to fulfill our sacred duty, certain that the gods had blessed every step of our path.

CHAPTER TWELVE

BLUEPRINT OF THE SACRED: MAPPING THE YAJNA'S PATH

Both Parmanand and I were immensely pleased with our master plan. The support we received from the sages and the establishment of Brahminabad-Harappa as a supply center bolstered our confidence. With everything meticulously arranged, we turned our focus to the next crucial milestone: attending the meet on Magha Purnima at Kalibangan.

As we journeyed towards Kalibangan, a sense of accomplishment and hope accompanied us. The preparations were in place, the support of the community was strong, and the blessings of the Saptarishis and sages guided our path. The upcoming meet on Magha Purnima would be pivotal, bringing together the greatest minds and spiritual leaders to finalize and bless our plans. By the time Magha Purnima arrived, we had returned to the ashram with everything we needed.

Upon reaching Kalibangan, I could feel the anticipation in the air. The ancient city, rich in history and archaeological significance, was the perfect setting for such an important gathering. The Magha Purnima meet was a grand event, drawing sages, scholars, and devotees from far and wide. Parmanand and I presented our detailed plans to the assembled gathering, speaking of the sacred rituals, the chosen sites for the yajna and supply center, and the collective efforts that had brought us this far. The audience listened intently, their eyes reflecting the same hope and determination that we carried.

Our master plan carried the design legacy of Kukkutarma–Mohenjo-Daro's Citadel, reflecting its importance both religiously and culturally. The Citadel, positioned prominently on a mound, included several exceptionally well-built independent residences and structures for saints, such as a notable hall, which would serve as a space of religious significance. It served as the focal point for religious activities, particularly the yajna, a ritual offering to the Gods—Agni (Fire), Saraswati (Water), and the Sun.

The city of Kukkutarma–Mohenjo-Daro, located a yojan away from the Sindhu-Indus River, would be protected by artificial barriers. The city was laid out with remarkable regularity into approximately a dozen blocks, or "islands," from north to south and from east to west, subdivided by straight or doglegged lanes.

The central block on the western side was artificially built up to a dominating height of half a Rajju (20 to 40 feet), using mud and mud bricks, fortified by square towers of baked brick. Buildings on the summit included an Elaborate Bath or Tank surrounded by a veranda, likely used for ritual purification; a Large Residential Structure for priests and important figures; a massive Granary for storing food supplies; and two Aisled Halls of Assembly used for gatherings and ceremonies.

The Citadel was evidently the religious and ceremonial headquarters of the site. It was central to the religious life of Kukkutarma–Mohenjo-Daro. The yajna ritual was a significant part of religious practices, performed on a specially designed platform with a circular fire pit at its center, with seating for sixteen participants, each with a specific role.

This Rajju-tall citadel represented a centralized form of authority among the inhabitants. It symbolized not just religious and ceremonial leadership but also the organized social structure and advanced urban planning. The Citadel was more than a religious center — it was a hub of community life.

The upper level of Kukkutarma–Mohenjo-Daro was dedicated to spiritual and religious activities. Central to this was the yajna, the sacred offering to Agni, Saraswati, and the Sun.

On the lower level, the city's infrastructure was meticulously planned to support a thriving urban community. Residences were built around central courtyards, facilitating communal living. These spaces encouraged social interaction and religious gathering. Granaries stored grain to ensure a steady food supply. Cow herds were integral, providing dairy for sustenance and ritual offerings. Wells were placed strategically across the city, and dedicated personal wells were assigned to various clans and gotras, preserving the purity required by tradition.

The yajna platform, two dhanushas deep and one dhanusha wide, was positioned prominently, slightly elevated above the approach stairway to emphasize its spiritual prominence. Sixteen participants had specific roles: four Speakers offered prayers; four Wood Placers ensured steady fire; four Ghee Pourers made offerings; and four Scribes recorded the rituals. Presiding over the ceremony was the Chief Priest, who corrected pronunciations and rectified any ritual errors.

The second part of our plan focused on Brahminabad-Harappa, designed with a grid-like layout similar to Kukkutarma–Mohenjo-Daro. It was divided into sectors for residential, religious, and administrative functions.

Though 300 krosha (about 643 km) away, Brahminabad-Harappa was directly connected to the yajna at Kukkutarma–Mohenjo-Daro. The latter was a one-time sacred ritual site; the former, a permanent supply and logistical center. Its location on the Ravi River enabled efficient transport via waterways.

Residential areas in Brahminabad-Harappa were planned with standardized baked bricks and grid patterns, allowing for drainage and hygiene. Many homes featured private wells and bathrooms. Large granaries, near the river and agricultural fields, highlighted its role in supporting the yajna city.

Brahminabad's citadel, an elevated zone, housed key public and religious buildings. It became the center of governance and spiritual assembly. Its elevation protected it from floods and invaders.

As Parmanand and I unveiled our master plan, the assembly of maharishis and sages was silent in focused attention. Every detail was meticulously thought out — from sacred locations to urban layout — and our reverence for ancient traditions permeated our presentation. We spoke not only of logistics but of reviving Saraswati, of rebuilding sanctuaries, and of uniting past and future.

After deep and insightful deliberation, their respect for our mission became evident. The sages unanimously endorsed our plan. It was a moment of immense honor, validating both our work and the vision we shared.

Then came a decision that would forever change the course of our journey.

The maharishis resolved to bestow upon me the extraordinary powers of the Saptarishis. This divine authority was entrusted to me so that I might oversee and execute the plan to revive the sacred River Saraswati. The magnitude of this honor was overwhelming. Their trust affirmed not just belief in our vision, but belief in me.

As the responsibility settled on my shoulders, I felt a surge of gratitude and resolve. I began searching for a spiritually significant occasion on which to formally accept these powers — a moment that would mark a new chapter in our sacred mission.

Joy surged within me. Soon, I would receive the powers of those who had long guarded the cosmic balance, the seers of the beginning of time. The realization that I was stepping into their lineage filled me with both reverence and awe. I stood at the threshold of something far greater than myself — a mission not just for our people, but for the very soul of creation.

CHAPTER THIRTEEN

<u>THE ETERNAL TORCHBEARER: SANATANI'S JOURNEY BEGINS</u>

In the serene stillness of the ancient forest, where the sun cast its golden rays through the dense canopy, I sat amidst the sacred grove, where the Saptarishees convened. The air was thick with the scent of blooming jasmine, the symphony of nature providing a soothing backdrop. It was here, in this divine setting, that my transformation began—a transformation that would redefine my very existence.

The Saptarishees, the revered sages of the age, surrounded me, their eyes closed in deep meditation. The energy in the grove was palpable, charged with an ancient power that transcended time. As I knelt before them, I felt the weight of their collective wisdom pressing down upon me, a burden and a blessing in equal measure.

A vibrant fire was lit before me, its flames dancing and crackling as the ancient hymns filled the air. The Rishis sat behind me, their voices resonating in unison, a powerful chorus that invoked the sacred verses. I could feel the heat of the fire on my face, but today, the flames seemed different—more intense, more alive. The fire was not just burning; it was reaching, striving toward the heavens, its vibrant colors shifting and flickering as if infused with a deeper purpose.

As I knelt before this sacred fire, an undefined energy surged through me. It was as though the very essence of the hymns was entering my being, transforming me from within. The Rishis chanted with a solemn reverence, their voices carrying the weight of creation itself, as if they were giving birth to something new—something sacred.

I felt a profound calm settle over me, a freshness that sharpened my focus on the mission that lay ahead. Yet, as the flames licked higher, I began to notice something more. My body was changing, responding to the ancient words that filled the air. It was as if I was being remade, each hymn shaping me into something stronger, something more resilient.

As the chants grew louder, I started to grasp the gravity of their words. They spoke of life and death, of powers that would now reside within me. The realization came slowly, but it hit me with the force of a revelation—I was to carry life and death in my hands. The responsibility was immense, yet it felt as if I was born for this very purpose.

Then, Rishi Vishvakarma, the divine architect, stepped forward and recited specific hymns dedicated to the Sun. His voice was firm, yet filled with a gentle power that resonated deep within me. As he spoke, I felt a warmth spread across my body, not from the fire, but from within me. He granted me a boon, one that would forever alter my existence.

"With the first ray of the Sun," he intoned, "any injury, cut, or bruise on your body shall vanish, as if it had never been. This gift will remain with you always. No matter where you are, no matter what happens, your body will be renewed with the dawn, as fresh as the next day."

The words echoed in my mind, and I could feel the truth of them settling into my very bones. The fire before me roared higher, as if acknowledging the transformation that was taking place. I knew then that I was no longer just Dhananter. I was becoming Sanatani - a being reborn in the sacred flames, entrusted with powers that spanned life and death, bound by the eternal cycle of the Sun.

As the hymns reached their crescendo, I felt the last remnants of my old self slip away. In their place was a new purpose, a new identity, forged in the fire and blessed by the Sun. I knew that whatever lay ahead, I would face it with the strength and resilience granted to me this day. The fire, the hymns, and the blessings of the Rishis had marked the beginning of my eternal mission.

When the Saptarishees opened their eyes, it was Rishi Kashyapa who first spoke, his voice calm yet resonant, carrying the weight of timeless knowledge. "Dhananter," he began, addressing me by the name I had carried all my life, "the time has come for you to shed your old identity. From this moment forward, you shall be known as Sanatani."

The name Sanatani echoed through the grove, a symbol of my new identity and the timeless nature of the mission I was to undertake. With the utterance of this name, I felt a profound change within me. The powers granted to me were immense control over life and rebirth, the ability to oversee all religious events at Kukkutarma-Mohenjo-Daro, and the responsibility to ensure that spiritual practices remained pure and in alignment with the divine order.

But these powers came with a heavy responsibility, one that required a deep understanding of self-control. The Saptarishees emphasized this as they continued to speak. Rishi Kashyap's words resonated with me: "It is through self-control that one achieves the highest state of being. Our powers, though divine, demand the discipline of the soul. For without self-control, power is but a fleeting shadow, dangerous and untamed."

As they spoke of the importance of mastering the mind, speech, and body, I realized the enormity of the task before me. The mind, as Rishi Vashisht explained, was the most formidable adversary. It was like a chariot without a driver, pulled in all directions by the horses of desire. To master it, I would need to discipline my thoughts, my emotions, and my very being.

The other Saptarishees added their wisdom to this teaching. Rishi Atri spoke of the 'two sets of five'—the Jnanendriyas, the sensory organs of perception, and the Karmendriyas, the organs of action. These were the tools through which the mind interacted with the world, and to control them was to achieve true freedom.

As I absorbed their teachings, I knew that the journey ahead would be arduous. The challenge of mastering the mind was immense, but it was the path to true liberation. I felt a renewed sense of purpose, a determination to rise to this challenge, knowing that my journey was not just about acquiring power, but about attaining self-mastery and harmony with the divine.

With each passing day, under the guidance of the Saptarishees, I inched closer to mastering the Manomayakosha—the mind and its desires. Through meditation, self-discipline, and the wisdom imparted by the seers, I began to transform the turbulent force of my mind into a vessel of peace and enlightenment, guiding me toward my ultimate destiny.

Yet, as I walked this path, the memories of Dhananter began to fade, leaving behind only the essence of my Brahmanical lineage and the name of my village. The rest was erased, replaced by the weight of my new identity as Sanatani and the mission that lay before me.

A pivotal aspect of this mission was the revival of the River Saraswati. It was believed that at the end of the grand yajna, when the Saraswati would begin to flow again, I could decide the course of my life's journey. Parmanand, though a close associate, was not given any specific powers. He was placed under my guardianship, serving as a diligent supporter in my overarching mission.

As Sanatani, I had become the living embodiment of the continuity and preservation of ancient knowledge, entrusted with a responsibility that spanned millennia. The legacies of Kukkutarma—Mohenjo-Daro—and Brahminabad—Harappa, with their unparalleled achievements in urban planning, advanced engineering, and meticulous social organization, now rested in my hands. These great civilizations, which had once been the pride of humanity, held within them not just material progress but profound spiritual and cultural wisdom. Through my guidance, their essence would endure, shaping future generations and leaving an indelible mark on the course of civilizations yet to come.

With this surge of determination, I fully grasped the magnitude of my task. The expectations placed upon me were immense, yet I felt the collective strength of all those who had come before me and stood beside me. The weight of history pressed upon my shoulders, but it also empowered me. I knew that my actions would ensure the purity of the spiritual practices birthed in the sacred cities of Kukkutarma—Mohenjo-Daro—and Brahminabad—Harappa. Under my stewardship, the timeless wisdom of the Saptarishees would continue to guide humanity, offering a beacon of knowledge and enlightenment amidst the changing tides of time.

As the golden hues of sunset bathed the sacred grove in a warm glow, I set forth on this sacred journey. My heart swelled with a deep sense of purpose, for I carried with me not just the knowledge of the ancients but the indomitable spirit that now resided within me as Sanatani. This journey would be more than a mere personal endeavor; it was a testament to the enduring wisdom of the Saptarishees and the divine mission they had entrusted to me. Their spirit, which had shaped the cosmos and guided humanity for eons, now pulsed through me, infusing my every step with purpose and resolve. And so, I embarked upon this path, knowing that I was not alone but carried within me the strength of those who had shaped the universe itself.

CHAPTER FOURTEEN

THE SACRED PREPARATIONS

With the final approval in hand, we returned to Brahminabad-Harappa, to begin the preparations in earnest. The yajna was set to take place at the confluence of the Saraswati and Sindhu-Indus was at a distance of a thousand Kos, that site too now bustling with activity as people from various regions gathered to contribute to the sacred mission. Massive construction activities began simultaneously in Brahminabad-Harappa and Kukkutarma-Mohenjo-Daro. Time was short, but the enthusiasm of the common people made the impossible possible. They joined the movement wholeheartedly, and their collective effort allowed us to rapidly construct the necessary infrastructure and supportive measures.

At Brahminabad-Harappa, which was designated as the supply center, large granaries were built to store food for the supply to the yajna place. People from all across the region began pouring their grains into these granaries, and before we knew it, the granaries were filled to capacity. The speed at which everything came together was nothing short of miraculous. Boats were prepared to transport the grain to Kukkutarma-Mohenjo-Daro, where a magnificent township was taking shape. The citadel was under construction, and everything was falling into place as if guided by divine hands.

Parmanand worked tirelessly, shuttling between Brahminabad-Harappa and Kukkutarma-Mohenjo-Daro. His dedication was evident in every detail, particularly in his innovative idea to place

Kund-water tank directly below the administrative room of the Principal of the Yajna, Rishi Vashisht. The bath was accessible by independent stairs, allowing Rishi Vashisht and Rishis of the day to take a ritual bath before leaving for the hymns at the yajna—a symbolic gesture that linked purity with divine leadership.

As the day of the yajna approached, the atmosphere became charged with a sense of sacred purpose. The rituals were conducted with meticulous precision and deep devotion. The confluence site, now the focal point of spiritual energy, resonated with the chants that invoked the blessings of the gods. Returning to Brahminabad-Harappa, the preparations intensified. The site near Sahiwal Brahminabad-Harappa became a hive of activity, with resources and volunteers streaming in from every direction. The community united, driven by a shared hope for the revival of the Saraswati.

Brahminabad-Harappa was the first to be fully prepared, its granaries filled to the brim with grains contributed by people from far and wide. Boats stood ready to transport these supplies to Kukkutarma-Mohenjo-Daro. The transformation of Kukkutarma-Mohenjo-Daro was extraordinary. The town gleamed like a jewel, its infrastructure now complete. Houses were ready, wells were operational, and the citadel stood tall. The Yajna Platform, a structure of rich construction, provided a vantage point from which the Rishis could overlook the Sindhu-Indus River on the eastern side.

The township of Kukkutarma-Mohenjo-Daro, constructed in a single monumental effort, was a testament to the meticulous planning and coordination of thousands of skilled laborers. Their dedication had created a magnificent infrastructure for a grand event. The inhabitants of Kukkutarma-Mohenjo-Daro, familiar with the challenges of water management, had designed sophisticated drainage systems and water management techniques—an ingenious response to the constant struggle for survival in a land where rivers had dried up.

Kukkutarma-Mohenjo-Daro, the City of Cockerel—was more than just a settlement; it was a place of profound significance. The city's infrastructure had been designed to accommodate thousands for this sacred event, a testament to the spiritual devotion and organizational capabilities of its inhabitants. The prayers recited here would be remembered for generations, transmitted as stuti, the sacred hymns. Srutis means "that which is heard." These texts are considered the most sacred and eternal. Srutis texts are believed to be divine revelations, holding absolute and unquestionable truth.

"The city of Kukkutarma-Mohenjo-Daro was one of the largest settlements of the Saraswati Sindhu Valley under my command, it became more than just a city—it became a symbol of what human ingenuity and organization could achieve."

"The city was laid out in a grid pattern, with streets running north-south and east-west, creating a well-organized urban plan. The streets were wide, paved, and often included covered drains to manage the waste—a sanitary marvel for its time. Each block was carefully planned with residential and two story buildings, ensuring a seamless flow of daily life."Further, "The residential areas were just as impressive. Houses were made of baked bricks, and many had multiple stories. They were equipped with their own wells and bathrooms, connecting to the city have advanced drainage system. Each house, no matter how humble, reflected a standard of living that was remarkably high for its time." "Imagine walking down those streets, seeing the bustling markets, the artisans at work, the children playing. It was a vibrant, living city."

"At the heart of Kukkutarma-Mohenjo-Daro was the Kund-Great Bath, a water tank that served as a place for ritual purification. This was created on the exclusive advice of Parmanand. This structure alone speaks volumes about the importance of cleanliness and religious practices in our daily lives. The water was supplied from the nearby Sindu-Indus River and stored in the brick made wells standing tall at various places of the townships and outflow of water channeled through sophisticated brick-lined drains."

"And then there was the granary," "a massive storage facility that ensured the city's food security. The granary was strategically placed near the river, facilitating easy transport of grain by boat.

Its design included air ducts for ventilation, preventing spoilage and ensuring that the city never faced famine."

As the day of the yajna drew near, the land buzzed with a vibrant energy, a tangible excitement that pulsed through the air. The grand yajna was approaching, and everyone involved felt the weight and significance of the event. At the heart of these preparations was Rishi Vashisht, the most jubilant and respected of all. As the principal orchestrator and Purohit of the yajna, his role was pivotal.

In the quiet of the ashrams, the Rishis gathered, clad in their simple robes, deep in meditation. Their minds were focused on the monumental task ahead, their bodies cleansed through fasting, their spirits aligned with the divine. Hours were spent in silent contemplation, the ancient mantras whispered in rhythmic cadences, preparing their souls for the sacred duty. The preparations for the Suktas, the hymns meant to invoke divine blessings, reached their peak.

The Rishis, accompanied by their loyal gotra followers, meticulously practiced the Suktas. The melodies, passed down through generations, were intoned with care, each note and syllable resonating with ancient power. They knew that at the break of dawn, during the revered Usha-Dawn vela, their voices would rise in unison to greet the first rays of the Sun, invoking the blessings needed for the revival of the Saraswati River.

Brahmins from all over the land prepared with equal fervor. Driven by faith and devotion, they journeyed to the sacred site, their hearts filled with reverence and their minds focused on the divine purpose. They arrived in throngs, each one carrying the sacred texts that held the prayers of their ancestors.

Parmanand and I oversaw every aspect, ensuring that the rituals were carried out with the utmost reverence. The sacred texts were studied with care, and the necessary herbs and offerings were gathered. The atmosphere thrummed with anticipation as the confluence of the Saraswati and Sindhu was prepared to receive the divine energies.

The yajna site was a sight to behold. Sacred spaces were meticulously cleansed and sanctified. The ground was adorned with intricate patterns drawn from rice flour and turmeric, symbols of prosperity and purity. Flowers of every hue decorated the space, their fragrance mingling with the scent of incense, creating an atmosphere of peace and sanctity.

On the auspicious day of the yajna, the site was filled with devotees, sages, and scholars. The air resonated with the sound of sacred chants and the fragrance of burning incense. Standing at the forefront, I led the rituals with unwavering devotion. My heart was filled with a deep sense of responsibility and a fervent prayer for the success of our mission.

Rishi Vashisht's unique position as the principal Purohit was crucial. From his room, a place of both tranquility and strategic importance, he could oversee all activities at the citadel level. A set of stairs from his quarters led down to the sacred bath, allowing him to perform his purification rituals with ease. Another staircase ascended directly to the yajna platform, symbolizing his connection between the earthly and the divine. Everything was under his watchful eye, every detail meticulously monitored to ensure the success of the prayers to the river Saraswati.

The event was not just a ritual; it was a profound act of devotion, a call to the divine to restore what had been lost. And in that moment, as the first light of the new day bathed the earth, there was a sense of renewal, a promise of divine intervention that would bring the sacred river back to life. We knew that the true test lay ahead, but for now, we allowed ourselves a moment of quiet satisfaction. The preparations were perfect, the prayers sincere, and the faith unshakable. The rest was in the hands of the divine.

The sunset today was unusually bright, with a deep orange hue, as if the Sun God himself was sending blessings for the gathering that will take place tomorrow. It's as if the Sun was anticipating the prayers that will be offered to the deities, prayers that will continue until the long-awaited arrival of the Saraswati River. Once the Saraswati flows again, the yajna will conclude, and from that moment on, the Sun God will oversee everything.

Through the vibrant sunset, it felt as though a cosmic message was being delivered to us. Feeling moved, I called Parmanand to my side and expressed my gratitude for his tireless efforts by embracing him warmly. The sages who were present blessed us both, recognizing the significance of the moment. With their blessings, we felt ready for the grand event the next day.

CHAPTER FIFTEEN

<u>THE INAUGURAL SACRED HYMNS</u>

On the auspicious day of the yajna, the site was filled with devotees, sages, and scholars. The air resonated with the sound of sacred chants and the fragrance of burning incense. Standing at the forefront, I led the rituals with unwavering devotion. My heart was filled with a deep sense of responsibility and a fervent prayer for the success of our mission. As the first light of dawn began to pierce the horizon, the yajna place came alive. The sacred fire, Agni, was kindled with mantras and offerings, its flames leaping in anticipation. Around the fire, the Rishis took their places, each a pillar of spiritual strength and wisdom. The Brahmins stood in silent prayer, their eyes closed, their minds focused on the divine task ahead.

The moment the first ray of the Sun kissed the earth, a deep silence fell over the gathering. Then, as if on cue, the Rishis began their recitation. One by one, they stepped forward, their voices blending with the dawn chorus. The Suktas, ancient and powerful, flowed from their lips like a river of divine nectar, each note a prayer, each syllable a call to the divine. The melodies filled the air, a divine symphony that transcended the physical realm and touched the very essence of the cosmos. The Brahmins joined in, their voices rising in harmonious chorus, a collective plea for the revival of the sacred Saraswati. The prayers echoed across the land, resonating with the very soul of the earth.

As the notes of the Sukta faded into the morning air, a profound silence enveloped the gathering. The Rishis and Brahmins, their hearts full of reverence and hope, bowed in gratitude, their prayers offered to the heavens. The preparations were complete, the prayers recited. Now, with unwavering faith and devotion, they awaited the blessings of the divine for the revival of the sacred Saraswati.

As the day drew to a close and the first rays of twilight began to fade, the sacred lands of Kukkutarma-Mohenjo-Daro were bathed in the golden glow of the setting sun. The Brahmins, hailing from diverse Gotras, gathered at this ancient site, their voices rising in unison as they chanted hymns that would echo through the ages. These hymns, composed and recited with deep reverence, were not merely words but the very essence of a civilization deeply rooted in spirituality and devotion.

The Brahmins, as the composers of these hymns, were the custodians of ancient wisdom and knowledge. They passed down the sacred verses from generation to generation, ensuring that the spiritual and cultural ethos of their society remained intact. The hymns recited at Kukkutarma-Mohenjo-Daro were the collective effort of Brahmins from various Gotras, who had inhabited the banks of the sacred Saraswati River for centuries. Often referred to as Rishis, these Brahmins were the seers and priests who chanted the hymns during the yajna, drawing from the rich tapestry of Saraswat Brahmin inhabitants along the river belt.

As they chanted, their voices rose in unison, carrying the essence of a civilization that revered the gods, honored their ancestors, and sought divine blessings for the revival of the sacred Saraswati River. The chants of the Brahmins echoed through the ancient ruins, weaving a tapestry of spirituality, culture, and devotion that bound them to their roots and their gods.

Rishi Vashisht was a centered man, his calm demeanor and profound wisdom making him the ideal leader for such an important event. His mind was solely focused on one goal: to please the river goddess Saraswati and pray for her to flow again as she had for millions of years. His pride in his heritage was evident, especially in his acknowledgment of Sanatani, who belonged to his own gotra, Vashisht. This connection added a personal dimension to his dedication and commitment.

Rishi Vashisht looked at me intently and instructed me to address the gathering, providing guidance and plans for the smooth operation of the yajna. I called Parmanand to stand by my side, ready to assist me in case I missed any important details or considerations for the entire duration of the yajna.

As I stepped onto the platform and gazed at the massive gathering before me, tears welled up in my eyes. A deep sense of fulfillment washed over me—I knew that I had accomplished what I was trained for. The sight of such a sacred assembly gave me a strong feeling that our united efforts would indeed bring about the desired results.

With my hands folded in a gesture of pranam, I bowed to the entire gathering, acknowledging their presence and the significance of this moment. "The assembly at Kukkutarma-Mohenjo-Daro," I began, my voice resonating with the weight of history, "was a grand event that brought together people from all walks of life. The Brahmins, hailing from different Gotras, were specially invited from the banks of other prominent rivers. Their collective prayers and rituals were encapsulating their spiritual and cultural ethos."

I paused, allowing the significance of my words to sink in. "The Brahmins gathered to recite hymns, offering their prayers to the deities for the flowing of the River Saraswati. This was no ordinary opening event; it is a convergence of spiritual leaders, artisans, laborers, and common folk, all united in their devotion and purpose."

I could see the understanding dawning in the eyes of my listeners as I continued. "Among the thirty thousand people who had gathered, there were Brahmins, scholars, craftsmen, merchants, farmers, and laborers. Each played a crucial role in the grand ceremony. The Brahmins, known for their knowledge of Vedic hymns and rituals, were the spiritual leaders. They came from different regions, bringing with them their unique traditions and practices."

"The artisans and craftsmen," I explained, "were responsible for building the intricate structures and altars needed for the rituals. They constructed platforms, yajna vedi (sacrificial altars), and shelters for the attendees. The merchants and farmers provided the necessary supplies, including food, ghee, wood, and other ritualistic items."

"The yajna," I described with a sense of reverence, "was the central part of the ceremonies at Kukkutarma-Mohenjo-Daro. At the heart of the platform was a round area designated for lighting the sacred fire. Sixteen participants will be involved in the ritual: four speakers offering prayers, four placing wood in the fire, four pouring ghee, and four spectators documenting the offerings."

"The chief priest," I continued, "oversaw the entire ceremony, ensuring correct pronunciation of the mantras and rectifying any errors in the offerings as needed. The participants sat around the fire, reciting hymns and making offerings to the Gods of Fire (Agni), Water (Saraswati), and the Sun. The ritual aimed to purify and renew the community, seeking divine intervention for the revival of the Saraswati River."

As I finished my tale, the importance of the Brahmins' role in preserving and passing down their spiritual heritage was clear. Their hymns, rituals, and devotion had formed the bedrock of a civilization that revered the divine and sought to maintain a harmonious connection with the forces of nature. The echoes of their chants, carried on the winds of time, continued to inspire and guide the descendants of those ancient seers and scholars.

In the quiet that followed, I reflected on the profound impact of those days at Kukkutarma-Mohenjo-Daro. The land had come alive with a sacred energy, a tangible vibration that pulsed through the very air. As the days drew closer to the grand yajna, the preparations for the Suktas across the globe reached a fevered pitch. The ancient hymn, known to hold the power of divine invocation, was to be recited with melodious precision, filling the atmosphere with spiritual resonance.

The sacred land buzzed with vibrant energy, a tangible excitement that pulsed through the air. The preparations for the Suktas, the ancient hymns meant to invoke divine blessings, were in full swing. The grand yajna was approaching, and every soul involved felt the weight and significance of the event. At the heart of these preparations was Rishi Vashisht, the most jubilant and respected of all. As the principal orchestrator and named Purohit of the yajna, his role was pivotal.

My passion for the subject was evident as I leaned forward, recounting the rituals to be perform at Kukkutarma-Mohenjo-Daro. "The rituals are elaborate and meticulously planned. The Brahmins, who were experts in Vedic rituals, will lead the ceremonies with unwavering devotion. Each ritual, each chant, will be performed with the utmost precision, ensuring that the divine energies were invoked in the correct manner."

The engraved seals and clay tablets prepared and distributed among the Rishis will be a marvel of organization. Each Rishi knew his role in the yajna, with the prayer timings and days meticulously marked on the seals. This ensured that the vast congregation of Brahmins, scholars, and devotees could worship and revere the divine forces that governed their lives without confusion or delay.

Paid my sincere tributes to the Rishis gathered. The rishis, clad in their simple robes, they sat in deep meditation, their minds focused on the monumental task ahead. Their bodies were cleansed through fasting, their spirits aligned with the divine. Hours were spent in silent contemplation, the ancient mantras whispered in rhythmic cadences, preparing their souls for the sacred duty.

Each Rishi, accompanied by their loyal gotra followers, meticulously practiced the Sukta. The melodies, passed down through generations, were intoned with care, each note and syllable resonating with ancient power. They knew that at the break of dawn, during the revered Usha-Dawn vela, their voices would rise in unison to greet the first rays of the Sun, invoking the blessings needed for the revival of the Saraswati River.

All Brahmins prepared with equal fervor. Driven by faith and devotion, they journeyed to the sacred land, their hearts filled with reverence and their minds focused on the divine purpose. Clad in pristine white dhotis, they arrived in throngs, each one carrying the sacred texts that held the prayers of their ancestors.

The yajna place was a sight to behold. Sacred spaces were meticulously cleansed and sanctified. The ground was adorned with intricate patterns drawn from rice flour and turmeric, symbols of prosperity and purity. Flowers of every hue decorated the space, their fragrance mingling with the scent of incense, creating an atmosphere of peace and sanctity.

In the hush that followed, a sense of unity and purpose settled over the land. The sacred task was not just a ritual, but a profound act of devotion, a call to the divine to restore what had been lost. And in that moment, as the first light of the new day bathed the earth, there was a sense of renewal, a promise of divine intervention that would bring the sacred river back to life. Rishi Vashisht knew that the true test lay ahead, but for now, he allowed himself a moment of quiet satisfaction. The preparations were perfect, the prayers sincere, and the faith unshakable. The rest was in the hands of the divine.

The inauguration day of the yajna was coming to an end. From the following dawn, the regular preset prayers would be offered with the rising sun. As the sun dipped below the horizon, casting its warm glow over Kukkutarma-Mohenjo-Daro, the Brahmins stood united in their chants, invoking the gods and goddesses with a fervor that resonated through the ancient ruins. The relics of a religious character, though few in number, hinted at a profound spiritual connection that transcended time and space. These large structures, built by generations, bore witness to the enduring legacy of a spiritually driven society—a society whose purpose in constructing such monumental edifices was to connect with the divine through prayer, ritual, and reverence.

Rishi Gritsamada was chosen to be the first to offer his prayers the next day. All eyes were on him, filled with anticipation and reverence. He stood calm and well-prepared, fully aware of the immense responsibility he carried. Tomorrow, he would begin the sacred efforts to revive the Saraswati River, a task that had been envisioned for so long.

As everyone dispersed, there was a palpable sense of hope in the air. They were on the brink of witnessing something extraordinary—prayers that had only been imagined until now. The next day's offering by Rishi Gritsamada would not just be a ritual; it would mark the opening of new gates for civilization, a turning point that would resonate through time.

CHAPTER SIXTEEN

GRITSAMADA: THE FIRST VERSES

Gritsamada stood at the center of the courtyard, his presence commanding both respect and awe. The air was thick with the scent of sandalwood and jasmine, and the soft murmur of prayers echoed in the background. Disciples and followers from near and far had assembled eager to witness the recitation of the hymns. Gritsamada, the revered sage recited the sacred verses. This event was not just a ritual but a celebration of divine knowledge and cosmic order. The Composers were Gritsamada Shaunahotra (later Gritsamada Shaunaka), Somahuti Bhargava, Kurma Gritsamada. They recite the 43 Suktas and took many days. As Gritsamada began to chant, his voice resonated with a deep, melodic timbre. The hymns were attributed to various rishis, including Gritsamada himself, and are dedicated to the Agni, the fire god, and Indra, the king of gods. The sacred verses celebrate the divine forces and their benevolent presence in the world. "Agni, the divine priest, the god, the invoker, true, most brilliant," chanted Gritsamada, his voice carrying the weight of centuries-old wisdom. He invoked Agni, the fire deity, who is the mediator between the gods and humans. Agni was not just a physical flame but a symbol of purity, transformation, and divine knowledge. As the words flowed, the gathered devotees could almost feel the warmth and light of Agni's presence enveloping them. Rishi Gritsamada and other sages, extol various deities, primarily focusing on Agni and Indra. These hymns praise the divine attributes and roles of these gods, emphasizing their importance in Yagyas -sacrificial rituals and their power to bestow blessings, protection, and prosperity upon devotees. Sukta 1: Rishi Gritsamada praises Agni, the fire god, as the bright presence in Yagyas, protector of homes, fulfiller of wishes, and a source of wisdom and prosperity. Sukta 2: Agni is lauded for his vital role in Yagyas, likened to a cherished calf, praised for bringing wealth, children, and favorable conditions for dawn. Sukta 3: Agni is acknowledged for his pervasive presence in the sacrificial altar, inviting gods to Yagyas and bestowing wealth, intelligence, and bravery. Sukta 4: Rishi Somahuti Bhargava extols Agni's swift actions, nurturing flames, and protective qualities, ensuring prosperity and bravery for worshippers. Sukta 5: Agni is venerated as a vigilant protector, aware of offerings, central to Yagyas, and deserving of hymns and sacrifices for satisfying gods. Sukta 6: Agni is invoked to accept offerings, bestow wealth, bring rain, and protect devotees, highlighting his deep knowledge and divine messenger role. Sukta 7: Agni is described as a nurturer and protector, praised for bringing wealth, strength, and capability to devotees through his grace. Sukta 8: Agni, depicted as a fire horse, is praised for bringing rain, destroying enemies, and providing protection and prosperity to worshippers. Sukta 9: Agni is honored as a brilliant, strong, and nourishing deity, fulfilling duties, protecting devotees, and bestowing wealth and food. Sukta 10: Agni is venerated as a luminous, immortal figure, protecting all worlds, spreading fire, and providing shelter, wealth, and protection through Yagyas. Sukta 11: Dedicated to Indra, the hymn praises his bravery in defeating Vritra, requesting his favor and protection. Indra is celebrated for his role in the Yagya, his thunderbolt's power, and his ability to provide wealth and protection. Worshippers seek Indra's blessings, wealth, and brave offspring, promising to praise him in their Yagya. Sukta 12: Indra is revered for his strength and heroic deeds, such as killing Vritra, stabilizing the earth, and supporting the sky. He is praised as the giver of wealth, protector of devotees, and conqueror of enemies. Worshippers seek his acceptance of Soma and blessings for sustenance, promising to sing his praises. Sukta 13: This hymn honors Indra for orchestrating Soma's journey from rain to river. Indra is praised for his creation of the world, protection of vegetation, and destruction of demons. Worshippers highlight his worthiness of praise, requesting divine donations, blessings of children, and consumption money. Sukta 14: The hymn calls for offering Soma to Indra, praising him for defeating various demons and fulfilling devotees' wishes. Indra's connection to the luxuries of sky, earth, and space is highlighted, and worshippers seek wealth and great children, promising to praise him in their Yagya. Sukta 15: Indra's powerful deeds and the influence of Soma are celebrated. Indra is praised for stabilizing the solar system, protecting sages, and ensuring safe river crossings. Worshippers seek his blessings, wealth, and children, promising to praise him in the Yagya. Sukta 16: Indra is honored for his strength, knowledge, and enemy-slaying capabilities. The hymn requests Indra to protect devotees, provide wealth, and fulfill their wishes. Worshippers promise to praise Indra with beautiful chants and seek his exclusive blessings. Sukta 17: Worshippers praise Indra for his joyous consumption of Soma and his role in defeating enemies and establishing cosmic order. They request wealth and fulfillment of desires, promising to praise Indra in their Yagya. Sukta 18: This hymn describes a sacred sacrifice performed at dawn, seeking to satisfy Indra in all three realms. Worshippers ask for Indra's companionship and blessings, promising continuous praise and hoping for victory in wars. Sukta 19: Indra is praised for consuming joyful offerings and using his thunderbolt to bring rain, obtain cows, and illuminate the sun. Worshippers seek strength, food, residence, and happiness, promising to praise Indra with their children. Sukta 20: Indra is likened to the creator of the world and praised for building a chariot and presenting food. The hymn celebrates Indra's readiness for penance, his role in defeating enemies, and creating earth and water. Worshippers request wealth and promise to praise Indra in their Yagya, seeking his blessings and protection. Sukta 21: Indra is celebrated for his invincibility and role as the conqueror of the world, wealth, and nature. The hymn praises Indra's victories, charity, ability to destroy enemies, and provision of rain and guidance. Worshippers seek Indra's protection, wealth, fame, and happiness, filling their days with joy. Sukta 22: Lord Indra is praised for his immense power and contributions to the Yagya. Indra's victories over evildoers, his strength from Soma, and his virtuous actions are highlighted. Worshippers acknowledge his knowledge of food and strength, asking for opulence and perfection. Sukta 23: Dedicated to Brahminspati (Brahaspati), this hymn praises his divine attributes, protection, and ability to destroy enemies and obstacles. Brahminspati is lauded for granting wealth, protecting devotees, and ensuring prosperity. Worshippers seek his blessings, promising to sing his praises in the Yagya. Sukta 24: Rishi Gritsamada Bhargava and Shonak praise Brahmanaspati (Brihaspati) for his wisdom, heroic deeds, and ability to remove obstacles. Brahmanaspati is acknowledged for bringing rain, revealing the sun, and ensuring fertility. Worshippers seek wealth, protection, and happiness through his blessings. Sukta 25: Rishi Gritsamada Bhargava and Shonak invoke Brahmanaspati for divine favor and protection. The hymn emphasizes the power of the sacrificial priest and the benefits of Brahmanaspati favor. Worshippers seek victory, prosperity, and nourishment through Brahmanaspati blessings. Sukta 26: This hymn emphasizes the power and blessings bestowed upon those who praise Brahmanaspati. Worshippers are encouraged to confront enemies, maintain strength, and offer ghee-laden offerings for abundant wealth. Brahmanaspati protects from sin and enemies, guiding devotees on an easy path. Sukta 27: Rishi Kumro, Gritsamada, and Gritsamada offer hymns to the Adityas, focusing on Mitra, Varuna, Aryama, Bhaga, Daksha, and Ansha. They seek refuge, protection, and divine happiness from these deities. The Adityas are praised for their vigilance, non-violence, and ability to sustain the world. Sukta 28: Varuna is lauded for his glory, benevolence, and role in sustaining the world. Worshippers seek liberation from sins, protection from fears, and resources for a prosperous life. Varuna's ability to remove obstacles and ensure prosperity is emphasized. Sukta 29: Hymns are offered to the Vishwadevas, seeking protection and the removal of guilt. Worshippers appeal to Varuna for strength, happiness, and refuge from enemies. The hymn highlights the gods' unwavering friendship and the removal of sins and bondages. Sukta 30: Rishi Gritsamada, Bhargava, and Shonak direct hymns to Indra, praising his attributes and heroic deeds. Indra is celebrated for defeating Vritra, guiding rivers, and securing wealth. Worshippers seek Indra's protection, prosperity, and recognition as brave warriors, invoking Saraswati and the Maruts for additional support. Sukta 31: Rishi Gritsamada, Bhargava, and Shonak offer hymns to the Vishwadevas. The human body is likened to a chariot, and Varuna, Aditya, Rudra, and the Vasus are invoked for protection. The gods are asked to safeguard the chariot, representing human spirit and sustenance. Indra and the Maruts are also called upon for refuge, strength, and prosperity. The hymn highlights the unity of gods and their role in providing wealth and happiness through yajna. Sukta 32: Hymns are directed to Dhavaprithvi and Perbrati, invoking the protection and blessings of heaven and earth. Indra is asked to prevent enemies' illusions and to provide safety and joy. The night goddess is praised for her grace and ability to grant wealth and protection. Various divine figures, including Saraswati and Indrani, are invoked for comprehensive protection and blessings for prosperity and well-being. Sukta 33: The Rishis pray to Rudra, seeking blessings, protection, and prosperity. They ask for happiness, long life, and strength for their children. Rudra is praised for his wealth, power, and ability to remove sins and diseases. The hymn seeks Rudra's mercy, protection, and happiness, asking him to keep away sin and provide rain and healing. Sukta 34: Prayers are offered to the Maruts, seeking strength, protection, and prosperity. The Maruts are described as fierce and powerful, bringing rain and defeating enemies. They are praised for their generosity and strength, and the hymn requests their protection and support for yajna. The Maruts are also invoked to drive away enemies and provide wealth and strength to the devotees. Sukta 35: The deity Apanpat is invoked for sustenance, beauty, and divine favor. The hymn praises Apanpat role in increasing water and sustaining life. Apanpat is asked to provide wealth, protect devotees, and grant blessings for prosperity and well-being. The hymn also highlights the connection between water and life, seeking Apanpat continuous favor. Sukta 36: Indra and Madhava are invoked for divine presence, satisfaction, and strength. The hymn praises Indra's power and ability to bring rain and prosperity. The worshippers seek Indra's favor and protection, asking for blessings and strength for yajna. Indra is also asked to accept offerings and provide wealth and happiness to the devotees. Sukta 37: Prayers are directed to Dravingodha's for strength, fulfillment, and divine favor. The hymn praises Dravingodha's role in providing food and wealth through yajna. Worshippers seek protection from enemies and request blessings for prosperity and strength. Dravingodha's also invoked to ensure the success of yajna and provide continuous support. Sukta 38: Savita is invoked for light, wealth, and divine protection. The hymn praises Savita's role in sustaining life and providing light. Worshippers seek Savita's blessings for prosperity, protection, and fulfillment of desires. Savita is also asked to ensure the success of yajna and provide continuous support and guidance. Sukta 39: Ashwini Kumars are invoked for protection, strength, and divine favor. The hymn praises Ashwini Kumars' role in providing health and prosperity. Worshippers seek their blessings for protection from violence and old age, and for continuous support. Ashwini Kumars are also asked to ensure the success of yajna and provide wealth and strength to the devotees. Sukta 40: Somapushno and Aditi are invoked for protection, prosperity, and divine favor. The hymn praises their role in providing wealth and sustaining life. Worshippers seek their blessings for prosperity, protection, and well-being. Somapushno and Aditi are also asked to ensure the success of yajna and provide continuous support and blessings. Sukta 41: Indra, Vayu, Mitra, Varuna, and Parbharti are invoked for strength, prosperity, and divine favor. The hymn praises their role in sustaining life and providing wealth. Worshippers seek their blessings for prosperity, protection, and well-being. The deities are also asked to ensure the success of yajna and provide continuous support and guidance. Sukta 42: Kapijjal and Indra are invoked for guidance, protection, and welfare. The hymn praises their role in providing wisdom and protection. Worshippers seek their blessings for safety and prosperity, and ask for continuous support. Kapijjal and Indra are also asked to ensure the success of yajna and provide wealth and strength to the devotees. Sukta 43: The deity Kapinjal and Indra are honored, likening the natural harmony between the divine and the earthly to birds searching for sustenance. The hymn praises the divine words of Kapinjal and requests his blessings for virtue and welfare. Worshippers seek continuous support and promise to sing praises in the yajna along with their descendants. These hymns speak of the harmony between the divine and the earthly. Birds searching for sustenance utter melodious words like praisers, akin to the Som singers reciting the Gayatri chhanda and Trishtup chhanda. Kapinjal enchants listeners with his recitations of these divine words. The verses highlight the bond between the celestial and the mortal, celebrating it through the ages.

Gritsamada stood at the center of the courtyard, his presence commanding both respect and awe. The air was thick with the scent of sandalwood and jasmine, and the soft murmur of prayers echoed in the background. Disciples and followers from near and far had assembled eager to witness the recitation of the hymns. Gritsamada, the revered sage recited the sacred verses. This event was not just a ritual but a celebration of divine knowledge and cosmic order. The Composers were Gritsamada Shaunahotra (later Gritsamada Shaunaka), Somahuti Bhargava, Kurma Gritsamada. They recite the 43 Suktas and took many days.

As Gritsamada began to chant, his voice resonated with a deep, melodic timbre. The hymns were attributed to various rishis, including Gritsamada himself, and are dedicated to the Agni, the fire god, and Indra, the king of gods. The sacred verses celebrate the divine forces and their benevolent presence in the world.

"Agni, the divine priest, the god, the invoker, true, most brilliant," chanted Gritsamada, his voice carrying the weight of centuries-old wisdom. He invoked Agni, the fire deity, who is the mediator between the gods and humans. Agni was not just a physical flame but a symbol of purity, transformation, and divine knowledge. As the words flowed, the gathered devotees could almost feel the warmth and light of Agni's presence enveloping them.

Rishi Gritsamada and other sages, extol various deities, primarily focusing on Agni and Indra. These hymns praise the divine attributes and roles of these gods, emphasizing their importance in Yagyas -sacrificial rituals and their power to bestow blessings, protection, and prosperity upon devotees.The air was thick with the sacred fragrance of ghee and sandalwood, and the golden flames of Agni danced fervently at the heart of the Yagya. The chants of the Rishis echoed like thunder, their voices rising and falling like waves, each verse a bridge between earth and heaven.

It began with Agni — the radiant fire, the divine messenger. I saw how the priests, led by Rishi Gritsamada, invoked him with such reverence. Agni was more than a mere flame; he was life itself. He was called the protector of homes, the one who fulfilled wishes, and the source of wisdom and prosperity. His brilliance was like that of a cherished calf, a symbol of nourishment and wealth. I saw the devotees offer oblations, seeking his protection, strength, and rain. Agni's flames rose, fierce and swift, a reminder of his unstoppable power to destroy darkness and purify all.

But the hymns did not stop with Agni. Soon, the praises shifted to Indra, the mighty king of the gods. His presence was like a storm rolling across the heavens. The Rishis called upon him, reminding all of his legendary victories over the demon Vritra, how he stabilized the earth and poured rain from the skies. They spoke of his unyielding strength, his connection to Soma, the divine elixir that filled him with invincible might. I saw the people raise their voices, promising to praise him in every Yagya, seeking his blessings for wealth, strength, and children.

Indra was the hero of the cosmos, but he was not alone. Brahmanaspati (Brihaspati) was next, the divine priest, the guide who led souls on the path of truth. His wisdom was like a steady light in the darkness. The Rishis spoke of his ability to remove obstacles, bestow wealth, and protect the righteous. The sacred fire rose higher as they called for his blessings, asking for a prosperous life and a Yagya free of sin.

Then the Adityas were invoked — the cosmic guardians, led by Mitra, Varuna, and Bhaga. I watched as the hymns spoke of their vigilance, their ability to maintain cosmic order, and their mercy. Varuna, the great upholder of truth, was praised for his power to forgive sins and ensure the balance of creation. Rudra was invoked as well — fierce yet compassionate, a healer with the power to destroy sin and disease.

I saw the Maruts, the storm gods, thunder across the sky in the hymns. Their strength, their wild beauty, and their role in bringing rain were celebrated. Apanpat, the sustainer of life through water, was called upon, as were Indra and Madhava for divine strength. The people sang to Dravingodha for wealth and the success of the Yagyas.

Then came Savita, the divine inspirer, his light pouring down like a golden dawn. The Ashwini Kumars, the divine physicians, were invoked for health and protection. Somapushno and Aditi were praised as the guardians of life, bestowing prosperity upon all.

The hymns became a chorus of divine names — Indra, Vayu, Mitra, Varuna, Kapijjal, and Kapinjal. Each had their moment of glory in the sacred verses. The fire leapt higher with each name, and the air shimmered with divine presence. The worshippers sought guidance, protection, and wealth. Their voices promised praise, sacrifice, and unwavering devotion.

I watched it all, my heart swelling with awe. The Yagya was more than a ritual — it was a bridge between the mortal and the divine, a dance of devotion, and a testament to the eternal bond between humanity and the gods. The hymns, those ancient words, were not just sounds. They were life itself, a whisper of eternity amidst the crackling flames of Agni.

These hymns speak of the harmony between the divine and the earthly. Birds searching for sustenance utter melodious words like praisers, akin to the Som singers reciting the Gayatri chhanda and Trishtup chhanda. Kapinjal enchants listeners with his recitations of these divine words. The verses highlight the bond between the celestial and the mortal, celebrating it through the ages.

CHAPTER SEVENTEEN

<u>VISHWAMITRA'S DIVINE HYMNS</u>

The great sage Vishwamitra was about to recite the sacred verses .This was a momentous occasion as Vishwamitra was renowned not only for his profound wisdom but also for his journey from being a warrior king to an enlightened sage. His family and disciples deeply rooted in the Vedic traditions played a crucial role in preserving and propagating the sacred knowledge.

The courtyard of Vishwamitra was adorned with fresh flowers, sacred symbols, and the fragrance of incense wafting through the air. Disciples and devotees had gathered, their faces reflecting a blend of reverence and anticipation. The morning sun cast a gentle glow, illuminating the scene with a divine aura.

Vishwamitra stood at the center, his tall figure radiating an aura of calm authority. His followers were by his side, ready to join him in his recitation. The unity and devotion of the disciples were palpable, setting the tone for the sacred ritual. Speculation surrounded Vishwamitra role in the recitation, as it was conducted under the Yagya purohit Maharishi Vashisht, with whom Vishwamitra had a long history of enmity. Vishwamitra taken up as Composing after the conclusion of Rishi Gritsamada Shaunahotra, Somahuti Bhargava & Kurma Gritsamada. Vishwamitra was second in line and recite the 62 Suktas and took many days. .

As Vishwamitra began to chant, his voice was a harmonious blend of strength and serenity. The verses are primarily dedicated to Agni, Indra, and the Maruts, reflecting the multifaceted aspects of the divine. With each intonation, Vishwamitra voice seemed to bridge the earthly realm with the celestial.

"Agni, you who illumine the heavens, accept our offerings, and bestow upon us your blessings," he chanted. The hymns to Agni celebrated the fire god's role as the divine messenger, carrying the prayers and offerings of humans to the gods. Agni was invoked not only as a physical flame but as the embodiment of divine energy and transformation.

Shakti, with her serene and composed presence, joined her husband in the recitation. Her voice, clear and melodious, complemented Vishwamitra, creating a symphony of sacred sounds. Their children, well-versed in the Vedic hymns, followed suit, their young voices adding a touch of innocence and purity to the ritual.

The verses then turned to Indra, the king of gods, and the Maruts, the storm deities. "Indra, the mighty, the valorous, the slayer of Vritra, we invoke you with our prayers," intoned Vishwamitra. The hymns to Indra extolled his strength, bravery, and generosity. Indra, the wielder of the thunderbolt, was revered as the protector of the righteous and the destroyer of evil forces.

As the recitation progressed, the moment everyone had been waiting for arrived. Vishwamitra voice took on a deeper, more solemn tone as he began to chant the Gayatri Mantra, one of the most sacred and revered hymns in the Vedic tradition. The mantra, composed by Vishwamitra himself, is found in is a universal prayer for enlightenment and wisdom.

ॐ भूर् भुव: स्व:तत्सवितुर्वरेण्यंभर्गो देवस्य धीमहिधियो यो न: पुरचोदयात्।

"Om Bhur Bhuvaḥ Swaḥ, Tat Savitur Vareṇyaṃ, Bhargo Devasya Dhīmahi, Dhiyo Yo Naḥ Prachodayāt," chanted Vishwamitra, his voice resonating with divine energy. The Gayatri Mantra, dedicated to Savitar, the Sun deity, is a prayer for spiritual awakening and insight. It seeks to illuminate the mind and soul, guiding one towards the path of righteousness and truth.

The assembled devotees joined in the recitation with their eyes closed in deep concentration, repeated the mantra with utmost reverence. Their voices merging into a unified chant that echoed through the courtyard. The power of the mantra, combined with the collective devotion of the participants, created an atmosphere charged with spiritual energy. The simplicity and profundity of the Gayatri Mantra encapsulated the essence of the Vedic teachings, emphasizing the pursuit of knowledge, truth, and divine wisdom.

As the recitation of the Gayatri Mantra concluded, Vishwamitra offered a final prayer, seeking the blessings of the gods for peace, prosperity, and enlightenment. "May the divine light of Savitur illuminate our minds and hearts, guiding us towards eternal truth and wisdom," he prayed. The devotees, their hearts filled with a sense of spiritual fulfillment, bowed in reverence. The recitation especially the Gayatri Mantra had touched their souls, leaving them with a profound sense of connection to the divine.

Gather around, a Yajna where the ancient flames danced, and the heavens themselves seemed to listen. It was a grand spectacle, a divine gathering where the sacred fire, Agni, raised high, its brilliance touching the sky, and the air vibrated with the hymns of the Rishis. The gods themselves were invited to partake, and the blessings they bestowed were beyond measure.

In those early moments, it was Agni who stood at the heart of the Yajna. The priests, with reverent hands, kindled the sacred fire, and as the flames leapt upward, the hymns rang out, each word a prayer, each note a plea. They praised Agni, the radiant flame, the divine messenger, who carries our offerings to the gods. I saw the seven rivers stir with his presence, their waters swelling as if touched by his sacred glow. Agni was the father of the world, they chanted, a protector of all born from water, a warrior against darkness, and a source of radiant strength.

As the Yajna continued, Agni was called upon not just as a flame but as the divine Vaishvanara, the all-encompassing fire. The hymns praised him as a loving son, an immortal carrier of offerings who brought joy to the gods. His brilliance illuminated the earth and sky, his warmth a comfort, his light a guide. In his presence, even the fiercest of enemies seemed powerless. The priests called upon him to grant wealth, long life, and prosperity to those who honored him.

But it was not just Agni who was honored in that sacred gathering. Soon the hymns shifted, and the mighty Indra was invoked. I saw the priests raise their arms, their voices raising in fervor, calling upon the thunder-wielding god, the slayer of Vritra, the liberator of the rivers. Indra, they sang, was the lord of strength, a fierce warrior who shattered the darkness and brought forth the waters of life. He was the great protector, whose chariot roared across the sky, whose might none be able to withstand.

Soma, the sacred drink, was prepared for Indra, its divine essence stirring the god's strength. They sang of his triumphs, of how he shattered mountains; slew the demons, and bestowed wealth and victory upon his devotees. It was a sight to behold — the offerings of Soma, the rhythmic chants, and the rising flames — all seemed to merge into a single divine song, a melody that touched the heavens.

Then the rivers were honored, those sacred waters that nourish the earth. The priests sang of the Vipasha and Shutudri, their waters flowing freely because of Indra's might. In their praises, the rivers were more than waters; they were divine beings, their flow a symbol of grace and abundance. The Yajna celebrated them, for they were life-givers, sustaining the fields, filling the lakes, and purifying the land.

But this was not all. In the final chants, the Vishwadevas , the universal gods were invoked. Their presence seemed to fill the air with a sacred energy. The hymns called upon Mitra, the lord of contracts; Varuna, the guardian of cosmic law; Brihaspati, the divine priest; and the Ashvins, the twin healers. Usha, the radiant dawn, was praised as the bringer of light, and Pūṣā, the protector of travelers, was honored with gratitude.

I saw the fire's glow reflected on the faces of the priests, their eyes closed in devotion, their voices unwavering. The air was thick with the scent of ghee and sacred herbs, and the sky seemed to shimmer with a golden light. As the Yajna reached its crescendo, the flames rose higher, and the hymns grew louder, a powerful chorus of divine praise.

The gods were pleased, I tell you. The air felt lighter, the sky brighter, and the hearts of all who were present swelled with joy and reverence. The Yajna was not merely a ritual; it was a bridge between the mortal and the divine, a moment when heaven touched the earth.

Such was the Yajna I witnessed. A gathering of gods, a dance of flames, and a hymn of eternal devotion ,a moment that lives on in my soul, a tale I now share with you.

As the sun reached its zenith, casting a radiant glow over the plains, the sacred abode of Vishwamitra remained enveloped in a tranquil and divine atmosphere. The hymns had not only honored the ancient traditions but had also reinforced the eternal bond between the mortal and the divine. This bond, celebrated through the sacred verses, would continue to inspire and guide future generations on their spiritual journey.

The last day's Rishiver Vishwamitra recitation had concluded, but the echoes of the sacred chants lingered in the air, a reminder of the timeless wisdom enshrined and the eternal quest for enlightenment embodied in the Gayatri Mantra.

CHAPTER EIGHTEEN

<u>VAMADEVA'S SACRED RECITATION</u>

The dawn broke gently over casting a soft, golden hue across its well-planned streets and impressive structures in the area. The air was thick with anticipation as the people of Kukkutarma-Mohenjo-Daro gathered, their hearts and minds open to the divine words that were about to be spoken. At the highest point of the citadel, a platform had been prepared, adorned with garlands of marigold and fragrant incense.

A land where once the Saraswati River flowed with sacred fervor witnessing a day full of great spiritual significance, for the sage Vamadeva would recite the sacred hymns. Vamadeva, a sage renowned for his deep spiritual insight and devotion, would be joined by his Brahmanical family and followers in this divine recitation.

Vamadeva residence, a modest yet serene abode, was adorned with garlands of fresh flowers and sacred symbols. The scent of sandalwood and camphor filled the air, mingling with the faint murmurs of prayers. Devotees and disciples from far and wide had gathered eager to partake in the spiritual experience. The atmosphere was one of reverence and anticipation. Vamadeva stood at the center of the courtyard, his tall and lean figure exuding a sense of calm and wisdom.

As the first light of dawn broke over the horizon, the ashram of Vamadeva was enveloped in an aura of sanctity. The morning air was crisp and pure, carrying the scent of blooming lotuses and the sound of rustling leaves. Vamadeva, an embodiment of wisdom and devotion, sat at the head of the assembly. Raising his hands to the heavens, Vamadeva began with an invocation to the Saptarishees, the seven great sages who had entrusted the sacred knowledge to him. His voice, resonant and powerful, echoed across the citadel, blending harmoniously with the natural sounds of the Indus flowing nearby.

"O Saptarishees, guardians of eternal wisdom, Bless this moment, bless these people, as we embark on a journey of sacred recitation, May your divine presence guide us through." His eyes, deep and serene, reflected the wisdom of ages as he began the sacred chant.

"Agne, yasya samidham grnanno visvany aryah," Vamadeva intoned, his voice resonating with a mystical cadence that seemed to transcend the physical realm. The first Sukta praised Agni, the god of fire, who was the mediator between humans and gods. The flames of the sacred fire danced in harmony with his voice, as if responding to the invocation.

As Vamadeva began the recitation, his voice was deep and resonant, carrying the weight of ancient wisdom. The hymns were attributed to various seers. Vāmadeva himself is considered the principal seer of many of these hymns. The verses celebrate the deities Agni, Indra, the Ashvins, and other cosmic forces, highlighting the intricate relationships between the gods and the natural world.

"Agni, the divine priest, the god of fire, the invoker, true, most brilliant," intoned Vamadeva. The hymns dedicated to Agni emphasized his role as the intermediary between the gods and humans. Agni was not merely a physical flame but a symbol of divine knowledge, purification, and transformation. As Vamadeva voice echoed through the courtyard, the listeners could almost feel the warmth and presence of Agni enveloping them.

The sun was beginning to set over, casting a golden hue across the bustling streets and the majestic Sindhu-Indus River. The hymns then shifted to the praise of Indra, the mighty warrior and king of the gods. "Indra, the invincible, the mighty, the protector of the righteous," chanted Vamadeva. The verses extolled Indra's strength, valor, and his role as the vanquisher of Vritra, the demon of drought. Indra's might and generosity were celebrated, painting vivid images of cosmic battles and divine triumphs.

As the recitation progressed, the verses also honored the Ashvins, the twin gods of health and medicine. "Ashvins, the healers, the swift, the bringers of dawn," chanted Arundhati, her voice filled with devotion. The hymns to the Ashvins highlighted their benevolence, their miraculous healing powers, and their role in restoring balance and harmony.

As Vamadeva recited the Mantras, the connection to the Indus River became palpable. The sacred waters, flowing since time immemorial, seemed to respond to his words, their gentle ripples mirroring the rhythm of the hymns. The river, a lifeline for the people of Kukkutarma-Mohenjo-Daro, now served as a conduit for the divine wisdom being imparted. With each passing Sukta, the energy in the air grew more intense

These hymns reflect the profound spiritual insights of the Vedic sages, emphasizing the essential role of divine forces in ensuring the prosperity, protection, and well-being of humanity. The hymns celebrate the interconnectedness of the cosmic and human realms, where the deities play a central role in maintaining harmony and granting blessings to those who honor them through rituals and prayers.

The final Suktas reached a crescendo, a powerful invocation of cosmic forces and divine entities. The Mantra, a verse of profound significance, echoed across the citadel, leaving a lasting impression on all who heard it. The atmosphere in the courtyard was charged with spiritual energy. The rhythmic chants, the deep intonations, and the profound meanings of the verses created a transformative experience for all present.

Vamadeva descended from the platform, his mission fulfilled. The sacred knowledge had been imparted, and the divine connection between the people, the river, and the cosmos had been reaffirmed. The Kukkutarma-Mohenjo-Daro, with its rich history and deep spirituality, had once again become a beacon of divine wisdom. The recitation at the bank of the Indus was not just a moment in time but a timeless event, a merging of the past, present, and future. It was a reminder of the eternal truths that bind us all, the sacred wisdom that guides us, and the divine presence that watches over us. In the heart of Kukkutarma-Mohenjo-Daro, the echoes of Vamadeva pronouncement would resonate for generations to come, a testament to the enduring power of the Vedic hymns.

BHARDWAJA'S SACRED HYMNS

The city of Kukkutarma-Mohenjo-Daro, renowned for its grand citadel and intricate streets, once again became a center of spiritual and cultural convergence. People from far and wide gathered at the top of the citadel, where a platform adorned with vibrant flowers and aromatic incense awaited the day's sacred rituals. Below, the Sindhu-Indus River flowed serenely, its waters glistening under the morning sun, a timeless witness to the ancient ceremonies about to unfold.

Bharadwaja, the esteemed sage celebrated for his profound wisdom and mastery of Vedic knowledge, ascended the platform with a dignified calm. Dressed in simple yet elegant saffron robes, his presence exuded a tranquil authority. The assembled crowd, sensing the gravity of the occasion, fell into a hushed silence, their hearts and minds open to the sacred wisdom about to be shared.

Bharadwaja began with an invocation to the divine forces and the Saptarishees, seeking their blessings and guidance for the recitation. His voice, rich and resonant, carried through the air, intertwining with the sounds of the natural world.

"O divine forces, custodians of eternal knowledge, Bless this moment, bless these seekers,
As we embark on this journey of sacred hymns, May your divine presence guide us and enlighten our path."

Bharadwaja's recitation commenced each Sukta a hymn of deep reverence and each Mantra a verse of cosmic significance. The

75 Suktas, encompassing 765 Mantras, flowed from his lips with rhythmic precision and profound insight. The people listened intently, their spirits elevated by the sacred vibrations.

Deities addressed besides Indra and Agni include the Vishvadevas, Pushan, the Asvins, Ushas (Dawn), the Maruts, Dyaus and Prthivi (Heaven and Earth), Savitar, Brhaspati, and Soma-Rudra. The rivers mentioned in the sixth Mandala are the Sarasvati, Yavyavati, and Hariupiya. One of a sukta is entirely dedicated to Naditama Sarasvati.

The Hymn to Agni "O Agni, the divine fire, the purifier of realms,
You who illuminate the dark paths,
Accept our offerings, guide us with your light,
May your eternal flame dispel the shadows of ignorance."

The Praise of Indra "Indra, the mighty, the conqueror of chaos,
Wielder of the thunderbolt, protector of the righteous,
Grant us strength, bestow upon us your courage,
May your power shield us from harm and guide us to victory."

The Waters of Life "O waters, the essence of all that lives,
You who nurture and sustain the cosmos,
Flow through us with your purifying grace,
Bless us with your clarity and wisdom, as we seek your truth."

Bharadwaja recited the Mantras; the connection to the Sindhu-Indus River became palpable. The sacred waters, flowing since time immemorial, seemed to respond to his words, their gentle ripples harmonizing with the rhythm of the hymns. The river, a lifeline for the people, now served as a conduit for the divine wisdom being imparted.

The Depth of Wisdom With each passing Sukta, the depth of Bharadwaja's wisdom became more apparent. His voice carried the weight of ancient knowledge, each Mantra a key to understanding the cosmos and the divine forces at play. The 765th Mantra, a verse of profound significance, echoed across the citadel, leaving a lasting impression on all who heard it.

The Eternal Truth "In the eternal cycle of creation and dissolution, we find our purpose, our place, our path, through the wisdom of the ancients, we transcend, Becoming one with the cosmos, eternal and infinite."

In the concluding Suktas, Rishi Bharadwaja's hymns resound with the reverence of divine forces that bestow light, protection, and prosperity upon the world. His voice rises in praise of Usha, the radiant dawn, the divine light that dispels darkness and grants wealth. Usha is not just a luminous force but a liberator, freeing the cows that symbolize abundance and bestowing prosperity upon the worshippers. From the glow of dawn, Bharadwaja's hymns turn to the Maruts, the fierce storm gods, whose thunderous presence brings rain, fertility, and prosperity. Their protective might, harnessed in the winds and rain, is invoked for the welfare of all, ensuring the sustenance of life.

The hymns then honor Mitra and Varuna, the cosmic protectors who uphold the divine order. These twin guardians, vigilant and wise, maintain the balance of the universe, ensuring peace and prosperity. Indra and Varuna are celebrated as valiant warriors, bestower of wealth, and guardians of Yajnas, the sacred rituals that connect the earth with the heavens. Bharadwaja sings of Indra and Vishnu, the lords of Soma, whose divine strength not only expands the cosmos but also grants wealth and divine blessings to those who honor them. Even the heavens and earth are revered as the eternal shelter, the sources of abundance and protection for all beings.

The divine invocation then turns to Savitadev, the radiant deity who nurtures all creation, ensuring the growth and prosperity of life. Indra and Soma are exalted as fierce warriors who destroy enemies and shower wealth upon their devotees. Brihaspati, the divine priest and the first among gods, is praised for his wisdom and strength, which secure victory in battles and ensure the success of Yajnas. The hymns invoke Soma and Rudra, the bearers of strength and protectors, who grant happiness and safety to the worshippers. Finally, Bharadwaja's voice venerates the implements of war, acknowledging their power to secure victory, protect the righteous, and ensure the success of battles. Together, these hymns weave a sacred tapestry of divine protection, cosmic harmony, and prosperity, reflecting the Vedic vision of a world blessed and safeguarded by the gods.

As Bharadwaja concluded the recitation, a deep sense of peace and fulfillment settled over the crowd. The sun had begun its descent, and the first stars appeared in the evening sky, a reminder of the vast universe that lay beyond. The people dispersed, each carrying with them the sacred words that had been spoken, their hearts and minds forever transformed.

Bharadwaja descended from the platform, his mission fulfilled. The sacred had been imparted, and the divine connection between the people, the river, and the cosmos had been reaffirmed.

The recitation at the bank of the Indus was not just a moment in time but a timeless event, a merging of the past, present, and future. It was a reminder of the eternal truths that bind us all, the sacred wisdom that guides us, and the divine presence that watches over us. The echoes of Bharadwaja's pronouncement would resonate for generations to come, a testament to the enduring power of the Vedic hymns.

CHAPTER TWENTY

<u>VASHISHT'S PIOUS HYMNS</u>

The dharma city was once again the focal point of a significant spiritual event. The platform at the highest point of the citadel was decorated with elaborate floral arrangements and incense, creating an atmosphere of reverence and devotion. The people gathered in great numbers, drawn by the promise of divine intervention to revive the dying Saraswati River. The Sindhu-Indus River flowed nearby, its waters reflecting the hopes and prayers of the gathered crowd.

Vashisht, the revered sage known for his profound spiritual insight and mastery of Vedic knowledge, ascended the platform with a serene dignity. Dressed in simple yet dignified white robes, his presence commanded respect and awe. The crowd fell silent, their hearts and minds open to the sacred wisdom he was about to impart.

Vashisht, as the purohit and principal overseer of the yajna, stood at the heart of the sacred gathering. The air was thick with the scent of burning ghee and the sound of ancient mantras reverberated through the surroundings. Every person present, from the learned Rishis to the common folk, was engaged in a unified prayer to the mighty Saraswati, beseeching the river to rise and flow once more.

Today, however, was different. Vashisht, who had been guiding others in their devotions, was about to offer his own personal prayer. With a deep sense of reverence and responsibility, he stepped forward to the sacred fire. His mind was clear, his heart resolute. As he raised his hands to the heavens, silence fell over the assembly. The moment had come for Vashisht to invoke the ancient powers, calling upon the divine to breathe life back into the sacred river, the lifeline of their civilization.

The intensity of his prayer reflected the collective hope and desperation of the people. Every word he uttered was a plea for the rebirth of Saraswati, for her waters to once again nourish the land and sustain the souls who depended on her. Vashisht's voice, filled with both authority and humility, reached out across the realms, seeking the divine grace to fulfill the sacred task.

Vashisht began with an invocation to the divine forces, seeking their blessings and guidance for the recitation. His voice, rich and resonant, echoed through the air, intertwining with the natural sounds of the surroundings.

"O divine forces, guardians of the cosmos, Bless this moment, bless these seekers, as we seek to revive the sacred Saraswati, May your divine presence guide us and bless our endeavor."

Vashisht's recitation each Sukta a hymn of deep reverence and each Mantra a verse of cosmic significance. The 104 Suktas, encompassing 841 Mantras, flowed from his lips with rhythmic precision and profound insight. The people listened intently, their spirits elevated by the sacred vibrations, hoping for the revival of the Saraswati.

"O Saraswati, the river of wisdom and knowledge, you who flow with the essence of purity, Revive and nourish the land and its people, May your waters bring life and prosperity once more."

The connection to the Sindhu-Indus River and the dying Saraswati became even more profound as the recitation continued. The sacred waters of the Sindhu-Indus, flowing since time immemorial, seemed to respond to Vashisht's words, their gentle ripples harmonizing with the rhythm of the hymns. The people's prayers and hopes were carried by the Indus, seeking to reach the Saraswati and breathe new life into its fading waters.

This second last hymn, dedicated to the deity of Frogs (symbolizing rain), compares frogs to devoted worshipers who stay awake all year, praising Parjanya, the rain god. As the rains arrive, the frogs croak joyfully, likened to calves calling to their mothers. They gather near water, symbolizing the harmonious natural cycles. The hymn celebrates the frogs' role in bringing wealth, extending lifespan, and blessing the land with abundance during the rainy season.

Thefinal hymn fervently calls upon Indra, Soma, Agni, and the Maruts to destroy demons that thrive in darkness. These deities are invoked to eliminate the demonic forces that threaten the righteous. The hymn vividly describes the cosmic battle, urging the gods to use their might to subdue and eradicate these malevolent beings, ensuring the safety and prosperity of the devotees. It emphasizes the need for protection against falsehood and evil, calling for the complete destruction of the demons by Indra's thunderbolt, thereby safeguarding the worshipers and their righteous endeavors.

As Vashisht concluded the recitation, a deep sense of peace and fulfillment settled over the crowd. The sun had begun its descent, and the first stars appeared in the evening sky, a reminder of the vast universe that lay beyond. The people dispersed, each carrying with them the sacred words that had been spoken, their hearts and minds forever transformed.

Vashisht descended from the platform, his mission fulfilled. The sacred knowledge had been imparted, and the divine connection between the people, the rivers, and the cosmos had been reaffirmed.

The recitation at the banks of the Sindhu was not just a moment in time but a timeless event, a merging of the past, present, and future. It was a reminder of the eternal truths that bind us all, the sacred wisdom that guides us, and the divine presence that watches over us. In the heart of people, the echoes of Vashisht's pronouncement would resonate for generations to come, a testament to the enduring power of the Vedic hymns and the hope for the revival of the Saraswati.

CHAPTER TWENTY-ONE

<u>THE MOTHER GODDESS</u>

The sun hung low in the sky, casting a melancholic glow over the once-thriving banks of the Saraswati River. The sacred waters that had sustained life for generations had long since dried up, leaving behind a barren landscape that mirrored the despair in the hearts of its people. Mohenjo-Daro, a bustling hub of Rishi and sages, now stood as a silent testament to the wrath of nature and the capriciousness of the Gods.

As I stood by the banks of what was once the mighty Saraswati, the weight of our collective failure pressed heavily upon my heart. The sun hung low in the sky, casting a melancholic glow over the barren landscape. The once-thriving riverbed, now dry and desolate, seemed to mock our efforts, a cruel reminder of the life that had slipped away from us.

I remember how Rishi Vashisht, our revered elder, had acted as the Purohit for the Yajna. His prayers were the last hope for reviving the Saraswati. We had all poured our hearts into the ceremony, believing that our devotion and the power of the ancient mantras would compel the gods to answer our pleas. The square, usually alive with the sounds of daily life, was filled instead with the soft murmurs of despair, as the realization dawned that our efforts had been in vain. The heavens remained indifferent, and the river did not reflow from the Himalayas to the sea.

The gathering of Rishis after the Yajna was a somber affair. The failure weighed heavily on all of us, but none more so than on Parmanand and me. We had been inseparable throughout this journey, sharing a bond forged by our common goal. We had meticulously prepared every aspect of the Yajna, creating seals and markings that were implemented for the first time on earth. But now, as I looked into Parmanand's eyes, I saw the same grief and hopelessness that I felt within myself.

"Our efforts were in vain," I whispered, unable to hold back the tears that welled up in my eyes. "The gods have turned a deaf ear to our prayers."

Parmanand's voice trembled as he replied, "We have given everything we had, and yet, we stand here with nothing. How do we face our people? How do we tell them that our mother river is gone forever?"

The supplies from Harappa had dwindled, and food was scarce. The once plentiful harvests were now a thing of the past. In desperation, some of the inhabitants had resorted to eating fish from the remaining water bodies at the dying Saraswati banks, a practice once considered unthinkable. The Saraswata Brahmins, who had thrived on the banks of the river for countless generations, were now facing the harsh reality of migration.

Rishi Vashisht, sensing the growing despair, rose to address the assembly. His voice, though aged, carried the weight of wisdom and authority. "Brothers and sisters, the time has come for us to make a difficult decision. The Saraswati, our lifeline, is no more. We must accept this reality and find a new path. Our ancestors have faced challenges before, and we must draw strength from their resilience."

His words, though painful, were true. We knew that migration was inevitable. The bond we shared with the Saraswati was not just of sustenance but of identity and heritage. To leave this land was to leave a part of ourselves behind. The rishis nodded in agreement, though their hearts were heavy. They knew that migration was inevitable. The world's largest migration, as it seemed, was about to begin. Each Rishi would lead their followers to different directions, seeking new lands where they could rebuild their lives.

Among the gathering, there was a palpable sense of loss. The bond they shared with the Saraswati was not just of sustenance but of identity and heritage. It was a connection that ran deeper than the river itself, intertwining with their very souls. To leave this land was to leave a part of them behind.

As the sun dipped below the horizon, casting long shadows over the square, the Rishis began to disperse. Some wept openly, while others held their grief in silence. The pain of separation from their sacred river was profound, but there was a flicker of hope in the hearts of the younger rishis. They believed that, just as the Saraswati had once given them life, they would find new rivers, new lands, where they could continue their traditions and keep the spirit of their ancestors alive. Parmanand and I lingered a while longer, gazing at the distant outline of the dried riverbed. We knew that our journey would be arduous, but we also knew that our faith and determination would guide us.

The great migration was about to begin, and with it, a new chapter in the history of the Saraswata Brahmins. Our hearts were heavy with sorrow, but our spirits remained unbroken. The legacy of the Saraswati would live on, not in the waters of the river, but in the hearts and minds of those who carried its memory forward.

The news of the failed Yagya had spread like wildfire through the lands of Kukkutarma-Mohenjo-Daro. The once-bustling city was now cloaked in a somber silence, its people struggling to come to terms with the loss of their lifeblood, the Saraswati River. . It was in this atmosphere of collective grief that Guru Vashisht, the revered elder and spiritual guide, announced a momentous gathering to be held on the next Purnima.

As the moon waxed full, casting its silvery light over the ancient city, the rishis and their followers gathered in the central square. The air was thick with anticipation and sorrow, the enormity of their impending migration weighing heavily on their hearts. Guru Vashisht stood at the center, his presence a pillar of strength for all who looked upon him.

"Brothers and sisters," he began, his voice resonating with a blend of authority and compassion, "we have gathered here to bid farewell to the life we have known, and to each other. The failure of our Yagya was not due to any lack of effort or devotion on our part. It is the will of Ishwar that we must now accept the inevitable and move on. The Saraswati, our mighty river, is no more. Her death is akin to the death of a part of our own selves."

A murmur of agreement rippled through the crowd. The pain of this acceptance was evident in every face, young and old alike. They had all contributed tirelessly to the success of the Yagya, and now, despite their best efforts, they had to face the harsh reality of their situation.

"I request all of you," continued Guru Vashisht, "to mark this farewell gathering with extraordinary conduct. We must honor the Saraswati not only for the life she provided but also for the wisdom and culture she nurtured. Though her waters no longer flow, her spirit will live on. From this day forward, Saraswati will be revered as the Goddess of Knowledge and Music.

The hymns we hold in our smriti will be the new river through which her essence flows, passed down through generations as a tribute to her eternal legacy." The tradition of adopting the surname "Saraswati" by many rishis signifies a deep connection to the revered river Saraswati and the goddess of knowledge, Saraswati Devi. By incorporating "Saraswati" into their names, these rishis not only honored their spiritual heritage but also made a vow that future generations would continue this legacy. This practice symbolizes the continuity of wisdom, spiritual purity, and the eternal quest for knowledge, attributes closely associated with both the river and the goddess Saraswati. It reflects the rishis' commitment to preserving and perpetuating their cultural and spiritual lineage through successive generations.

The announcement brought a renewed sense of purpose to the gathering. Though their hearts were heavy with grief, they found solace in the idea that the spirit of Saraswati would continue to guide them. Guru Vashisht's vision gave them a way to honor their beloved river and carry forward its memory.

"I request all of you," Guru Vashisht continued, "to prepare an idol of Saraswati. The best of these creations will be accepted as the final idol of our beloved Goddess Saraswati. Let this be a tribute to her, a symbol of our undying reverence. Rishi Vishvakarma, known for his exceptional skill in the arts, is preparing an idol. However, I invite everyone with knowledge and talent in the arts to contribute their work, dedicated to our Mother Goddess Saraswati."

The crowd listened intently, their minds already envisioning the task ahead. This was not just about creating an idol; it was about channeling their grief and reverence into a lasting tribute that would stand the test of time. The artisans among them, inspired by the call, began to discuss their ideas, their sorrow momentarily set aside by the spark of creativity.

As the night wore on, the gathering dispersed, each person carrying with them a sense of purpose and a determination to honor Saraswati in the best way possible. The following days were filled with the sounds of crafting and creation, as every artisan poured their heart and soul into their work. The spirit of the Saraswati seemed to flow through their hands, guiding their creations.

As we prepared for the days ahead, Guru Vashisht's words echoed in my mind: "From this day forward, Saraswati will be revered as the Goddess of Knowledge and Music. The hymns we hold in our smriti will be the new river through which her essence flows, passed down through generations as a tribute to her eternal legacy." And so, with a heavy heart but a resolute spirit, I joined my fellow Rishis, ready to face the uncertain future and carry the memory of Saraswati into new lands.

The days leading up to the next Purnima weighed heavily on our shoulders, each moment a reminder of the immense task that lay ahead. Much work was still to be done, and though our minds understood the urgency, our hearts were far removed, lost in the sorrow of what we had witnessed.

As Parmanand and I walked towards our ashrama, our steps were slow and hesitant, like those of a small child who had just learned to walk. The weight of our failure pressed down on us, making each step feel like a burden. The path that once seemed familiar now felt alien, as if the very ground beneath us had shifted in some irreparable way.

An unbreakable silence hung between us, a silence that spoke of our shared grief and the unspoken fears that neither of us dared to voice. The usual banter that had accompanied our journeys was absent, replaced by a heavy, oppressive quiet that mirrored the desolation in our hearts.

When we finally reached the ashrama, the sight of its once comforting walls did little to ease the ache within us. The place that had been our sanctuary now felt like a reminder of all that we had lost. We stood at the entrance for a moment, neither of us willing to break the silence, both of us reluctant to enter a space that had once been filled with purpose and now seemed hollow.

Inside, the ashrama was just as we had left it, yet everything felt different. The tools and scriptures that had once been the focus of our days now seemed distant, as if they belonged to a different life. The fire pit, where we had performed countless rituals, was cold, its ashes a stark reminder of the Yajna that had failed to bring Saraswati back to life.

Finally, Parmanand spoke, his voice barely above a whisper. "What do we do now, Sanatani?"

I looked at him, seeing the weariness in his eyes, the same weariness that I felt in every fiber of my being. "We prepare for the Purnima," I replied, though the words felt hollow. "Guru Vashisht has given us a task, and we must see it through."

He nodded, but the spark of determination that usually accompanied such resolutions was missing. We both knew that this was not just another ritual or task; it was our way of honoring Saraswati, of finding some sense of closure in the midst of our loss.

As we began to set our minds to the preparations, the silence between us remained a companion to our grief. But beneath that silence, there was a faint flicker of resolve, a shared understanding that we would carry on, not just for ourselves, but for the legacy of the Saraswati, and for those who would come after us.

The days ahead would be difficult, but as we set to work, we knew that this Purnima would be different. It would be a time not just of ritual, but of reflection, of mourning, and of finding the strength to continue in the face of overwhelming sorrow.

. It was in this atmosphere of collective grief that Guru Vashisht, the revered elder and spiritual guide, announced a momentous gathering to be held on the next Purnima.

CHAPTER TWENTY-TWO

THE FAREWELL

On the next Purnima, Kukkutarma-Mohenjo-Daro was transformed into a vibrant display of artistic expression. The square, once a place of gatherings and commerce, now served as a sacred ground, adorned with idols of Saraswati, each unique and meticulously crafted. Guru Vashisht and the other rishis walked among them, their eyes filled with admiration and pride. Among the idols, one stood out—a figure of Saraswati, crafted by the divine hands of Rishi Vishvakarma. This figure, along with a statue of me, Sanatani, was more than just an idol; it was a testament to our shared heritage, the strength of our community, and the deep spiritual connection we all shared with the goddess.

In a solemn and grand ceremony, the final idol of Saraswati was selected with the utmost care. This idol was the perfect embodiment of the goddess's grace, wisdom, and divine serenity. Crafted to capture the very essence of Saraswati, she who is revered not only as the goddess of knowledge but also as the muse of arts and learning, the idol radiated a quiet power that resonated with all who beheld it.

As the beautifully sculpted earth idol was placed in its new sanctum, the rishis led the gathered devotees in reciting sacred hymns. These hymns were not chosen lightly; they were meticulously selected to invoke and preserve the spirit of Saraswati, ensuring that her divine presence would remain alive and vibrant for generations to come. The air was thick with the melodious chant of mantras, creating an atmosphere of spiritual elevation and reverence.

Saraswati's transformation into the "mother of the Vedas" was not just symbolic; it signified the expansion of her domain to encompass all forms of artistic expression. No longer just a river goddess, she had become a celestial figure, embodying the flood of illumination and inspiration. Celebrated as the chief of the sixteen Vidyādevis, or goddesses of knowledge, each representing different branches of learning and the arts, Saraswati's influence was profound and far-reaching.

Her importance was so great that a special festival, Basant Panchmi, was dedicated to her. This festival, marking the onset of spring, was a time when devotees paid homage to Saraswati, seeking her blessings for wisdom, learning, and artistic talent. During this festival, people placed books, musical instruments, and art materials before her idol, symbolizing their dedication to acquiring knowledge and skill.

Saraswati's association with dhi, or inspired thought, and her role as the goddess of speech and the Word (vāch or vāk), further highlighted her importance in the Vedic tradition. The Vedic poets, inspired by the sounds of the river Saraswati, praised her as the "inspirer of hymns," making a natural connection between her and the creative process of composing sacred texts.

Her constant association with speech and inspiration made her not only a symbol of knowledge and learning but also a guardian of the arts. Saraswati's presence in the lives of her devotees was a source of enlightenment and cultural enrichment. The reverence for Saraswati reflected the deep-rooted belief in the power of knowledge and the arts to uplift and transform human consciousness.

Thus, the installation of her idol and the accompanying rituals symbolized the eternal flow of wisdom and the unending quest for knowledge—much like the river Saraswati herself, which once flowed mightily, inspiring and nurturing the minds and spirits of those who dwelled along its sacred banks.

Though they were on the brink of a great migration, the people of Kukkutarma- Mohenjo-Daro left with a sense of hope and purpose. The river that had given them life would now live on in their songs, their stories, and their hearts—a river of knowledge flowing eternally through the annals of time.

As I stood before the gathered crowd, their eyes reflecting the flickering light of the evening fire, I knew it was time to share the final leg of our journey. This was not just a story of migration but a deep dive into the history and evolution of the Saraswata Brahmins, a community intrinsically tied to the ancient River Saraswati and its eventual transformation.

"Saraswata Brahmins were not originally a distinct group by birth," I began, my voice steady and resonant, capturing the attention of everyone present. "Initially, Brahmins were made, not born, based on their knowledge and spiritual prowess. The Saraswata Brahmins, in particular, were deeply connected to the River Saraswati. Their existence and prosperity depended on the river's flow. When the river changed its course or dried up, it is going to lead to mass migration, chaos, disease, famine, and a decline in population."

The crowd listened intently, their faces illuminated by the warm glow of the fire, as I continued, "For thousands of years, the Saraswata Brahmins experienced cycles of prosperity and decline. They thrived on the banks of the Saraswati for millennia, but the drying up of the river marked a significant turning point. This failed event will lead to mass migrations in various directions, with the Saraswata Brahmins establishing new settlements and civilizations without any reference to their origin."

I paused, allowing the weight of my words to sink in before adding, "The conditions for the Saraswata Brahmins deteriorated due to changes in the river's course, disturbing our economic and religious life and creating chaotic conditions. We attempted to revive our mighty river through a grand Yagya here, dedicated to the deities of Water, Agni, and Sun. Despite their fervent prayers, the Yagya failed, and Saraswati did not rise to our aid."

My voice carried a tone of solemn reverence as I continued, "The failure of the Yagya will lead to a mass migration of Saraswat Brahmins and other community members. As we move to new areas, we are carrying with us the Vedas in smriti as presented during the Yajna. We transformed our reverence for the river into the worship of Saraswati as the Goddess of Knowledge and Learning, symbolizing the unending flow of wisdom and education."

My eyes gleamed with passion as I spoke of the Saraswat Brahmins' cultural and religious contributions. "The Saraswata Brahmins were instrumental in preserving and transmitting Vedic knowledge. The term 'Brahmin' encompasses those who know God, possess Vedic knowledge, and serve as priests, teachers, and intellectuals. The Saraswata Brahmins demonstrated leadership and innovation in addressing survival challenges and managing their society. This act symbolized their resilience and hope for a future where Saraswati's essence would continue to flow through education and wisdom."

I added, "The part of Saraswat Brahmins' migration moved westward, integrating with Sumerian and Mesopotamian civilizations, while others moved eastward. I was under the guardianship of Rishi Agastya, who decided to go south through the sea route. The other clans had reservations about traveling by sea, so they took various routes by land, reaching the banks of other rivers. Their history is a testament to their struggle for existence and adaptation to new environments. The Saraswat Brahmins' legacy is a record of their resilience, adaptability, and spiritual devotion. Their journey from the banks of the Saraswati to various parts of the Indian subcontinent will reflect their enduring spirit and commitment to preserving their heritage."

As the sun set, casting long shadows across the ancient structures of Mohenjo-Daro, I knew that the story of the Saraswat Brahmins, much like the flow of the River Saraswati, would endure. It was a testament to the power of human resilience, spirituality, and the timeless pursuit of knowledge and enlightenment.

Rishi Agastya had entrusted me with a solemn and significant duty—one that tied me indelibly to the ancient city of Kukkutarma-Mohenjo-Daro. His instructions were clear: I was to remain in the city until the last person had departed, ensuring the final closure of an era. As a further command, he decreed that sixteen people and their families were to remain in Kukkutarma-Mohenjo-Daro permanently, safeguarding its memory and legacy for future generations. Once I had fulfilled this task, I was to journey south to Bharatavarsa, where Rishi Agastya awaited my report. However, this was not the end of my connection to this sacred place. Agastya ordered me to return here every twenty-five years, ensuring a continuous link with the past, preserving the spirit of the ancient civilization.

I was born with a singular purpose: the revival of the Naditama Saraswati. I carry within me the assurance that the life cycles granted to me by the Saptarishees will not cease until I witness the flowing waters of the Saraswati once more. My mission is not merely one of duty, but of destiny. I am here to remain on this earth, enduring through the ages, to witness the moment when the Saraswati reclaims her rightful place as a living river.

Before my departure, Parmanand and I made offerings to Kukkutarma-Mohenjo-Daro, leaving behind symbols of our presence and connection to this ancient city. I left my Brahmin figure, an idol that would serve as a symbolic presence in Kukkutarma for the infinite years to come. It was not just an image of me but a reminder of the sacred duty and the eternal bond I shared with this place. Parmanand, too, left a remarkable gift: a copper sculpture of a girl, an artistic marvel symbolizing the first introduction of copper to humanity. He remarked that such a magnificent gift—the "Dancing Girl"—should remain here, rooted in the history and legacy of Kukkutarma, rather than being carried with him.

And so, after ten days of waiting, when every last inhabitant had left the city and the ancient streets had fallen silent, our mission in Kukkutarma-Mohenjo-Daro came to a close. But its spirit remained, through the presence of our gifts, through the families who stayed, and through the vow I made to return—every twenty-five years—until the Saraswati flowed once more.

Parmanand and I walked through the silent ruins of Mohenjo-Daro, our footsteps echoing off the ancient stones. The once bustling streets, now deserted, served as a stark reminder of the great migration that had taken place. The structures, though worn by time, stood resilient, a testament to the architectural brilliance and enduring spirit of our ancestors. The gifts we left behind—a figure and a copper girl—were symbols of our deep respect and reverence for the rich heritage we had inherited.

As we approached the sixteen guardians who remained, their faces reflected a mixture of sorrow and understanding. They knew, as we did, that the legacy of the Saraswata Brahmins was not bound to a single river, but to the wisdom and knowledge that we carried within us—wisdom that would continue to guide us, even as we journeyed far from our ancestral home.

I addressed them with a solemn resolve. "The Saraswati may have dried up, but the essence of what she represented lives on within us. Our journey does not end here. It is our duty to carry forward the legacy of our ancestors, to spread knowledge and enlightenment wherever we go. Every 25th year, I shall return to this place. You must remain here, and pass this commitment to your future generations. Remember, one day, Saraswati shall flow again. Until then, you are the true sons of Saraswati. Those who have migrated from her banks cannot claim that title."

With these words, the chapter of this last leg of our journey came to a close. Though the Saraswata Brahmins were now dispersed across distant lands, we remained united in our pursuit of wisdom and our commitment to preserving our heritage. The story of our journey, and the resilience we showed, would be told for generations to come—a testament to the enduring spirit of the Saraswata Brahmins. As Parmanand and I embarked on our new journey, the story of the Saraswat Brahmins and their unyielding spirit continued to echo through time, a reminder of our enduring quest for knowledge and enlightenment. The path ahead was uncertain, but the legacy of Saraswati would guide us, as it had guided our ancestors before us.

CHAPTER TWENTY-THREE

THE QUEST FOR THE TRUTH

The days following the mass departure from Kukkutarma-Mohenjo-Daro were marked by a solemn quiet that seemed to envelop the ancient city in a shroud of melancholy. The once-bustling streets, now deserted, echoed the silence of a civilization on the brink of a great transformation. With the last of the people gone, Parmanand and I prepared ourselves for the journey northward—a journey that would take us through the arid lands and desolate villages that lay in the shadow of the great mystery: the drying up of the Saraswati River.

As we began our journey northward, the reality of our task began to settle in. The lands we traversed were parched and barren, a stark contrast to the fertile plains that had once been nourished by the mighty Saraswati. Villages that had once thrived on the river's bounty now lay in ruins, their inhabitants long gone in search of more hospitable lands. The desolation was a constant reminder of what had been lost, fueling our determination to uncover the truth.

Weeks turned into months as Parmanand and I pressed on, driven by a desire to understand the demise of the river that had once been the lifeblood of our civilization. Along the way, we encountered scholars, sages, and seers, each offering their own theories and wisdom. Some spoke of the changing climate, of droughts that had sapped the river of its strength. Others pointed to the shifting of tectonic plates, suggesting that the very earth beneath our feet had shifted, redirecting the river's course or causing it to disappear altogether.

As we pieced together these fragments of knowledge, a picture began to emerge—a complex interplay of natural forces that had conspired to bring about the Saraswati's extinction. The river's demise was not the result of a single event but a culmination of various factors: prolonged droughts, tectonic shifts, and possibly even the changing patterns of the monsoon winds. Each of these elements had played a role, weakening the river over time until it could no longer sustain its flow.

Our journey was arduous, the terrain unforgiving, but our resolve never wavered. Each step we took brought us closer to the truth, and each conversation with a learned sage added another piece to the puzzle. Along the way, we shared our story, recounting the history of our people and the lessons learned from our migration. It was a story that resonated with those we met, a tale of resilience in the face of adversity and a testament to the enduring spirit of the Saraswata Brahmins.

Finally, after months of travel and countless discussions, we reached our conclusion. The drying up of the Saraswati was not merely a natural phenomenon; it was the result of a series of interconnected events that had unfolded over centuries. Climatic changes had reduced the rainfall that once fed the river, while tectonic shifts had altered its course, causing it to retreat underground or dissipate into the desert sands. The river's extinction was a slow, inexorable process, one that mirrored the gradual decline of the civilization that had once flourished along its banks.

Armed with this knowledge, Parmanand and I returned to Kukkutarma-Mohenjo-Daro, ready to share our findings with the guardians of the land. As we stood before the sixteen guardians who had been left behind, we recounted our journey and the conclusions we had reached. The guardians listened in silence, their faces reflecting a mixture of sorrow and understanding. They, like us, had known that the river was lost, but now they understood why.

"The drying up of the Saraswati was not the work of the gods, nor was it a punishment for our sins," I explained. "It was the result of natural forces beyond our control. But the essence of what the river represented lives on within us. The wisdom, the knowledge, and the culture that flourished along its banks—these are the true legacy of the Saraswati, and it is our duty to carry them forward."

With these words, the chapter of our investigation came to a close. The Saraswata Brahmins, though dispersed, remained united in their pursuit of wisdom and their commitment to preserving their heritage. The story of our journey would be told for generations to come, a testament to our resilience and the enduring spirit of the Saraswata Brahmins.

Then, as we prepared to depart, the unexpected happened—Parmanand expressed his wish to stay in Kukkutarma-Mohenjo-Daro for the rest of his life. His words struck me like lightning. Parmanand, my closest companion, my shadow, had always stood by my side in these years of quest and discovery. The thought of continuing my journey without him felt foreign, unsettling. For a moment, I was overwhelmed. We had weathered every storm together, and his presence had been a constant source of strength.

But as I looked into his eyes, I saw the determination and peace that came with his decision. He was resolute; his heart firmly rooted in the ancient soil of Kukkutarma, where he felt his purpose could best be fulfilled. I had no choice but to honor his wish. Though it pained me to leave him behind, I knew his decision was driven by the same cause we both served. With a heavy heart, I accepted his choice and resolved to continue my journey alone, to fulfill my duty to Rishi Agastya and reach the southern part of Bharatavarsa.

As I embarked on the next leg of my journey, I realized that our quest was far from over. The Saraswati River may have dried up, but the knowledge, wisdom, and culture it had nourished would continue to flow. Those like Parmanand who stayed behind, and those who shared our dedication to the cause, would carry forward the torch of enlightenment and truth. My journey, like the river itself, would not be defined by an end, but by continuity. It was an eternal quest for knowledge and understanding, one that would echo through the ages, just as the spirit of the Saraswati would live on, carried forward by those who remained devoted to its revival.

135

CHAPTER TWENTY-FOUR

THE MANUSCRIPT

Hundreds of years had passed since the Saraswat Brahmins first left the sacred banks of the River Saraswati. The once-vibrant river, which had been the lifeblood of their civilization, had long since dried up, leaving behind a barren landscape and memories of a glorious past. Yet, the legacy of the Saraswat Brahmins endured, carried forward by those who had pledged to preserve their sacred knowledge.

I, Sanatani, had become a frequent visitor to Agastya Peeth, the revered ashram founded by the great Rishi Agastya. Despite the passage of time, my commitment to periodic visits to Kukkutarma-Kukkutarma-Mohenjo-Daro never wavered. I held onto the hope that the river might one day flow again, but as the centuries passed, that hope had dimmed. I had already lost Parmanand, whom I had been addressing as Sulakhan since the end of the Yajna, and the weight of time bore heavily upon me.

On one of my visits to Kukkutarma-Mohenjo-Daro, I was shocked to see that the major structures of the ancient city had collapsed. The once-grand edifices now lay in ruins, a stark reminder of the relentless march of time. Alone, I began my painstaking search for any sign of the Brahmins who had stayed behind.

I scoured the ruins, hoping to find them alive, perhaps hidden away in some untouched corner of the city. But as I dug through the debris, my hope turned to despair. Their skeletons were found buried under the rubble of rooms and stairs, their lives claimed by a sudden and devastating earthquake. The sheer force of the earthquake had destroyed the structures, toppling walls and burying everything beneath. The Brahmins, steadfast in their duty, had no chance to escape. Their remains were a stark reminder of the city's tragic end and the devotion of those who gave their lives to protect it.

With a heavy heart, I searched for the families of the sixteen inhabitants left behind but found no trace of them. It was painful to stand among the ruins, the silence only broken by the wind whispering through the fallen stones. As I paused, my gaze distant, memories flooded back, and I began to recount the past.

"It was during my search for our scattered families," I began, "amidst the winding rivers and treacherous terrains, that I encountered a moment that will forever remain etched in my soul. As I was crossing a river, a voice from behind called out, compelling me to stop? I turned and saw a grand boat, its occupants lying prostrate before me, in reverence. When they rose, I recognized them as my own kin—survivors of a tragedy that had claimed the lives of our guardians of the land."

"They told me how an earthquake had torn the land asunder, taking the lives of those on shore. But by some divine grace, they had been spared, for they were on the water, celebrating the Basant festival. 'Baba,' they called me, their voices heavy with resolve, 'we will remain on these boats until the Saraswati flows once more. The land has betrayed us, but the waters have kept us safe. We, the tribe of Mohano have sworn in the name of Naditama Saraswati that we will earn our livelihood from waters only till the reflow of Saraswati. Promise us, Baba that you will visit us every 25 years, and that when the Saraswati flows again, your mission will be fulfilled.'"

Their words were a plea, a covenant of faith, and I could do nothing but vow to return to them every 25 years, wherever they might be. I knew then, as I know now, that their hope is intertwined with my journey, and only when the Saraswati runs free will my task be complete.

When I returned to Agastya Peeth, I recounted the tragic scene to Rishi Agastya. The sage, with his anteryami (inner vision), comforted me, telling me that the sixteen inhabitants had been buried and were now resting in peace. He instructed me not to disturb them on my future visits but to continue my visits every twenty-five years as dictated by the Saptarishees. I consented, understanding the wisdom in Agastya's words.

Rishi Agastya then instructed me to visit him on the next Basant Panchmi, hinting that he had news that would bring an unprecedented change. "Things are taking shape," Agastya said, "and I am hopeful that it will be ready even at the cost of my life."

On the day of Basant Panchmi, the atmosphere was festive, filled with the pleasant warmth of early spring. I arrived at Agastya Peeth, sensing the excitement in the air. However, upon reaching the ashram, I found Rishi Agastya bedridden. Despite his frail condition, the sage's eyes shone with a determined light. He handed me a manuscript titled "Rig Veda."

"These are the hymns from the Yajna," Agastya explained, "which were preserved in smriti. They have now been recorded in writing. The spoken words are now written, and I have completed this transformation of hymns from memory to written content on palm leaves."

My eyes welled up with tears as I held the manuscript. It was a monumental moment, the culmination of centuries of effort to preserve our sacred knowledge. I was overwhelmed by the significance of the first written manuscript of the Rig Veda, even though I could not read it.

Agastya, sensing my emotions, said, "Before you leave for Kukkutarma-Mohenjo-Daro, you must learn a written language here. Only then will the Rig Veda be a true companion to you, much like Parmanand was." He further instructed me to leave my saropa and headgear with him, as he would see through his anteryami eyes placing this manuscript there. I followed each instruction with care.

The Rigveda-Samhita was not just a collection of texts; it was the very essence of Vedic wisdom, a compendium of poetic, philosophical, and religious insights. The Rigveda was composed entirely of poems, known as 'Riks,' which praised the gods and captured the essence of ancient rituals and beliefs.

I agreed, recognizing the importance of understanding the language in which our sacred hymns had been written. I immersed myself in the study, guided by the scholars at Agastya Peeth. Days turned into months as I diligently learned the language, driven by a sense of duty and reverence for the sacred texts.

One evening, as the sun dipped below the horizon, Agastya gathered the disciples around a sacred fire. The air was thick with the fragrance of incense and the sound of chanting. "The Rigveda is not just a text," he said, his voice resonating with authority. "It is the heartbeat of our culture, the foundation of our spiritual heritage. Each Mantra, each Sukta, carries the wisdom of the ages." I, now deeply immersed in the teachings, felt a profound connection to the ancient seers who had composed these hymns. The journey had transformed me from a curious youth into a devoted guardian of Vedic knowledge.

Rishi Agastya then unveiled the first stone statue of Goddess Saraswati, destined to be placed at the Gangaikonda Temple. This exquisite statue depicted Saraswati carrying a kamandalu, or water pot, in her upper left hand, symbolizing the river, while her lower left hand held palm leaf manuscripts, representing the Vedas and inspired speech.

In Vedic symbolism, Saraswati transforms from being an impetuous river to embodying the powerful image of illumination and inspiration. She is revered as the "impeller of happy truths," who "awakens in the consciousness the great flood and illumines all thoughts." Saraswati is celebrated as "the best of mothers, best of rivers, and best of goddesses." She becomes the goddess of speech, the Word (vāch or vāk). The geographical location of the Vedic poets along the riverbanks, where the river's sounds permeated their ashrams, led to a metaphorical interpretation of the river's gurgling as inspired speech. Initially praised as an "inspirer of hymns," Saraswati's association with dhi, or inspired thought, solidified her role as the goddess of speech and inspiration, the vehicles of knowledge and learning.

When the time came for me to depart for Kukkutarma-Mohenjo-Daro, I felt a profound sense of purpose. With the manuscript in hand, I embarked on my journey, retracing the steps of our ancestors.

The journey was arduous, but the landscape was breathtaking. I traversed dense forests, crossed roaring rivers, and climbed towering mountains. Along the way, I recited Rigveda's most famous Suktas, such as the Nasadiya Sukta, which delved into the mysteries of creation, and the Purusha Sukta, which described the cosmic being from whose body the universe was formed. As I approached the ruins of Kukkutarma-Mohenjo-Daro, I felt a deep connection to the land that had once been the cradle of our civilization.

Standing amidst the ruins, I carefully placed the manuscript in a protected niche, offering a silent prayer to Goddess Saraswati. Agastya's Rishi eyes twinkled in divyadrishti with satisfaction as I placed the first copy of the manuscript there on the soil of Kukkutarma-Mohenjo-Daro. "You have fulfilled a sacred duty, Sanatani," Agastya said softly. "The preservation of knowledge is the highest form of devotion. The legacy will live on through the Rig Veda, guiding future generations."

This act, I felt, was a true tribute to the Goddess of Knowledge, a fulfillment of the legacy we had vowed to preserve. The Rig Veda, now recorded in writing, symbolized the unending flow of wisdom and the resilience of the Saraswata Brahmins.

My tears flowed freely as I stood there, feeling the presence of Parmanand and the countless others who had shared this journey. I knew that the written Rig Veda would endure, carrying our heritage forward into the future.

With a heart full of reverence and a renewed sense of purpose, I left Kukkutarma-Mohenjo-Daro, the manuscript now a testament to our enduring spirit. As I made my way back to Agastya Peeth, I felt a profound sense of peace, knowing that I had played a part in preserving the sacred knowledge for generations to come.

Upon my return, I discovered that Rishi Agastya had already departed for the heavenly abode. The head, despite his failing health, had been waiting for me but had left for Kashi-Varanasi to fulfill his duty of submerging the ashes of the great sage. I inquired about the Saropa and headgear I had left while departing for Kukkutarma-Mohenjo-Daro. A sadhak of the peeth informed me that the spiritual head carried with him a wooden box, which had been entrusted to him by Rishi Agastya with strict instructions not to open it. The box, now en route to Kashi-Varanasi, held an air of mystery and significance.

Determined to retrieve the box, I decided to travel to Kashi-Varanasi, the sacred city on the banks of the Ganga. Upon my arrival, I learned that the head came from Agastya Peeth had also passed away. Despite my efforts to locate the wooden box, my search proved fruitless.

Reflecting on the series of events, I sensed the hand of destiny at play. I accepted the outcome as the will of the divine, recognizing that some mysteries were meant to remain unresolved, their secrets guarded by the flow of time and the will of the gods.

From that day forward, my visits to Kukkutarma-Mohenjo-Daro were marked by a sense of completion and fulfillment. The manuscript, safely ensconced within the ancient city, stood as a beacon of our enduring spirit and dedication to the pursuit of knowledge.

As the years rolled by, I continued my visits, each time finding solace in the presence of the manuscript and the memories it held. I remained a steadfast guardian of the Saraswata Brahmins' heritage, my life a testament to their resilience and unwavering commitment to the eternal quest for knowledge and enlightenment.

CHAPTER TWENTY-FIVE

THE FIRE OF FATE

The journey to Kukkutarma-Mohenjo-Daro had always been one filled with anticipation and reflection. As I made my way through the familiar landscapes, my mind was preoccupied with thoughts of the tasks ahead. The weight of centuries of tradition and the responsibility of preserving our sacred knowledge lay heavily on my shoulders. Yet, I was determined to fulfill my duty, no matter the obstacles that lay in my path.

As I walked, the serene silence of the countryside was shattered by a sudden and jarring sound. A loud crash, followed by the agonizing cries of children and women, pierced the air. Without a moment's hesitation, I sprinted towards the source of the commotion, my heart pounding with urgency.

When I arrived, I was met with a scene of chaos and terror. A vehicle had smashed into a roadside barrier, its front crumpled like paper, and fuel was leaking from its ruptured tank. The car doors were locked, trapping a terrified family inside as the ominous smell of gasoline filled the air, signaling an imminent explosion.

There was no time to waste. With a nearby rock, I smashed the car's window and began pulling the passengers out one by one. The fear in their eyes only fueled my determination. Despite my efforts, those who had initially rushed to help fled in panic when they saw the leaking fuel, abandoning the family to their fate.

But I could not—would not—abandon them. The cries of the children, the desperate pleas of the mother, and the sight of their terror-stricken faces spurred me on. I continued to rescue them, pulling each passenger to safety. As I reached for the last person, my left leg became twisted and trapped in the wreckage.

And then it happened.

A massive explosion erupted from the fuel tank, sending a shockwave through the air. Flames engulfed the vehicle, and in that moment, I was caught in the inferno. The heat was unbearable, the flames relentless, but I did not utter a single cry of pain. My silence was not out of bravado but something deeper—an acceptance, perhaps, of whatever fate had in store for me.

Those who had gathered around recited verses from the Quran, their voices trembling with fear and reverence as they witnessed the scene. My body, consumed by the flames, became a spectacle of horror and awe. It was as if the fire had stripped away all that was mortal, leaving behind something beyond the understanding of those who watched.

The police arrived swiftly on the scene, their presence a reminder that life, despite its unpredictability, marches on. The crowd urged them to rush me to the hospital, their pleas tinged with desperation. The doctors, upon seeing my severely burnt body, declared that I had suffered 99% burns and had no hope of survival. The lead inspector, assuming I would not make it through the night, left two constables to keep watch and departed, believing their task was simply to ensure my passing.

But fate had other plans.

The next morning, when the constables checked on me with a burial shroud (kafan) in hand, they found my hospital bed empty. Panic spread through the hospital like wildfire. The staff and guards searched frantically, unable to comprehend how a man who should have been on the brink of death could vanish without a trace. A guard reported that the man bought by the policemen previous night had left the hospital uninjured at dawn, walking away as if nothing had happened.

The news of my mysterious disappearance spread quickly, causing a ripple of fear and superstition throughout Sindh. Rumors of a ghost, a spirit returned from the dead, began to circulate, fueling the panic. I, unaware of the chaos I had left in my wake, continued my journey to Kukkutarma-Mohenjo-Daro, my mind focused solely on the task at hand.

Upon reaching Kukkutarma-Mohenjo-Daro, I was apprehended by the local guards who had been alerted by the police. They were wary, their eyes filled with suspicion as they handed me over to the Sindh police. I was questioned, interrogated, but the answers they sought were not the ones I could provide. They were searching for explanations that lay beyond the realm of human understanding.

Frustrated by their inability to extract anything useful from me, they transferred me to a secret agency led by General Sattar. The General regarded me with a mix of curiosity and doubt. He sought to unravel the mystery of my survival, to understand the forces at play, but even he could not grasp the true nature of my existence.

As I sat before him, I knew that my journey was far from over. The path I walked was one paved with trials and tribulations, but it was also one of purpose and destiny. The fire that had engulfed me had not consumed my spirit. Instead, it had forged me into something stronger, something unbreakable.

My journey to Kukkutarma-Mohenjo-Daro had taken an unexpected turn, but I knew that the true test lay ahead. The manuscript, the legacy of the Saraswata Brahmins, awaited me. And with it, the fulfillment of a promise made to those who had placed their trust in me. In the face of fire and fear, I had emerged unscathed, a testament to the power of faith and the indomitable will to fulfill one's duty. The road ahead was uncertain, but I was ready to face whatever challenges came my way.

The incidents after my meeting with General Sattar are well known to all of you. His questions, his attempts to unravel the mystery of my survival, and the events that followed have become part of the tale that now weaves itself into the fabric of our collective memory. But today, I stand before you not to recount what you already know, but to reaffirm something far more profound—my unwavering faith in the reflow of the Saraswati.

For centuries, the Saraswati has been more than just a river to our people. She is the lifeblood of our civilization, the source of our wisdom, the mother of our sacred texts. When her waters dried up, it was as if a part of our very soul had been lost. The migrations that followed, the dispersal of our knowledge and our people, were a wound that has never fully healed.

But I have not walked this path, lived these lives, and carried this knowledge merely to witness the passing of an era. No. My purpose, and the purpose of all those who came before me, has always been to ensure the return of what was lost. The reflow of the Saraswati is not a distant hope or a myth to cling to—it is inevitability. And I stand here today as a living testament to that faith.

I have seen the signs, felt the currents shift beneath the surface of the earth. The prayers of the Rishis, the yajnas performed over millennia, have not gone unheard. The Saraswati will flow again, and when she does, it will be not just a river restored, but the revival of an ancient truth that has been waiting to emerge.

The waters of the Saraswati are tied to the essence of who we are as a people. Her reflow will signal the awakening of the wisdom that has been dormant, the resurgence of the spirit that has guided us through the ages. And so, I stand here before you today, not as a man who has merely survived the trials of time, but as one who has lived to witness the reawakening of our greatest legacy.

I reaffirm my faith in the reflow of the Saraswati. I urge you all to carry this faith within you as well, for it is this collective belief, this shared commitment that will see her waters rise again.

In the silence that follows, let us remember that we are not just spectators of history—we are its creators. The Saraswati's return will mark the beginning of a new chapter, not just for us, but for the world. And when her waters flow once more, they will carry with them the stories, the wisdom, and the spirit of a civilization reborn.

So, let us stand united in this faith. The Saraswati will rise, and when she does, we will be ready. We will be there to greet her, to welcome her back into the heart of our land, and to honor the journey that has led us to this moment.

As I stand before you now, dear friends, scholars, and seekers of truth, the culmination of my journey is upon us. Thousands of years have passed since the first step of this sacred path was taken, a path etched not only in time but in the very soul of our existence. The journey to Kukkutarma—what you know as Mohenjo-Daro—was not just one of distance, but of transformation. And so, I speak today not merely to recount events, but to leave you with the understanding of what it means to be a bearer of the sacred knowledge entrusted to me.

The journey through the familiar yet ever-changing landscapes was filled with anticipation, my mind burdened by the weight of centuries of tradition, the responsibility to safeguard our ancestral wisdom, and the hopes of countless souls. This task was not mine alone but was entrusted to me by the Rishis themselves, the bearers of eternal truth who foresaw the needs of future generations.

But along this journey, as it often happens, life reminded me that destiny weaves in unexpected ways. The incident with the crash—the cries of terror, the inferno that engulfed me—was not simply a test of courage but a symbol of something greater. Fire, often a destroyer, became my rebirth. In that moment, consumed by flames, the mortal veil began to fall away. As the world recited prayers and witnessed what should have been the end of my earthly form, I was forged anew, not merely as a man, but as something far more.

I continued to Kukkutarma-Mohenjo-Daro, the city of old that now stands like a monument to the times gone by. The guards, the police, and even the formidable General Sattar sought answers—answers that would make sense in the world they knew. But I could offer none that would fit within their understanding, for the truths I carried were far beyond the reach of ordinary inquiry. The questions they asked were bound by the limits of time and space, but my journey, my duty, transcended such confines.

And now, as I stand here, having placed the final manuscript—the sacred legacy of the Saraswata Brahmins—in its rightful place, I feel the weight of the millennia lift slightly from my shoulders. Yet I know that the task is not done. My journey may have spanned eons, but it has not ended.

You, who sit before me today, have listened attentively to the story of my trials, of fire and fear, of survival against all odds. You have heard of the migration from the banks of the Saraswati, of the knowledge that must be preserved for future generations. But even as I speak, I know that there are truths I cannot share with you. Truths about my identity, the lives I have lived, and the secrets buried deep within the annals of time.

Some knowledge is not for all to bear. The cosmic design, the divine purpose that guides our existence, is too vast, too profound, for human minds to fully comprehend. The migrations, the exodus from the Saraswati's banks, the events that unfolded—these are but glimpses of a much larger picture, a design that spans the very fabric of our history. And so, I leave you with what you need, but not more.

You, the scholars and sages before me, who have dedicated your lives to understanding the sacred texts and ancient wisdom, may wrestle with the silence I leave behind. You may ponder whether the true reasons for the Saraswati's drying up and the massive migrations have been fully revealed. You may debate whether the deeper mysteries remain hidden. And perhaps they do.

But some things are meant to stay veiled, until the time is right.

As I conclude, I look into your eyes, seeing the reflection of your desire for knowledge. But there is a part of me that knows—knows that to reveal all would disrupt the balance of our world, would place burdens too heavy for even the most learned to bear. And so, I end with this simple yet profound truth:

"I am Sanatani, the guardian of our sacred knowledge. My journey has not ended—it has only just begun."

With those words, I step down from this platform, knowing that what I have shared today will stir your hearts and minds. You will ponder the implications of my story, debate the meaning of my survival, and wonder about the mysteries that lie ahead. But the deeper truths—the identities I have taken, the lives I have lived, the secrets of the universe—these will remain locked within me, waiting for the day the world is ready to receive them.

For the journey of Sanatani, the protector of our ancient wisdom is eternal. And the revelations that wait will come only when the world, too, has walked its path and is ready to embrace the fullness of the truth. Until that time, I continue on my way, guided by the eternal light of the Rishis and the wisdom of the ages.

CHAPTER TWENTY-SIX

THE DIPLOMATIC CALSS

All eyes turned towards General Sattar as he was sitting at a corner of room. The atmosphere was tense, and Sattar felt the weight of the situation pressing down on him. His embarrassment was palpable as he prepared to confront the man who had defied death and sparked a wave of fear and curiosity across the region. To add to his unease, his true identity as a general in the Pakistan Army had been exposed, despite his cover as a military attaché at the Pakistani Embassy under a bogus name.

Sattar's secret life had been meticulously concealed, his true identity known only to a select few. The exposure of his dual role not only jeopardized his current mission but also risked diplomatic repercussions. He now stood in the spotlight, with his credibility and authority on the line.

Clearing his throat, he tried to steady his nerves. "Sanatani you are silver for us. You are our asset," he began his voice steady despite the turmoil within; "you have been through an extraordinary ordeal. But there are questions that need answers. Who are you, truly? How did you survive the fire? How did you recover fully with the next dawn? What brought you to Mohenjo-Daro again and again?" You have told everything as per you but we don't head the flimsy stories. We still have to go in deep whether it's a covert operation by Abhimanyu or you're RAW because we don't believe on the fancy story told by you. My heart may accept your version but my professional training and responsibility call for further investigation from you.

Sanatani, looked up at Sattar with calm eyes. "I am but a traveler on a path lay out by destiny," he replied. "My survival is not for me to explain, but for the divine to reveal."

Sattar frowned, unsatisfied with the cryptic response. "You must understand the gravity of the situation. Your reappearances at our soil have caused widespread panic. We need clear answers."

Sanatani remained silent, his gaze unwavering. The tension in the room grew thicker, the pressure on Sattar mounting. He knew that the eyes of his peers and subordinates were on him, judging his every move. Frustration boiled over in Sattar's mind. He leaned forward, his voice dropping to a harsh whisper. "Do you realize what kind of situation you've created? People think you're some kind of ghost. There's chaos out there. I need to know who or what you are dealing with."

Sanatani's expression remained serene. "What happened to me is beyond your comprehension. My journey is guided by forces you do not understand."

Sattar felt a pang of frustration. "Enough with the riddles. We're not playing a game here. Lives are at stake, and you owe us the truth."

Sanatani sighed, sensing the futility of his cryptic responses. "I am a seeker, drawn to the ancient wisdom and sacred sites of our land. My survival... it is not something I can explain with mere words. There are forces at work that are far greater than you or I."

Sattar's eyes narrowed. "And these forces led you to Mohenjo-Daro?"

"Yes," Sanatani nodded. "There is something there that I must find. Something that is connected to the ancient past and holds great significance for our future."

Sattar leaned back, contemplating his next move turned towards the Abhimanyu. "You realize I cannot just let you go. We need to ensure you are not a threat. Until we understand more, you will remain under our watch."

Sanatani nodded, accepting his fate. "I understand. But know this, General Sattar: the path I walk is one of destiny. No matter how tightly you try to control it, fate has a way of unfolding as it is meant to."

As Sanatani was escorted out of the room, Sattar felt a chill run down his spine. The man had survived an ordeal that should have claimed his life, and his calm demeanor hinted at a depth of strength and knowledge that was beyond ordinary comprehension. Sattar knew that the days ahead would be challenging, not just for him, but for everyone involved in uncovering the truth behind Sanatani's miraculous survival.

With Sanatani in custody, Sattar rang to his team at Islamabad. "We need to dig deeper into this man's past. Find out everything we can about him. I want to know what he's searching for in Mohenjo-Daro and why."The team nodded, setting to work immediately. Sattar told them to go for a job, the weight of the situation still heavy on his shoulders. He couldn't shake the feeling that they were on the cusp of something much larger than any of them had anticipated.

Jaffar and Abhimanyu stood silently, observing the intense exchange between Sanatani and General Sattar. As the National Security Advisors (NSA) of their respective countries, they possessed a more mature and nuanced understanding of such situations. Their responsibilities extended beyond a single brigade or agency, encompassing the safety and security of entire nations. Their eyes met across the room, and they exchanged knowing smiles, a silent acknowledgment of the gravity of the situation and their shared responsibility.

After the tense meeting concluded, Abhimanyu and Jaffar moved to a quieter corner to discuss the next steps. The room emptied slowly, the lingering tension replaced by the sound of distant conversations and footsteps echoing through the corridors

"Given the current circumstances, I believe it would be prudent for Sanatani to be handed over to India," Abhimanyu began. "He is definitely not a RAW asset, but his safety and the clarity of his intentions are paramount."

Jaffar nodded thoughtfully, his gaze steady. "I understand, Abhimanyu. The situation demands a careful and considered approach. I will speak with the Prime Minister of Pakistan about this. If he agrees, your Prime Minister can make a formal request over the hotline."

General Sattar objected to leave Sanatani here. Abhimanyu used the hard term in declaring that Sanatani is not going anywhere now. He will be with us though technically you have to relieve him. But it is up to both of you that how this happen but for sure Sanatani is not going anywhere as long accomplishment of his mission. He requested Jaffar to talk to the PM of Pakistan and if he is agreed to, our PM makes a formal request to him over hotline. He also passed the directions that now General Sattar has no role in India, he should also go back to his secret agency. Jaffar nodded his head. A special Pak Air Force Aircraft landed at Delhi. Jaffar and General Sattar were ready to step in when the black Lamborghini car entered the port and Abhimanyu came out of Car. He wholeheartedly shakes hands with Jaffar and Sattar. Wished for their Comfortable journey and stood there till the aircraft left the Delhi.

As night fell, Abhimanyu remained in his office, poring over reports and files. His thoughts kept drifting back to Sanatani's calm, enigmatic presence. Who was this man really? What secrets did he hold? And what destiny awaited them all at Kukkutarma-Mohenjo-Daro?

Abhimanyu Singh sat at his desk, his eyes fixed on the silent phone before him. The air in his office was thick with anticipation. He had been waiting for this call from NSA Pakistan Jaffar for what felt like an eternity. Today, Jaffar was expected to discuss Pakistan's role in the Sanatani-Silver affair. To the Pakistani authorities, he was known as Silver, but on the Indian side, they had come to accept him as Sanatani.

The clock ticked with an almost deafening rhythm, each second stretching out longer than the last. Abhimanyu's mind raced with the possible outcomes of this conversation. He had spent countless hours preparing for this moment, crafting proposals and navigating the intricate web of diplomacy and national security.

Finally, the shrill ring of the phone shattered the silence. Abhimanyu's hand moved swiftly, almost instinctively, to pick it up.

"Abhimanyu Singh speaking," he said his voice steady but with an undercurrent of urgency.

"Congratulations, Abhimanyu," Jaffar voice came through the line, clear and decisive. "The proposal given by you to hand over Silver to you has been accepted by the Prime Minister."

Abhimanyu's heart skipped a beat. He had hoped for this outcome, but hearing it confirmed was something else entirely. "That is indeed good news, Jaffar sahib. Much appreciated."

Jaffar continued, "Much time has been consumed as the Prime Minister was in discussion with the armed services chief, Home and Foreign Affairs Ministry. After thorough deliberation, he has cleared the move. Now the ball is in your court. The administrative clearances are with me, and you can now proceed with the operation."

Abhimanyu felt a wave of relief wash over him. "Thank you, Jaffar. I understand the gravity of this decision and the efforts involved. We will handle the next steps with the utmost care and precision."

"I trust you will, Abhimanyu," Jaffar replied. "This is a critical juncture for both our nations. Ensure that everything proceeds smoothly. We cannot afford any missteps."

Abhimanyu nodded, even though Jaffar couldn't see him. "Absolutely, we will coordinate closely with your team to ensure a seamless transition. Sanatani-Silver will be in good hands."

"Very well," Jaffar said. "I will send over the documents and clearances shortly. Good luck, Abhimanyu ."

"Thank you, Jaffar sahib. I will keep you updated on our progress." Abhimanyu felt a wave of gratitude and a deep sense of personal obligation as he thanked Jaffar sincerely. "Thank you, Jaffar sahib. This is not just a professional success but a personal obligation on me. Your cooperation means a great deal."

"You're welcome, Abhimanyu. Best of luck," Jaffar replied, ending the call on a sweet note.

The call ended, leaving Abhimanyu in a moment of reflective silence. He leaned back in his chair, allowing the magnitude of the situation to sink in. Silver, or Sanatani as he was known to them, was now his responsibility. The weight of this task was immense, but Abhimanyu was prepared. He had spent his career navigating such complex scenarios, and this would be no different.

Abhimanyu stood up and walked to the window, looking out over the bustling city. He felt a renewed sense of purpose. The delicate balance of international relations and national security hinged on the next steps he would take. There was no room for error.

Abhimanyu immediately picked up the phone again and sought an appointment with the Prime Minister. Within an hour, the meeting was scheduled. Abhimanyu knew there was no time to lose; every moment counted.

Entering the Prime Minister's office, Abhimanyu felt the gravity of the situation intensify. The PM, a seasoned statesman with an air of calm authority, greeted him warmly.

"Abhimanyu, I trust you have good news," the PM said, gesturing for him to sit.

"Yes, sir," Abhimanyu began, briefing the PM on the latest developments and outlining the future plan of action. "The first critical step is for you to speak with the Prime Minister of Pakistan and formally request the handover of Sanatani. This will solidify our diplomatic stance and ensure a smooth transition."

The PM nodded thoughtfully. "Very well, Let's get this done. The hotline should be ready."

After a brief wait, the hotline between the two Prime Ministers was established. The room was charged with anticipation as the PM of India initiated the conversation.

"Good evening, my friend," the PM of India began, his tone warm and congenial. After exchanging a few pleasantries and general gossip, he steered the conversation toward the matter at hand. "I must make a formal request regarding Silver-Sanatani. We request that you hand him over to us. I assure you, he will not be used for any political motives or diplomacy. His role will be purely humanitarian, and any significant insights from his inputs will be shared at the NSA level."

The PM of Pakistan listened intently, and then extended his good wishes. "I understand the importance of this matter. You have my word, and I extend my good wishes for Silver-Sanatani's future endeavors. As he is already in India, our role in this matter has come to an end."

"Thank you, my friend. This means a great deal to us," the PM of India replied, his relief palpable. "Let us continue to work together for the betterment of our nations."

With the formalities concluded, the call ended on a positive note. The PM turned to Abhimanyu, his expression serious yet relieved. "The path is clear now. Proceed with the next steps."

"Yes, sir," Abhimanyu replied, feeling a surge of determination. He knew the importance of this mission and the delicate balance it required. The successful transition of Silver, now Sanatani, was crucial.

Back in his office, Abhimanyu coordinated with his team, ensuring that every detail was in place. The administrative clearances were reviewed once more, and the final preparations were made.

As night fell, Abhimanyu knew that the hardest part of the mission was behind them, but the real work was just beginning. The journey of Sanatani had entered a new phase, one that promised hope and cooperation between nations.

Abhimanyu stepped out into the cool night air, the weight of his responsibilities settling comfortably on his shoulders. With the diplomatic hurdles cleared and the support of both governments secured, he was ready to lead Sanatani through the next chapter of his extraordinary journey.

He turned back to his desk and picked up the phone once more, dialing the number of his most trusted advisor. "We have the green light," he said when the call was answered. "Prepare the team. It's time to bring Sanatani home."

As the day progressed, Abhimanyu coordinated with various departments, ensuring that every detail was meticulously planned. The administrative clearances arrived promptly, just as Jaffar had promised. Abhimanyu reviewed each document with a critical eye, leaving nothing to chance.

By the evening, the plans were set in motion. The operation to bring Sanatani, to Delhi was underway. Abhimanyu knew that this was only the beginning. The path ahead was fraught with challenges, but he was ready to face them head-on.

With a deep breath, Abhimanyu stepped out of his office, ready to lead his team through this critical mission. The future of their nations depended on the successful execution of this plan, and Abhimanyu was determined to see it through.

CHAPTER TWENTY-SEVEN

<u>**THE REUNION**</u>

A special aircraft of the Indian Air Force touched down at Bangalore Airport, its sleek form cutting through the early morning mist. As the ramp lowered, two black cars rolled out, engines purring quietly, ready to embark on a journey to an undisclosed location. Inside one of the cars sat Abhimanyu Singh, his expression focused and intent. His phone was a constant companion, buzzing with updates and instructions as he coordinated the final details of their mission.

The convoy moved smoothly through the streets, their destination known only to a select few. Abhimanyu's mind raced with the implications of their task. He had to ensure everything was perfect, that every detail had been anticipated and accounted for. The significance of their mission was not lost on him.

As they entered the premises of the secluded compound, a sense of calm enveloped them. The area was serene, a stark contrast to the whirlwind of activity they had left behind. Abhimanyu stepped out of the car, taking a moment to appreciate the tranquility before heading inside.

In a quiet room, Sanatani awaited their arrival. His demeanor was composed, his eyes sharp with understanding. As Abhimanyu entered, Sanatani spoke, breaking the silence.

"The absence of Jaffar and Sattar indicates that you have taken the necessary diplomatic clearances from Pakistan," Sanatani said, his voice steady. "So now, I will be in your captivity."

Abhimanyu nodded, meeting Sanatani's gaze. "Yes, sir. We took all the clearances from them. But you are not here as a prisoner. Treat us as members of your team for your mission. Even the Prime Minister of India will be a buddy to you for your mission."

Sanatani's expression softened, a rueful smile touching his lips. "I understand. Let's proceed."

"We need to leave this place now," Abhimanyu continued. "We will move to Delhi for better connectivity and decision-making."

Sanatani stood from his chair, ready for the next phase of his journey. He had anticipated this moment and was prepared for what lay ahead. The cars started their engines once more, heading back to the airport under the cover of twilight.

The flight to Delhi was uneventful, the atmosphere in the cabin charged with a sense of purpose. As the plane landed at Delhi Airport around 8 PM, a robust security detail was already in place. The operation was running like clockwork, every element precisely timed and executed.

"You will stay with us at Rashtrapati Bhawan," Abhimanyu informed Sanatani as they disembarked. "Tomorrow morning, we will meet the Prime Minister. After that, we will determine the next course of action."

Sanatani nodded, appreciating the meticulous planning that had gone into this operation. His journey was far from over, but he felt a renewed sense of purpose knowing that his mission would continue under the careful watch of his new allies.

The convoy moved through the darkened streets of Delhi, the cities hum a distant backdrop to their quiet determination. As they arrived at Rashtrapati Bhawan, the grandeur of the historic building seemed to welcome them, a symbol of the weighty responsibilities they all carried.

Abhimanyu escorted Sanatani, ensuring he was comfortable and well-provided for. "Rest well, Sanatani. Tomorrow, we begin the next chapter of our mission."

Sanatani offered a tired but genuine smile. "Thank you, Abhimanyu. I look forward to it. I shall be personally thankful to you as you have scheduled my meeting with the Parmanand. Parmanand has took, more than 100 births to reach here. "

As the night settled over Delhi, Abhimanyu felt a sense of accomplishment mingled with anticipation. The day had been a success, but there was much work ahead. Tomorrow would bring new opportunities, new decisions, and new paths to tread. But for tonight, Abhimanyu allowed himself a moment of quiet reflection, the weight of the day's events finally lifting as he prepared for the journey ahead.

The morning sun cast a golden glow over Delhi as Abhimanyu and Sanatani made their way to the Prime Minister's Office. The air was crisp, filled with a sense of anticipation. Today was a day of great significance, not just for Sanatani but for the entire nation. They were on the brink of a mission that could change the course of history.

As they entered the grand hall of the PMO, Abhimanyu's mind was focused, his thoughts on the critical conversation ahead. Sanatani, calm and composed, walked beside him with an air of quiet dignity.

The doors to the Prime Minister's office opened, and they were ushered inside. The room was spacious, filled with light and the subtle hum of power. Moments later, the Prime Minister entered, his presence commanding and yet humble. He approached Sanatani and, in a gesture of deep respect, performed a pranam, prostrating fully before him.

Sanatani's eyes softened with recognition and a hint of amusement. "Parmanand," he said his voice resonant with warmth and authority.

The Prime Minister's cheeks turned a shade of pink, and a radiant smile spread across his face. His eyes sparkled with a light that seemed to come from within. In that moment, he was not just the Prime Minister but Parmanand, a soul who had taken more than a hundred births to reach this position. He acted as if he understood his destiny and the significance of his presence in this era.

"Sanatani ji," the Prime Minister began, his voice filled with reverence, "it is an honor to meet you. I understand now the purpose of my journey and my presence here. We are to complete the mission of re-flowing the mighty river Saraswati."

Sanatani nodded his expression serious. "Indeed, Parmanand. The river Saraswati holds the key to our civilization's resurgence. It is not just a physical task but a spiritual one. The role you played at Mohenjo-Daro was crucial, and now, as the Prime Minister, you are in a unique position to make this vision a reality."

The Prime Minister stood straighter, his resolve evident. "I am ready, Sanatani ji. Whatever needs to be done, we will do it. The resources of this nation are at your disposal."

Abhimanyu watched the exchange, feeling a deep sense of pride and responsibility. This mission was more than just a task; it was a calling, a divine purpose that transcended lifetimes.

"Sanatani," Abhimanyu interjected, "we have the support of the government and the people. The scientific community is ready to assist, and we have mapped out the potential sites for the river's resurgence. With your guidance, we can achieve this monumental task."

Sanatani turned to Abhimanyu, a look of appreciation in his eyes. "You have done well, Abhimanyu. The preparations are thorough. But remember, this is as much a spiritual journey as it is a physical one. The re-flow of Saraswati will require the harmony of mind, body, and soul."

The Prime Minister, now fully embodying his role as Parmanand, nodded in agreement. "We will ensure that every step is taken with reverence and precision. Let us begin this journey together."

With the initial pleasantries and formalities concluded, they delved into the specifics of the mission. Maps were spread out on the table, discussions on logistics, environmental impacts, and the cultural significance of the Saraswati flowed freely. Each detail was meticulously planned, each potential obstacle identified and addressed.

As the meeting progressed, the sense of unity and purpose grew stronger. They were not just leaders and officials; they were stewards of a sacred mission, bound by a shared history and a common goal.

By the time the meeting ended, the foundation for their mission was firmly in place. The Prime Minister, Abhimanyu, and Sanatani stood together, ready to embark on this historic journey. The re-flow of the Saraswati was no longer a distant dream; it was a tangible goal, within their grasp.

As they left the PMO, the significance of the day resonated deeply within them. The future held challenges, but with determination and divine guidance, they knew they would succeed. The mighty Saraswati would flow again, bringing life and prosperity to the land, and fulfilling a destiny that had been written in the sands of time.

CHAPTER TWENTY-EIGHT

<u>THE RIVER OF WISDOM</u>

The Prime Minister of India, seated in his ornate office, leaned forward, a spark of curiosity in his eyes. Across from him sat Sanatani, now known as a revered scholar for his deep understanding of Vedic texts. The Prime Minister broke the silence with a question that had long intrigued him.

"Sanatani, I've always been fascinated by the mention of rivers in the Rig Veda, especially the Saraswati. It's intriguing how frequently it is referred to, more than any other river. Can you shed some light on this?"

Sanatani smiled, appreciating the Prime Minister's interest in ancient wisdom. "Sure, Prime Minister. The Saraswati holds a unique position in the Rig Veda. Its mentions are numerous, perhaps nearly fifty times. This river isn't just a geographical entity; it's a multifaceted symbol with profound spiritual significance."

The Prime Minister nodded, urging him to continue. "I understand it has various aspects. Could you elaborate on these?"

Sanatani leaned back, his eyes reflecting the depth of his knowledge. Firstly, the Saraswati is depicted as a mighty river flowing across the land, much like the Ganga or the Sindu/Indus. Verses such as the Nadi-stuti celebrate this aspect, listing it among other significant rivers. It's described as originating from the mountains and flowing to the ocean, symbolizing its grand presence and importance."

"That's quite poetic," the Prime Minister remarked. "But I also read that it is sometimes visualized as descending from the heavens. How does that fit in?"

"Indeed, Prime Minister. This brings us to its second aspect, the Saraswati as a river-deity. The Vedic seers, in their reverence, considered her descent from the mountains as a divine act. Verses invite her from the heavens and the high mountains to participate in sacrifices, highlighting her celestial origins."

"So, she is both a river and a deity. How do these roles overlap?" the Prime Minister inquired, his interest piqued.

"In the Vedic worldview, these roles are intertwined and not strictly compartmentalized. Saraswati is revered as 'nadītamā' (best of rivers) and 'devītamā' (best of goddesses. The verses praise her as the best of mothers, rivers, and goddesses simultaneously. This dual identity enriches her symbolic presence."

"It's fascinating how the Vedic seers integrated these aspects. What about her role in learning and intellect?" the Prime Minister asked, leaning in closer.

"Her association with intellect and speech is another vital facet," Sanatani explained. "Initially, this connection appears in her role as an Apri deity, invoked during sacrifices to aid in the ritual's intellectual and spiritual efficacy. Verse speaks of Saraswati as prompting our intellect towards higher thoughts. Over time, this evolved, and she became the goddess of learning and fine arts, a role that is widely recognized today."

"So, her transformation into the goddess of learning was gradual?" the Prime Minister queried.

"Yes, it seems so. The Vedic texts primarily highlight her role in rituals and intellect. However, these foundations laid the groundwork for her later identification as the goddess of wisdom, speech, and the arts. This evolution reflects the dynamic nature of Vedic deities, who often embody multiple roles and attributes."

"And what about her physical course? Does the Rig Veda provide details on where she flowed?" the Prime Minister asked, clearly captivated by the narrative.

"The Rig Veda gives a clear geographical context. It describes her journey from the mountains to the ocean. This indicates a vast, powerful river, comparable to the great rivers we know today. Additionally, her mention between the Yamuna and the Sutlej in the Nadi-stuti hymn provides clues about her location, suggesting she flowed through the northwestern part of the Indian subcontinent around Shivalik hills," Sanatani detailed.

"But if she was so mighty, why is there so much debate about her identification today?" the Prime Minister wondered aloud.

"Ah, the mystery of the Saraswati physical disappearance has intrigued scholars for centuries," Sanatani replied. "Geological and hydrological studies suggest that climatic changes and tectonic movements might have altered her course or dried her up. However, her spiritual and cultural legacy remains powerful, embodying the essence of knowledge and purity."

The Prime Minister leaned back, a thoughtful expression on his face. "Thank you, Sanatani. Your insights not only clarify the historical and spiritual significance of the Saraswati but also highlight the rich, interconnected tapestry of Vedic culture. It's clear why she holds such an esteemed place in our heritage."

Sanatani smiled a glint of satisfaction in his eyes. "It was my pleasure, Prime Minister. Understanding the Saraswati indeed understands a vital part of our ancient wisdom and cultural heritage."

As the conversation concluded, the Prime Minister felt a renewed sense of connection to his nation's ancient past, enlightened by the profound wisdom of the Vedic texts and the timeless reverence for the river Saraswati. Now, both of them were to join a gathering in PMO.

The room was filled with scholars, historians, and dignitaries, all eager to hear the tale that Sanatani had meticulously seen. But today, he had more than a story to share; he had a mission to propose. However, Prime Minister requested Sanatani to share the basic relationship of a river, deity in front of gathering which includes the scientists, Engineers, Seers and representatives from the intelligence and armed forces.

"Honorable Prime Minister," Sanatani began his voice steady and resonant, "I am honored to share with you a chapter from our ancient history, a tale that not only highlights the cultural and spiritual richness of our ancestors but also underscores the profound reverence they had for the divine feminine. This is the story of how the Saraswati River was adopted as the goddess Devi Saraswati in the ancient city of Kukkutarma/Mohenjo-Daro."

Sanatani paused, allowing the anticipation to build before continuing.

"In the ancient city of Kukkutarma/Mohenjo-Daro, every dwelling echoed with the presence of the divine feminine, manifested in the form of female figurines adorning the sacred spaces of the inhabitants. Each family revered its own kul Devi, a guardian mother goddess who watched over them with love and protection. The world has seen the recovery of a multitude of Mother Goddess figurines from every excavated site hints at the widespread worship of the divine feminine during the glorious days of the Sindhu/Indus Valley civilization.

Among the treasures unearthed at Kukkutarma/Mohenjo-Daro was a standing figure of the Mother Goddess, now displayed at the National Museum in New Delhi. This terracotta figurine, ornately adorned with chokers, necklaces, and bangles, exuded a sense of divine grace and maternal love. The elaborate headgear, intricate jewelry, and finely crafted attire spoke of the reverence and devotion accorded to the Mother Goddess, a symbol of fertility, protection, and abundance.

The large terracotta figurine, measuring 23 by 8.5 cm, showcased the technical mastery of the Rishi Vishvakarma in clay modeling and baking. The thick red slip coating not only added luster but also protected the surface from erosion, preserving the divine essence of the Mother Goddess for eternity. Adorned with intricate necklaces and a fan-shaped headdress reminiscent of oil lamps or incense trays, the figurine radiated a sense of sacred beauty and spiritual power.

As the ancient plowed their fields and crafted their wares with skill and precision, the worship of the Mother Goddess remained a central aspect of their religious beliefs. Every village, every home, had its own guardian mother, a Mata or Amba, revered for her blessings of children, health, and prosperity. The female figurines found at Kukkutarma/ Mohenjo-Daro, nursing infants with love and care, symbolized the nurturing and protective qualities of the divine feminine that permeated every aspect of daily life. The female figurines stood as symbols of religious power and divine grace. With their hands raised in reverence, their legs pressed together in a stance of strength and stability, these figurines embodied the essence of the Mother Goddess, the giver of life and sustenance. The intricate double volute headdresses, decorated and painted black, added a touch of mystique and elegance to these sacred representations of the divine feminine.

One fateful period, the sages of the Saptarishees gathered in a solemn assembly at Kukkutarma/ Mohenjo-Daro to perform a grand yajna, a fire sacrifice, intended to invoke the blessings of the divine for the prosperity of their land. As the sacred flames danced and the air filled with the fragrant smoke of burning herbs and ghee, the sages chanted ancient hymns, their voices rising in harmonious unison.

However, despite their fervent prayers and meticulous rituals, the Yagya failed to yield the desired blessings. The sages, deeply troubled by this turn of events, sought the counsel of the revered sage Rishi Agastya. It was he who, with his profound wisdom and insight, perceived that the river Saraswati, a lifeline for the civilization, needed to be honored and elevated to the status of a deity.

In an inspired vision, Rishi Vashisht saw the river Saraswati as a divine mother, nurturing and sustaining all life with her sacred waters. He proposed that the failed Yagya be transformed into a ceremony of adoption, wherein the river Saraswati would be consecrated as Devi Saraswati and the goddess of knowledge, music, art, and wisdom.

The sages and the people of Kukkutarma/ Mohenjo-Daro embraced Rishi's vision with reverence and devotion. They gathered the many figures of the Mother Goddess, each representing various aspects of the divine feminine, and presented them before the sacred fire. Among these figures, one stood out with unparalleled grace and majesty. Adorned with exquisite jewelry and an ornate headdress, this figurine radiated a serene and compassionate aura, embodying the essence of Devi Saraswati.

In a sacred ritual, Rishi Vashisht and the assembled sages invoked the divine presence into this chosen figure, consecrating it as Devi Saraswati. The river Saraswati, now honored as a goddess, was celebrated with hymns of praise and offerings of flowers and fruits. The people of Kukkutarma/ Mohenjo-Daro rejoiced, their hearts filled with gratitude and reverence for the divine mother who had accepted their devotion and blessed their land.

Sanatani concluded his narration, and the room fell silent, the weight of the ancient story resonating deeply with everyone present. The Prime Minister, visibly moved, nodded appreciatively.

But before the Prime Minister could respond, Sanatani leaned forward, his eyes blazing with conviction. "Honorable Prime Minister, the time has come for us to do more than merely honor our past. We must act to restore the glory of the Saraswati River. The task is monumental, but it is inevitable and essential for the revival of our cultural heritage and the sustenance of our land."

Sanatani straightened his posture, his voice authoritative and unwavering. "Honorable Prime Minister, I propose that you and I, together, embark on a mission to revive the Saraswati River. This is not just a matter of historical significance; it is a vital step for the future of our nation. By restoring the Saraswati, we will not only honor our ancestors but also provide a lifeline for our agricultural and cultural resurgence."

The room buzzed with murmurs of agreement and excitement. The Prime Minister nodded slowly, his expression serious yet thoughtful. "You speak with great passion, Sanatani. This is indeed a noble mission. Let us work together to make this vision a reality.

The re-flow of the Saraswati is a task we will undertake with determination and unity."

Sanatani smiled his heart swelling with pride and determination. "Thank you, Prime Minister. Together, we will bring the divine waters of the Saraswati back to life, and in doing so, we will rejuvenate the soul of our nation."

The commitment was made, and a new chapter in the history of their land was set in motion, driven by the timeless wisdom of the past and the unwavering resolve of the present.

The room was silent as Sanatani continued, "Our future is built on our present, which in turn is built on our past. These elements are intertwined, forming a continuous thread through time," Sanatani began. "By ignoring lessons from the past, we risk repeating the same mistakes in both the present and the future."Hence, the call to action: 'Awake, Arise & Flow, O Saraswati, be proud once more of thyself.' This should be India's motto for the next decade." It's time to explore and reach out to the roots of Saraswati culture from the present states of Himachal Pradesh, Haryana, Punjab, and Rajasthan."

Sanatani eyes gleamed with passion as he outlined his vision. "Everything is in place to help those who wish to revive Saraswati. Our noble ancestors have documented everything meticulously. The excavated artifacts reflect a glorious past, and with modern technology, science, and knowledge, we can achieve the goal of bringing Saraswati back to life."

He added, "When this circle is completed, India will raise to the top, offering a gift to humanity—a restored sense of purpose and spirit. India will become the divine leader of the world, spreading the principles of Sanatana Dharma."

"The first responsibility of reviving Saraswati lies with the Brahmin Saraswat community," Sanatani declared. "Thousands of years ago, the kings and people looked to us to protect the dying Saraswati. We failed then, but now we must prioritize this mission. I dream of seeing the flowing waters of the Saraswati and a replica of Kukkutarma/ Mohenjo-Daro, 'The Saraswat Brahminabad,' on the banks of Saraswati in Haryana or 'Sapta Saraswat' in Rajasthan."

The Rig Veda praises Saraswati, and its hymns pray for the river to sustain its inhabitants. The present discovery of the river's dry bed via satellite images debunked the myth of Saraswati and highlighted its importance in our Vedic times." "Saraswati's heritage is not dead; she lives, she flows, and she still has a role in shaping humanity's future," Sanatani asserted. "The Saraswat community must unite to revive the Saraswati culture and heritage. Renaming places and justifying our existence as Saraswata on earth is crucial to rejuvenate the Mother of Rivers, The Saraswati."

He concluded, "This mission is not just about reviving a river but about rekindling a cultural and spiritual renaissance. It's about honoring our ancestors, preserving our heritage, and ensuring that the wisdom and knowledge of the Saraswati civilization continue to inspire and guide future generations."

"Moreover, the time has finally arrived for the purpose of my life to reach its fulfillment—a purpose rooted in the revival and reflow of the Saraswati River. This mission has guided my every step, shaping my journey through trials and discoveries, and now, as the waters of Saraswati are destined to flow once more, I see the culmination of all that I have worked for. It is not merely a personal victory but a restoration of heritage, a rekindling of hope, and a tribute to the ancient wisdom that has endured through generations. My life's purpose will conclude on a positive note, symbolizing renewal, connection, and the resilience of a civilization waiting to be reborn."

The Prime Minister, moved by Sanatani's passionate plea, stood and extended his hand. "Sanatani, your vision is compelling and necessary. Together, we will embark on this mission to revive Saraswati. Let us begin this journey, not just for ourselves, but for the future of our nation and the world."

Sanatani shook the Prime Minister's hand, feeling the weight of history and the promise of the future in their grasp. The mission to revive the Saraswati River was no longer a dream; it was a shared commitment, a beacon of hope, and a testament to the enduring spirit of their people.

CHAPTER TWENTY-NINE

THE LANGUAGE OF THE SEALS

After meeting with Sanatani, many questions swirled in the Prime Minister's mind. Yet, a sense of comfort had settled over him after their discussion about the revival of the Saraswati River. Feeling the weight of the mission, the Prime Minister called for an urgent meeting. The National Security Advisor (NSA) arrived at the PMO, accompanied by Sanatani.

The Prime Minister stood, paying his respects to Sanatani, before instructing the NSA to leave the room. Once they were alone, the Prime Minister leaned back in his chair, his eyes keen with interest.

"Sanatani," he began, his voice measured, "the mission to revive the Saraswati River demands extensive work in archaeology and linguistics. We need to decipher the Indus seals and uncover the true nature of the Saraswati civilization. Can you assist us in unraveling these ancient symbols?"

Sanatani smiled humbly, a glint of wisdom in his eyes. "Prime Minister, the modern world has yet to interpret my creation correctly. You see, that is not a language as we understand it today. At that juncture, no written language existed. It was later, at Agastya Peeth, that Agastya transcribed the spoken hymns in writing. The Indus seals comprise slightly over 400 basic signs. Only 31 of these signs occur over 100 times, while the rest were not used regularly. In truth, these 400 symbols can be reduced to 39 elementary signs; the rest are merely stylistic variations and differences between scribes."

The Prime Minister nodded, his interest piqued. "So, what is the solution to this deciphering problem, as no universally accepted decipherment exists. No bilingual inscriptions have been found to compare the Indus Script with a known writing system."

"The solution lies in the small inscriptions," Sanatani explained. "Each seal or tablet typically records an average of six signs. The seals are revealing due to their pictographic nature. The signs are not alphabetical but largely pictographic. Traditional methods of present world analyzing recurring sign patterns have failed to unlock the meaning of this writing system, but the decipherment of the seal signs can still be pursued successfully."

Sanatani continued, "The Indus Script combines word signs and symbols with phonetic values. This type of writing system is known as 'logo-syllabic,' where some symbols express ideas or words while others represent sounds. Based on the identification of roughly 400 signs, it is unlikely that our Sindhu/ Indus Script were solely phonetic. However, if the hypothesis that the hundreds of signs can be reduced to just 39 is true, then the Indus Script could indeed be solely phonetic."

The Prime Minister listened intently as Sanatani elaborated. "Certain numerical values have been identified in the script. A single unit is represented by a downward stroke, while semicircles denote units of ten. The symbols inscribed on seals are archaeological proof of the activities that took place. Sanatani leaned forward, his voice steady and confident, as he began to explain the profound significance of the Sindhu/Indus seals. "These seals," he said, "serve as standardized formats that encapsulate the agenda of the day for sacred rituals. Each seal provides a wealth of information: the Rishi responsible for chanting the hymn, the deity being invoked, and the King or Kshatriya serving as the main offerer. They also detail the hymn's metre, the Swar or tone of the metre, and the precise timeline for the Rishi's performance at the yajna, specifying the required month, day, or kaala to complete the sacred chants. These elements collectively form a meticulous framework for preserving the sanctity and precision of the Vedic rituals."

These seals acted like tokens for the activities happening in Mohenjo-Daro. There may have been many priests and many mantras in one hymn, so permutations and combinations are necessary to understand the symbols. We can start by assuming that animals facing right indicate days leading up to the full moon (Purnima), while animals facing left signify days leading up to the new moon (Amavasya). Seals that are straight represent the days of the full moon and the new moon, respectively."

Sanatani's explanation captivated the room. He added, "By putting the Deity or Priest first in our permutations, we can start to make sense of these ancient symbols. The seals essentially captured the activities and rituals of the day, providing a structured agenda."

The Prime Minister, impressed by the depth of Sanatani's briefing, nodded thoughtfully. "Sanatani, your insights are invaluable. We must begin this task immediately. The revival of the Saraswati River and the decipherment of the Indus seals are intertwined missions. By understanding our past, we can reclaim our heritage and move forward with a renewed sense of purpose."

Sanatani smiled, his heart filled with a sense of fulfillment. "Prime Minister, together we shall unlock the secrets of the Sindhu/Indus seals and bring the Saraswati River back to life. This journey will not only honor our ancestors but also set the foundation for a prosperous future."

The commitment to decipher the Indus seals and revive the Saraswati River was now a shared mission, driven by the collective determination to honor the past and shape the future.

The Prime Minister, still intrigued by the insights Sanatani had shared, leaned forward, his curiosity undiminished. "Sanatani, there are brick tower-like structures at Kukkutarma/Mohenjo-Daro. Can you tell me more about those? What purpose did they serve?"

Sanatani nodded, his eyes gleaming with the excitement of a scholar eager to share his knowledge. "Prime Minister, those tower-like structures you refer to are indeed fascinating. They were not merely architectural marvels but were integral to the advanced urban planning and sanitation systems of our township. These towers were actually water tanks, ingeniously designed to supply water to the inhabitants."

The Prime Minister's interest deepened as Sanatani continued. "The water tanks were constructed with baked bricks, ensuring their durability and resistance to the elements. From these tanks, burnt earth pipes extended into the various rooms of the inhabitants. This system was highly advanced for its time, providing a steady supply of water directly to the kitchens and toilets within the rooms/homes."

Sanatani paused to let the Prime Minister absorb the information before elaborating further. "The purpose of these water systems was not just practical but also deeply cultural. The Brahmins, along with other classes, observed strict codes of purity and cleanliness. By having a reliable and separate water supply, they could maintain the sanctity of their living spaces, kitchens, and ritual areas without the risk of contamination from other activities."

He continued, "These water tanks and the associated plumbing systems reflect the sophisticated engineering skills of that time. The pipes were laid with precise gradients to ensure a consistent flow of water, and the tanks were strategically placed to optimize the distribution throughout the settlement. This also allowed for efficient drainage and waste management, crucial for maintaining the overall health and hygiene of the densely populated city."

The Prime Minister was visibly impressed. "Sanatani, it's astounding to think that such advanced systems existed thousands of years ago. How did you and your team manage to develop such intricate engineering techniques?"

Sanatani smiled. "We were remarkably innovative. We combined practical needs with our deep understanding of natural principles. The materials used, such as burnt bricks and carefully crafted pipes were chosen for their durability and effectiveness. The design of the water tanks and the layout of the plumbing systems were results of meticulous planning and a keen understanding of hydraulics, even if not formally articulated in the way we understand engineering today."

He added, "The kitchens and toilets in each dwelling were crucial aspects of daily life. The kitchens, regarded as sacred spaces where food was prepared with ritual purity, required a steady and pristine water supply. Toilets, which were typically attached to each house, were connected to a sophisticated drainage system that ensured waste was efficiently removed from the living areas. This separation of spaces for different functions helped maintain the health and spiritual well-being of the community."

The Prime Minister pondered this information, recognizing the complexity and foresight of the ancient urban planners. "It's incredible to see how these ancient systems laid the groundwork for modern urban planning and sanitation. Their emphasis on purity and efficiency is something we can still learn from today."

Sanatani nodded in agreement. "Indeed, Prime Minister. The lessons are timeless. The achievements in urban planning, water management and social organization reflect a society that valued innovation, health, and spiritual purity. As we work towards reviving the Saraswati River, we should draw inspiration from their ingenuity and commitment to holistic well-being."

He continued, "The water tanks and the plumbing systems are more than just remnants of a bygone era. They are symbols of a civilization that understood the importance of harmony between man, nature, and the divine. As we strive to bring the Saraswati back to life, we must also revive the spirit of innovation and respect for nature that characterized our ancestors."

The Prime Minister, deeply moved by Sanatani's words, spoke with renewed determination. "Sanatani, your insights have not only deepened my understanding of our ancient heritage but have also inspired me to approach our mission with a greater sense of purpose. We must ensure that our efforts to revive the Saraswati River honor the legacy of the Saraswati Civilization and contribute to the well-being of our nation."

The Prime Minister, with a touch of reluctance, asked Sanatani about the lasting significance of the Yajna and why, despite its ancient wisdom, the modern world often overlooks its profound insights. Sanatani responded with a serene smile and began to explain. He described the civilization commonly known as the Indus Valley or Harappan Civilization, which he referred to as the Saraswat Civilization, thriving along the Sindhu (Indus) River with prominent sites like Kukkutarma (Mohenjo-Daro), Brahminabad (Harappa), Kalibangan, and Lothal. Initially thought to be limited to regions such as Sindh, Punjab, Rajasthan, and Gujarat, this civilization's reach extended across the subcontinent—from Tamil Nadu to Vaishali in Bihar—and into modern-day Pakistan, Afghanistan, and parts of Iran, dating as far back as 7000 BCE.

Sanatani smiled, feeling a profound sense of fulfillment. "Thank you, Prime Minister. Together, we will bring the divine waters of the Saraswati back to life, drawing from the wisdom of our ancestors and the strength of our people. This mission will not only revive a river but also rekindle the spirit of innovation and harmony that has always been the hallmark of our civilization."The journey to revive the Saraswati River was not just a physical endeavor but a spiritual and cultural renaissance that would shape the future of their nation.

The meeting concluded with the Prime Minister saying, I wish you could be my personal guest, as we share a connection spanning thousands of years, we must adhere to protocols, and I apologize for that. Hopefully, you must be comfortable at Rashtrapati Bhawan. I will see you soon, but first, I need to attend to the day's pressing matters."Sanatani nodded in agreement, and the meeting dispersed.

CHAPTER THIRTY

<u>STRATEGIZING THE REVIVAL OF SARASWATI</u>

The grand conference room in the Rashtrapati Bhawan was abuzz with anticipation. Gathered around the large oval table were the Prime Minister, the Chief Ministers of Himachal Pradesh, Punjab, Haryana, Gujarat and Rajasthan, as well as top officials from the state irrigation and water departments. Also present were a high-profile officer from ISRO and a team of zoologists, all assembled to discuss the ambitious plan of reviving the Saraswati River.

The Prime Minister began the meeting with a clear and determined tone. "Ladies and gentlemen, we are here to discuss a project of national significance—the revival of the Saraswati River. This is not just a matter of historical and cultural importance, but also a critical step towards ensuring water security and agricultural sustainability for our states."

He gestured to the Chief Minister of Himachal Pradesh, signaling him to present first. "Our state has the potential to contribute significantly to this project," the Chief Minister began. "We have several rivers and streams originating from the Himalayas. By creating interconnections, we can direct some of this water towards the dried bed of the Saraswati. It will require meticulous planning and cooperation across state lines."

The Chief Minister of Haryana added, "Haryana is ready to collaborate. We have substantial canal networks that can be modified to facilitate this project. Additionally, groundwater recharging will be an essential aspect to ensure the sustained flow of water in the Saraswati."

The Prime Minister nodded in agreement and turned to the Chief Minister of Rajasthan. "Rajasthan's arid conditions make this project even more crucial for us," the Chief Minister said. "By reviving the Saraswati, we can enhance our water availability for both agriculture and daily use. We are committed to making the necessary investments and policy changes to support this initiative."

The Chief Minister of Punjab highlighted the seasonal nature of the Ghaggar River and expressed optimism that collective efforts could transform it into a perennial river. He quoted that Haryana has already declared the Ghaggar as the ancient Saraswati and emphasized that, currently, Rajasthan and Gujarat do not have a direct role in this matter. However, he acknowledged that if there will any changes regarding the course of the ancient Saraswati and if those states were involved, Punjab would wholeheartedly support such initiatives. He also mentioned that Punjab is open to contributing water from the rivers flowing through the state to support such a noble cause.

The Chief Minister of Gujarat expressed his unwavering commitment to the project aimed at reviving the ancient Saraswati River. He extended his gratitude to all the concerned states through which the Saraswati once flowed and is now about to flow again. The Chief Minister emphasized that while the entire nation would gain spiritual connectivity through this endeavor, it is ultimately the people of Gujarat who will benefit most tangibly from the restored water resources. This project, he noted, symbolizes not just the revival of a river but also the reawakening of a profound spiritual bond that unites all of Bharatavarsa.

The high-profile officer from ISRO then took the floor, presenting detailed satellite images and geospatial data of the region. "Using advanced imaging technology; we have identified the historical route of the Saraswati River. Our data indicates potential connection points where existing rivers and streams can be redirected. This map shows the most feasible routes for water flow."

The ISRO officer pointed to a large screen displaying the maps. "Here, in Himachal Pradesh, we see viable sources that can be channeled through Haryana and into Rajasthan, eventually feeding into the ancient Saraswati bed. The terrain analysis and flow simulations support this route as the most efficient."

The Prime Minister, impressed by the thorough analysis, asked, "What about the environmental impact? How do we ensure that this project benefits the ecosystem and does not disrupt existing habitats?"

One of the zoologists, an expert in aquatic ecosystems, responded, "We have conducted preliminary studies and can assure that the revival of the Saraswati will have positive ecological impacts. By creating new water bodies, we will enhance biodiversity, providing habitats for various species. Additionally, we plan to implement measures to protect and nurture the local flora and fauna, ensuring a balanced and sustainable ecosystem."

At this pivotal moment, the Prime Minister welcomed a special invitee from Pakistan to address the gathering. He acknowledged the significance of the occasion, noting how the efforts to revive the Saraswati River were now reaching their final stages. The Prime Minister highlighted that the origins of this great river trace back to present-day Pakistan, and he praised Pakistan for demonstrating an exemplary spirit of cooperation by granting India the freedom to undertake this monumental task.

He emphasized that Pakistan's gracious conduct in allowing this cross-border initiative would serve as a shining example of goodwill and collaboration for generations to come. The Prime Minister expressed his deep appreciation for this gesture, recognizing it as a symbol of shared heritage and a step towards fostering unity and understanding between the two nations.

Mohammad Faiz Husain, the globally renowned environmentalist, began his address by expressing gratitude to the Indian Prime Minister for his commitment to maintaining transparency and inclusiveness throughout this significant endeavor. He acknowledged the Prime Minister's promise to keep

Pakistan informed of every development and expressed his deep appreciation for this gesture of collaboration.

Turning to the Chief Ministers and guests, Husain conveyed his complete satisfaction and happiness at seeing all the states, despite their diverse languages and cultures, united in support of the project. He commended the collective spirit and readiness of every state to contribute in every possible way.

With a lighthearted remark to the Chief Minister of Gujarat, Husain noted that before Gujarat reaps the benefits, Pakistan will be the first to witness the river's revival, as the Saraswati will interact with the Indus at Sakkur before flowing eastward towards the Rann of Kutch. He highlighted that at Sakkur, the real confluence of waters from both countries—the Indus and the Saraswati—will take place, symbolizing an ancient bond that predates any religious divisions in the region.

"We were united when the Saraswati turned away from us, and we will be united again when she greets the Indus with her Himalayan waters," he proclaimed. He then extended Pakistan's wholehearted cooperation and support for this historic project, emphasizing the shared heritage and deep connections between the two nations.

The Prime Minister turned to the state irrigation and water department heads. "We need a detailed plan on how to implement these connections. This includes engineering designs, cost estimates, and timelines. We must also consider the legal and policy frameworks required to facilitate cross-state water transfers."

The head of Haryana's water department spoke up, "We will work closely with our counterparts in Himachal Pradesh and Rajasthan to draft a comprehensive plan. This will involve constructing new canals, upgrading existing infrastructure, and ensuring that water distribution is equitable and efficient."

The Prime Minister emphasized, "This project must be a model of inter-state cooperation and innovation. We will establish a joint task force with representatives from each state, ISRO, and environmental experts. Regular updates and transparent communication will be key issue to our success."

As the meeting progressed, the leaders and experts brainstormed various aspects of the project, from technical challenges to funding mechanisms. The atmosphere was charged with a sense of purpose and collaboration, each participant recognizing the significance of their endeavor.

Prime Minister stated, "The revival of the Saraswati River is a mission that will require our collective expertise, resources, and unwavering commitment. Let us pledge to work together to bring this ancient river back to life, ensuring a prosperous future for our people and honoring the legacy of our ancestors."

Sanatani, who had been observing the meeting, felt a deep sense of fulfillment. The seeds of his vision were taking root, nurtured by the dedication and unity of these leaders and experts. The journey to revive the Saraswati River was underway, driven by a shared commitment to reclaim their heritage and secure the future.

Then the Prime Minister introduced Sanatani as an eminent sage from Augusta peetha to provide a motivation and inspiration road map to come out from this exercise as flying colours.

Sanatani stood before the assembly, a gathering that included the Prime Minister, the chief ministers of the states connected to the river's ancient course, and a host of distinguished guests. The grand hall was filled with a sense of anticipation as Sanatani prepared to share his findings and vision for the revitalization of the Saraswati River. His mission was ambitious yet clear: to chart the ancient route of the Saraswati, reconnect the cities and regions it once nurtured, and ensure its sacred waters would flow once again.

With a deep breath, Sanatani began his voice steady and resonant. "Esteemed Prime Minister, honorable chief ministers, and distinguished guests especially from a neighboring Country Pakistan, today marks a significant milestone in our journey to rediscover and revive the Saraswati River. As described in our ancient texts, the Saraswati holds immense historical, cultural, and spiritual significance. It is originated in the Himalayas, flowing through what are now the states of Himachal Pradesh, Punjab,

Haryana, and Rajasthan, before discharging into the Rann of Kachchh in Gujarat. Our mission is to trace this ancient route and reconnect the dots that have been lost to time. During its flow, Saraswati should meet the Indus in the same way as thousands of year ago and should depart to Rann of Kutch carrying the Indus waters to merge with the sea.

He gestured to a detailed map projected onto a large screen, highlighting the proposed route of the Saraswati River. The Prime Minister informed me that research, supported by satellite imagery and archaeological evidence, has conclusively established that the river originated in the Himalayan region, specifically from the glaciers of Himachal Pradesh and Uttarakhand. It then flowed southwest, enriching the land and sustaining ancient civilizations along its course.

The northwestern part of India is currently drained by three major independent river systems: the Yamuna, Sutlej, and Ghaggar . The Yamuna and Sutlej are perennial rivers, while the Ghaggar is primarily an ephemeral river. The Sutlej River originates from the holy lake of Mansarovar in Tibet, flowing through the Himalayas and entering the plains near Ropar in Punjab, where it takes a sharp right-angled turn and flows westward for about 150 km before joining the Beas River near Firozpur. It is also joined by several smaller streams, such as the Sirsa Nadi, Siswan Nadi, Chikni Nadi, Bakhi Nadi, and Haripur Nadi, as it meanders through the region.

Meanwhile, the Tons River, originating from the Bandarpunch Glacier in the Garhwal Himalayas, joins the Yamuna River at Paonta Sahib. It meets the Giri River near Paonta, about 12 km upstream from the confluence of the Bata and Yamuna rivers. The Yamuna, once thought to be a major tributary of the Saraswati, was diverted through the Yamuna Tear Fault and originally flowed through the Bata River course to join the Markanda River. The Yamuna River itself begins at the Yamunotri Glacier, entering the plains near Yamunanagar in Haryana and displaying a typical rectangular drainage pattern indicative of its flow through a structurally controlled terrain.

The Ghaggar River originates from the Morni Hills in the Siwaliks and enters the plains near Ambala in Haryana. It flows for 175 km before joining the Saraswati at Rasula in Patiala district, Punjab. The combined river, known as the Ghaggar, continues through Sirsa in Haryana, and Hanumangarh and Ganganagar districts in Rajasthan, eventually passing through the Bahawalpur region in Pakistan, where its bed dries up near Sirsa. The Saraswati River rises in the Sirmur region of the Siwaliks, entering the plains at Adi Badri in Yamunanagar district of Haryana, and flows through Yamunanagar, Kurukshetra, and Karnal districts before merging with the Ghaggar near Rasula in Patiala district, Punjab.

The Ghaggar's flow along straight lines joined at sharp angles reflects the structural control of its unstable channel. The Markanda River, originating from Nahan in Sirmaur district of Himachal Pradesh, reaches the plains in Ambala and later joins the Ghaggar in Patiala district, serving as a natural divide between the Bata-Markanda complex and the Giri River.

Pointing to the regions on the map, Sanatani continued, "The river's journey, as described in Rigvedic literature, includes four major rivers: the Sindhu (Indus) and its tributaries, such as Vitasa (Jhelum) and Asikni (Chenab); the Shatadru (Sutlej) and its major tributaries, Vipasa (Beas) and Parasuni (Ravi); the Saraswati with its upper tributaries like Markanda, Ghaggar, Chautang, and Dangri; and the Drishadvati, potentially with Lavanavati as a tributary. Originating from the Himalayas, these rivers historically flowed across Rajasthan, Gujarat, and parts of Pakistan, eventually meeting in the Rann of Kachchh in the Arabian Sea. Today, only the Indus and Sutlej rivers continue to flow through the vast Indo-Gangetic alluvial plain, while the Saraswati and Drishadvati have dried up, their remnants buried beneath the sands of the Thar Desert.

The room was silent; the audience captivated by the river's storied past. Sanatani continued, "To reconnect the various dots of the Saraswati's path, we propose a multifaceted approach. The present administrators have rightly done extensive geological surveys, hydrological studies, and archaeological excavations. They have also traced the remnants of the riverbed, identify potential sources of underground water, and revive the flow where feasible."

"Excavations at key sites along the proposed route will uncover our ancient settlements, artifacts, and other evidence of the Saraswati's historical presence. These findings will provide invaluable insights into the river's past and guide our efforts to revive it. Pilgrimage routes will be established, connecting key sites and fostering a deeper connection with our past".""

Sanatani's voice grew more impassioned as he spoke of the future. "The revival of the Saraswati River is not merely an academic exercise or an environmental project. It is a journey to reclaim our heritage and reconnect with the essence of our civilization. As the waters of the Saraswati flow once more, they will bring with them the wisdom of the ages and the promise of a prosperous future." "I urge all of you present here to support this endeavor, to join hands in this sacred mission. Together, we can bring the Saraswati back to life, not just as a physical river but as a living testament to our enduring legacy."

CHAPTER THIRTY-ONE

<u>The Grand Plan for Saraswati's Revival</u>

The room erupted in applause, with leaders and guests rising to their feet in a unanimous show of support. The Prime Minister stepped forward, his voice filled with admiration. "Sanatani, your vision is inspiring, and your dedication is commendable. The government will provide all necessary resources and support to ensure the success of this monumental task. However, despite the vast amount of information at our disposal, there remains a significant gap—we have yet to identify the exact course of the revered Saraswati. All our technological analyses, excavation sites, archaeological findings, and even oral traditions point in different directions, leaving us unable to converge on a singular path. I request you, Sanatani, to focus specifically on which direction we should precede."

Sanatani smiled inwardly, recognizing the depth of the challenge ahead. He stood from his chair, and like a commander calling his troops to attention, he raised his hand, signaling for silence. The room quieted immediately, captivated by his presence. With a calm yet commanding voice, he began, "This is the cause of Saraswati, our *Naditama*, our *Devitama*. She cannot be restricted to a single direction or confined within a single path. Throughout millennia, the Saraswati has taken many courses, adapting to countless changes brought about by natural forces and human endeavors."

He paused, letting the weight of his words settle over the room. "Originally, she emerged from the peaks near Lake Mansarovar, only to later shift her origins to the Bandar Poonch area. From there, the Saraswati gathered the waters of the Yamuna, Giri, Tons, and Bata, flowing down to Kurukshetra, Sirsa, and into the valley segment of the Luni, between Pachpadra and the Rann of Kachchh. Yet, even this was not a constant; the river shifted westward, severing its connection with the Luni and forging new channels through the desert terrain of Jaisalmer district. Eventually, the river settled into the Hakra-Nara-Wahind-Raini course."

Sanatani's voice grew more passionate as he continued, "The Saraswati was forced to shift her course at least four times, driven westward by the encroachment of Aeolian sands on her southern route. These shifts created multiple courses for the river over the ages. The Oldest Course was Nohar-Surjansar-Samrau-Pachpadra, the earliest known path of the Saraswati, flowing through northwest India. The Second Course was Sirsa-Lunkarnansar-Bikaner-Samrau-Pachpadra, another ancient path shaped by geological and environmental changes.The Third Course was Nohar-Rangmahal-Suratgarh-Anupgarh-Sakhi-Hakra-Nara, a further westward shift as the river sought a new way to reach its destination.The Fourth Course was Jakhal-Sirsa-Hanumangarh-Pilibangan-Suratgarh-Anupgarh-Sakhi-Hakra-Nara, showing yet another transformation in the river's journey as it adapted to the desert's challenges and the Fifth Course was a shift at Anupgarh-Fort Abbas, where the river altered its path to join the Indus drainage basin rather than continuing independently to the Rann of Kutch."

He paused again, his eyes sweeping across the room, ensuring his message was fully absorbed. "This is why we cannot confine Saraswati to a single direction. Her journey was not a straight line but a dynamic, living path that changed as the land around her changed. To find her, we must explore all these routes, understand the geological shifts, the changes in topography, and the layers of history buried beneath the sands. The Saraswati is not just a river but a symbol of resilience, adaptability, and the enduring spirit of our civilization."

Sanatani's voice softened, filled with a reverence that seemed to touch every corner of the room. "I ask that we proceed with a multi-directional approach, respecting the river's many courses and the stories each path holds. Let us employ all available technologies, our collective wisdom, and above all, the spirit of unity in this sacred mission. For in finding the Saraswati, we do not just rediscover a river; we reconnect with our roots, our heritage, and the divine essence that flows through us all."

Recognizing the urgency of the moment, Sanatani sensed the need for a clear and actionable plan. He put forth his proposal to the assembly with a thoughtful demeanor. "In such circumstances," he began, "we can consider a strategic approach that involves integrating the waters at Adi Badri. This would serve as a critical confluence point for the revival of the Saraswati."

He continued, "The waters of the Giri, Bata, and Tons rivers should be directed towards Adi Badri. By carefully managing the water flow, especially at intersections such as the Markandeya and Bata, where the mountain level rises only 20 meters, we can reduce this height to flow the waters towards Adi Badri."A dedicated channel from Yamuna should be made to divert Yamuna waters towards Adi Badri.

Sanatani then outlined his dual-route plan. "From Adi Badri, we should pursue two distinct routes. The western branch will merge with the waters of the Ghaggar River . Sutlej dedicated channel will then feed into the Ghaggar. This way, the Ghaggar River will no longer be just a monsoon-fed stream but will have a perennial flow, enriched throughout the year. The water from this route will continue to replenish the dry bed of the Hakra River and ultimately meet the Indus River. This will ensure a continuous flow, reviving one of the ancient path of the Saraswati."

He paused, allowing the gathered leaders and guests to absorb the significance of his words before continuing. "The eastern branch should draw water from the Yamuna and its tributaries through a specially constructed channel at Adi Badri , which would then carry the flow towards western Rajasthan. This path acknowledges the historical reality that the once-mighty Saraswati met a sudden end due to geotectonic activities and climatic changes, transforming it from a perennial river flowing with grandeur into an ephemeral stream that eventually disappeared into the sands of the Thar Desert."

Sanatani's eyes gleamed with a blend of hope and determination. "However, by re-establishing this route, we can restore the Saraswati's flow, allowing it to traverse its ancient course. After meeting the Indus at Sakkur, the Saraswati will once again carry the combined waters of the Indus to the sea through Runn of Kutch. Furthermore, the Luni River, which flows through the arid regions of Rajasthan, can join this course, channeling its waters towards northern Gujarat and ultimately discharging into the Gulf of Khambhat on the Gujarat coast."

He concluded, "By integrating these waters, we aim not only to revive the Saraswati but also to restore the ancient hydrological balance that once sustained our ancestors. This approach will not only benefit the regions through which the river flows but will also enhance the ecological and cultural connectivity of our land, from the Himalayas to the sea. The Saraswati's revival will symbolize the restoration of a lost heritage and the rekindling of a collective spirit that transcends borders and generations."

The room fell silent, filled with a mix of awe and reflection. Then, gradually, nods of agreement spread like a wave among the gathered leaders and guests. The Prime Minister, visibly moved by Sanatani's insight and passion, stepped forward again. "Sanatani, your plan is as comprehensive as it is visionary. It offers a practical approach to reviving the Saraswati while respecting its historical and spiritual legacy. We must now work together to turn this plan into reality, ensuring that the Saraswati flows once more, not only as a river but as a symbol of our unity and resilience."

A moment of deep contemplation settled over the assembly, followed by a wave of renewed determination. The Prime Minister nodded, his face filled with resolve. "You are right, Sanatani. We will not be confined by any single path. Let us proceed with a broader vision and with the full force of our resources and spirit. Together, we will bring Saraswati back to life."

The applause that followed was louder, more fervent than before, a sign of their unanimous resolve to move forward with renewed vigor and purpose. The leaders and guests, inspired by Sanatani's vision, pledged their cooperation, setting the stage for the next steps in the grand endeavor to revive the ancient Saraswati River.

As the meeting concluded, Sanatani felt a profound sense of fulfillment. The journey ahead was challenging, but he knew that with the collective efforts of the nation and the blessings of the divine, the Saraswati River would flow again, a symbol of resilience and renewal.

In the days that followed, plans were set into motion. Teams of scientists, engineers, archaeologists, and volunteers began their work, guided by Sanatani's vision. Every day brought new findings, new insights, and new steps forward. Geological surveys were launched to map the ancient riverbeds, and advanced remote sensing technology was deployed to identify underground water channels. Archaeological teams began their excavations, uncovering evidence of ancient settlements and water management systems that bore testimony to the Saraswati's presence.

Progress was broadcasted to the world, with each milestone celebrated as a step closer to the river's rebirth. News networks, social media, and local communities were abuzz with excitement, sharing stories of the revived river and its significance for India's cultural and spiritual heritage.

Sanatani became a symbol of this movement—a figure who had a dedicated mission of his life cycles to restoring a lost river, and in doing so, rekindling the essence of a civilization that had thrived for millennia. His unwavering commitment and deep knowledge had inspired a new generation to explore, preserve, and honor their heritage.

The legacy of the Saraswati River, intertwined with the story of Sanatani, was a reminder that the essence of a people and their heritage could never truly be lost—only waiting to be rediscovered and celebrated. The leaders and guests, moved by Sanatani's words and the unity they felt in the room, knew that they were standing at the threshold of a monumental achievement.

And so, with a united spirit and shared determination, they set out to revive the Saraswati, confident that their efforts would not only restore a river but also renew the spirit of Bharatavarsa, reconnecting past, present, and future in one unbroken flow.

CHAPTER THIRTY-TWO

The Rebirth of 'Ambitame, Naditame, Devitame' Saraswati

Sanatani stood at the pinnacle of the Himalayas, his eyes filled with determination and reverence. He had liberated the sacred waters of the Saraswati, overcoming countless obstacles that had held them captive for millennia. With each step towards Adi Badri, Sanatani felt the weight of history and the hopes of his ancestors. The waters of the Saraswati, now free, flowed alongside him, their presence a testament to his unyielding resolve. As he descended the mighty peaks, the landscape began to transform, signaling his approach to the revered site of Adi Badri.

He reached Adi Badri from the verdant valleys of Himachal Pradesh and Uttarakhand. His journey, guided by the wisdom of the ancient rishis and the blessings of the divine, had led him to this pivotal moment.

Adi Badri, nestled at the foothills of the Himalayas, was a place of profound spiritual significance. It was here that the sacred waters of the Saraswati were to merge with other rivers, symbolizing the unification of ancient wisdom and contemporary aspirations. As Sanatani arrived, he was greeted by a congregation of saints, sages, and devotees from across India and the world.

Sanatani, declared the Yagya at the end of this Himalayan Yatra. He travelled from Mansarover , Bandar Poonch and the ice layers of Himalayan to reach at Adi Badri by the time Government agencies do the desired jobs for integrating the waters at Adi Badri.

On the day of the Yagya, the air was filled with anticipation. The sound of sacred chants and the fragrance of burning herbs created an atmosphere of reverence and hope. Sanatani, leading the rituals with unwavering devotion, felt the collective energy of all those who had supported their mission. They had gathered to witness and participate in a Yagya reminiscent of the grand rituals once performed at the Adi Badri.

They recited hymns from the Rig-Veda, which encapsulated the spiritual and cultural ethos of the time. The preparations for the Yagya were meticulous. The altar, adorned with sacred symbols and offerings, was set at the confluence of the rivers. The air was thick with the fragrance of sandalwood, incense, and the sound of Vedic chants. The saints, clad in traditional robes, began chanting the Rig Veda hymns, their voices resonating with divine energy. The verses, ancient and powerful, echoed through the valley, invoking the blessings of Agni, Varuna, and other deities.

As the Yagya commenced, Sanatani stood at the forefront, his heart overwhelmed with emotion. The sacred fire was lit, its flames dancing and flickering as if acknowledging the sanctity of the moment. Offerings of ghee, grains, and Soma were poured into the fire, symbolizing the union of human devotion and divine grace. The recitation of all the Mandalas spoken at Moahnjo Daro repeated in the same manner as thousands of years ago done.

There was profound stillness descended upon the gathering. The sacred chants reached their crescendo, a miraculous change began to unfold. The ground trembled gently, and the waters of the Saraswati began to flow once more, to be merging at Adi Badri in a harmonious embrace. A murmur of awe rippled through the crowd as the waters of the Saraswati began to flow once more. Sanatani's eyes welled up with tears as he watched the waters of the Saraswati merge with the rivers at Adi Badri. This was the moment he had been striving towards for thousands of years. The liberation of Saraswati's waters was not just a physical act but a spiritual renaissance. It signified the reawakening of a civilization, the fulfillment of a prophecy, and the realization of a dream that had spanned millennia.

The saints continued their chants, their voices rising in a crescendo of divine praise. The atmosphere was charged with an ethereal energy, as if the very cosmos were celebrating this sacred union. The Yagya, with its intricate rituals and profound symbolism, was homage to the great sacrifices of the ancient rishis and a beacon of hope for future generations.

The event was being live telecasted, watched by billions around the world. People from all walks of life, from the bustling cities to the quiet villages, were glued to their screens, witnessing the rebirth of the Saraswati. In the offices of the Prime Ministers of India and Pakistan, the scene unfolded on large digital displays, a reminder of the shared cultural and spiritual heritage of the subcontinent.

As the Yagya concluded, the saints and devotees chanted in unison, their voices blending with the sound of the flowing rivers. The sacred waters of the Saraswati, now free and revitalized, flowed towards Sakkur, guided by the spirit of Sanatani. The ancient river, once lost to time, was now a living testament to the enduring power of faith, perseverance, and divine grace.

Sanatani knew that his journey was far from over. The next leg of his pilgrimage would take him to Sakkur, where the Saraswati would merge with Indus. This final confluence was a vision that the ancient rishis had desperately wanted to witness. With renewed resolve, Sanatani prepared to continue his journey, carrying with him the blessings of the Yagya and the hopes of a civilization reborn.

Sanatani's heart swelled with a mix of pride and humility. He had fulfilled the ancient mission, but his journey continued. With each step he took towards Sakkur, he carried the collective dreams of countless rishis and the blessings of a billion people. The reflow of the Saraswati was not just a physical phenomenon but a spiritual renaissance, a reminder that the sacred and the eternal are never truly lost but merely waiting to be rediscovered.

The journey of the Saraswati, from its liberation in the Himalayas to its confluence at Sakkur, was a saga of hope, resilience, and divine intervention. And at the heart of this epic journey was Sanatani, the custodian of an ancient legacy, walking hand in hand with the sacred river towards a future where the past and present converged in a timeless embrace.

The Yagya was a grand success, bringing peace and prosperity to the land. Sanatani's journey not only fulfilled his responsibilities but also transformed him into a revered sage whose knowledge and compassion became legendary.

The revival of the Saraswati was a testament to the power of unity, dedication, and faith. The Saptarishees, watching from their celestial abodes, bestowed their blessings upon Sanatani, whose name became synonymous with wisdom, perseverance, and the eternal quest for harmony. His authority, granted by the Saptarishees, extended beyond the Yagya, as he continued to oversee the restoration and preservation of the Saraswati.

The story of their journey and the revival of the Saraswati was passed down through generations, a timeless tale of hope, unity, and the transformative power of faith and determination. The rejuvenated river brought prosperity and harmony to the land, fulfilling the ancient promise and restoring the sacred essence of life.

The rejuvenated river brought prosperity and harmony to the land, fulfilling the ancient promise and restoring the sacred essence of life. The story of Sanatani journey, and the revival of the Saraswati, was passed down through generations, a timeless tale of hope, unity, and the transformative power of faith and determination.

The legacy of their mission endured, inspiring future generations to cherish and protect the natural and spiritual treasures of their heritage. The Saraswati, once again a lifeline of the land, flowed as a testament to the power of dedication, unity, and the blessings of the divine.

Sanatani's journey began from Adi Badri, where the sacred waters of Saraswati were first liberated. He was leading the waters of the eastern branch. The pristine waters cascaded down the slopes, merging with tributaries and streams, bringing life to the landscape.

As he moved through Haryana and Rajasthan , the river's ancient path became more evident. The fertile plains, once fed by the Saraswati, revealed remnants of a glorious past. Excavations at sites like Kalibangan and Rakhigiri unearthed artifacts and structures that spoke of a thriving civilization sustained by the river.

In Rajasthan, the journey grew more challenging. The arid land bore the scars of time, but the underground flow of the Saraswati provided a glimmer of hope. Here, the Government worked tirelessly, constructing check dams and revitalizing wetlands to bring the river's life-giving waters to the surface.

CHAPTER THIRTY-THREE

<u>THE REUNION AT MOHENJO-DARO</u>

Sanatani made his way toward Sakkur with the eastern branch, determined to bring the sacred river's revival to its final and most significant chapter. A massive gathering awaited him at Sakkur, where thousands had assembled in anticipation of this historic event. Today, the barriers of faith and nationality seemed to dissolve into the flowing river. People of all religions, backgrounds, and beliefs stood together, united in purpose and spirit. There were no borders between the two nations that had long considered each other adversaries. The revival of the Saraswati had not only broken the physical barriers of the earth but had shattered diplomatic divides as well. Today, Sanatani walked a path that was seamless, unhindered by any division or difference.

At the western branch, the vision resonated with the ancient dream of reviving the Saraswati River, a river once revered in Vedic times for its life-giving waters transforming the western branch seasonal Ghaggar into an ever-flowing river, Sanatani words conjured an image of the river in its prime — clear, vibrant, and full of life. Now, the Ghaggar with the waters of the Saraswati was no longer seasonal but eternal, surged forward with newfound strength and vitality.

At the eastern branch, The River, clear and vibrant, surged forth, merging at Sakkur. These waters of eastern branch, carrying the legacy and blessings of an ancient past, merged seamlessly with the mighty Sindhu/Indus at Sakkur. Here, the confluence became a sacred junction, symbolizing unity and the harmonious blending of two great rivers, an echo of the land's spiritual and cultural heritage. From Here, the waters will destined to continue their journey southward with the blessings of seven sacred rivers, winding through the expanse of the Rann of Kutch. The journey through the Rann, a region of stark beauty and endless salt marshes, became a symbolic passage, carrying with it the aspirations, hopes, and blessings of the people.

The Mohano people, descendants of the ancient Sindhu/ Indus Valley Civilization, were there in great numbers. Their boats, traditionally carved and decorated with intricate designs, were freshly adorned with white cloths that fluttered in the breeze. The air was filled with the sound of their drums and their joyous chants. "Jai Jai Baba! You have done it! You are a true Sanatani!" they cried. "You have glorified the way of life that we now know as Hinduism, yet transcend beyond labels, beyond boundaries."

Sanatani's heart swelled with emotion as he watched the Mohano people, who had lived on their boats for thousands of years, bound by a vow to remain afloat until the Saraswati flowed again. Today, they were jubilant, their faces radiant with a newfound hope. As they chanted and danced on their boats, they seemed to embody the very spirit of the river—resilient, unyielding, and alive. The Mohano had embraced their past with open arms, and in this moment, they felt like the true keepers of the Saraswati's legacy.

The waters of the Indus and the Saraswati flowed together towards Kukkutarma/Mohenjo-Daro, carrying with them the collective spirit of the thousands gathered. This flow was more than just a reunion of rivers; it was a symbol of victory in a battle that had spanned thousands of years—a battle against nature's relentless forces, against time and the erosion of memory. The ancient Saptarishees, the seven great sages who had witnessed the original flow of the Saraswati, were present too; their ethereal forms visible only to those with pure hearts and deep faith. From the skies, they watched over the proceedings with subtle smiles, their presence a blessing over the gathering below.

The Mohano people, in their white garments, beat their drums rhythmically, a sound that echoed across the waters and seemed to make a path for the flowing river. It was a grand union, a blending of faiths and histories. The Mohano, now followers of Islam, stood shoulder to shoulder with thousands from across Pakistan, chanting the ancient hymns of the Rig Veda. Their voices rose in unison, creating a sound that transcended time, as if they were speaking directly to their ancestors and reclaiming their shared heritage. In this moment, they were all Sanatani, all connected to the same roots.

Tears streamed down the faces of the gathered crowd—tears of joy, of reconciliation, of a deep-seated recognition of their shared past. The Prime Minister of Pakistan, moved by the scene before him, declared that a new city would be built for the Mohano people, who had faithfully lived on their boats for thousands of years, honoring their vow until this very day.

Sanatani, the guardian of ancient wisdom, stood at the confluence of the Saraswati and Indus rivers. His journey had been long, spanning millennia, and now he returned to the sacred lands where it had all begun. The sight of Saraswati submerging into the Indus was a poignant reminder of the timeless flow of history, a merging of the past into the present.

Sanatani's footsteps led him to various locations at Kukkutarma/ Mohenjo-Daro.. As he walked through the ruins, memories of a bygone era filled his heart. He paid homage to the First Rishi Augusta written Rig Veda on palm leaves buried thousands of years ago by him, a testament to the enduring legacy of his people.

He visited the room where the eleven Dharma Rakshaks had laid down their lives to protect their sacred traditions. Their skeletal remains were a solemn reminder of their sacrifice. He also stood at the staircase where two of his loyal subordinates had been recovered, their spirits still guarding the ancient halls.

Ascending to the Great Bath, a symbol of ritual purity, Sanatani climbed the stairs to the room of the Yajna Purohit. Here, where grand Yajnas were once performed, he felt the echoes of the past rituals. Despite the ruins, the sanctity of the place remained.

Sanatani took the ashes from the ancient Yajna and placed them on his forehead, a mark of reverence and continuity. As he descended, he took a 360-degree view of the entire site, absorbing the essence of Mohenjo-Daro one last time. Passing a statue made in his likeness, he smiled, recognizing the tribute to his legacy. With a heart full of gratitude and reverence, Sanatani folded his hands and murmured prayers, recalling the noble deeds of the Saptarishees.

Sanatani, standing at the Citadel of Kukkutarma/Mohenjo-Daro, felt the gravity of the moment. He took a step forward and offered the sacred waters at the ancient yajna place, where rituals had been performed thousands of years ago. As he poured the water onto the sacred ground, a hush fell over the crowd. Sanatani closed his eyes, and in that moment, he could see the past and present merge seamlessly. He saw the ancient priests, the offerings to the gods, and the prayers that had once echoed in this very place. He realized he was the only person alive who had witnessed both the beginning and the conclusion of this ancient yajna, a spiritual ceremony that had spanned millennia.

The Saptarishees above, their subtle forms glowing with divine light, raised their hands in blessing. From the skies, they chanted Vedic hymns, their voices melding with those of the people below. "May the Saraswati flow eternal, may her waters bring wisdom, peace, and unity to all who come in her path," they blessed, their words a powerful force that reverberated through the air. Their blessing seemed to descend like a gentle rain, touching every soul gathered there.

On the ground, the Mohano people continued their celebrations, their drums beating louder, their chants growing more fervent. They danced on their boats, their movements graceful and filled with joy. The riverbanks were filled with people singing and swaying, and it seemed as if the very earth beneath their feet was vibrating with the energy of their collective happiness. For the Mohano, today was a reunion with their ancestors, a reconnection with their ancient roots. Even though their faith had transformed over the centuries, today they stood as one with their past.

As Sanatani turned towards the gathering, he could see the tears of joy flowing down the faces of the people. The waters of the Indus and Saraswati may have been deep, but they seemed almost shallow compared to the flood of tears that ran from the eyes of those witnessing this historic moment. Tears flowed without restraint—tears of joy, relief, and a profound sense of honor at being a part of these events.

Sanatani knew that the waters had to continue their journey. The newly united flow of the Sindhu/Indus and Saraswati turned eastward, heading towards the Rann of Kutch. Many in the gathering expected Sanatani to terminate his Yatra here. But he surprised them all when he declared that he would take the sea route, following the path of the legendary Rishi Agastya, to reach Agastya Peeth—his final destination. He embarked on his final journey to Augusta Peeth, choosing the same sea route once taken by Rishi Agastya.

The Mohano people, still filled with excitement and gratitude, pleaded with Sanatani to take one of their boats. He agreed, and they quickly prepared their finest vessel, adorning it with even more decorations and sacred symbols. As Sanatani climbed aboard, he turned back to face the ancient city of Kukkutarma/Mohenjo-Daro. He paused for a moment, gazing at what was once called the "Mound of the Dead." Today, it was alive—filled with people, with history, with faith, and with the flow of the sacred Saraswati. Mohenjo-Daro, no longer a mound of the dead, was vibrant and alive. The echoes of the past had merged with the present, creating a new story for the future—a story where rivers flowed freely, where people were united, and where the divine blessings of the Saptarishees watched over them all.

As the Saraswati flowed toward the sea, it represented not just the merging of rivers but the merging of civilizations, cultures, and spiritual beliefs. It was a river that flowed through time, connecting the ancient with the present, the spiritual with the physical, and the regional with the universal. The waters, rejuvenated by the contributions of many regions, flowed with a purpose, to reach the ocean, where they would offer themselves to the vastness of the sea — a tribute to the enduring spirit of the land and its people, forever seeking to reclaim their ancient heritage and ensure the river of Saraswati would flow eternally.

The boat set sail, moving slowly down the river. The waters sparkled under the bright sun, carrying the blessings of the Saptarishees and the hopes of countless souls. Sanatani stood at the helm, feeling the wind against his face, a sense of peace settling over him. He knew that his journey was not over, but this chapter was one of triumph. The river was alive once more, and with it, the spirit of the people, their faith, and their connection to a past that had never truly been forgotten.

Boarding a wooden boat, Sanatani sailed gracefully to the Konkan region, retracing the sacred paths once traversed by ancient sages. Upon reaching the Konkan seashore, he stepped out of the boat, his feet touching the earth with a quiet purpose. The Mohano people, who had accompanied him, broke into tears, pleading with him not to leave them. Sanatani, calm yet resolute, stood as a figure of both solace and determination, his eyes searching for the eternal phase of his journey. Slowly, he walked away, only to pause and turn back toward the wooden boat. The Mohano people, overwhelmed with a mix of jubilation and dread, cried louder, sensing deep within their hearts that this moment marked the end of their era with Sanatani. For generations, he had been their anchor, their most precious treasure, and now they faced the painful reality of losing him. With a serene smile, Sanatani raised his hands to bless them, offering the most profound *ashirwad*. Then, lifting both arms high, he bestowed his final blessings before turning to disappear into the mangroves. As his figure vanished into the dense foliage, the Mohano people erupted into a chorus of prayers. In a moment of profound transformation, they, who had embraced Islam over time, spontaneously recited hymns from the Rigveda, reconnecting with the spiritual essence of their origins. Inspired by Sanatani's departure, they began their own journey back to their ancestral roots, determined to honor the legacy he had safeguarded for them through countless generations.

As the boat sailed further into the horizon, Sanatani looked ahead to Agastya Peeth, knowing that every ripple in the water was a reflection of the countless souls who had come together to witness the rebirth of the Saraswati. He felt a deep satisfaction, a quiet joy, knowing that he had fulfilled his purpose. The Saraswati flowed once more, and with it flowed to the spirit of an eternal civilization.

CHAPTER THIRTY-FOUR

THE ETERNAL FLAME OF DHARMA

Sanatani's journey brought him to the lush, verdant lands of the Konkan region, where the western coastline of India met the vast, blue Arabian Sea. The wind carried the scent of salt and the song of the waves as he moved deeper into the heart of Bharatavarsa, towards Agastya Peeth. It was a journey marked not by haste but by a deep reverence for the land and its ancient traditions. Here, in the tranquil embrace of nature, he would take the final steps of his long and purposeful pilgrimage.

Upon reaching Agastya Peeth, Sanatani felt a profound stillness settle over him. The ashram, a sanctuary dedicated to the revered Rishi Agastya, stood as a testament to the sage's wisdom and his contributions to the ancient lore of Bharatavarsa. The head of the ashram, a venerable seer with eyes that seemed to pierce the veil of time, welcomed him with open arms. Sanatani approached the seer with a quiet dignity, his footsteps echoing the humility that had marked his journey.

With a deep bow, Sanatani removed his saropa—a long, flowing scarf symbolic of his spiritual status—and his headgear, which bore the marks of his many travels and trials. He handed them to the chief seer, who accepted them with a knowing smile and a nod of respect. The seer understood that Sanatani had completed his earthly mission and had come to the ashram to surrender the symbols of his worldly duties.

Sanatani spent the day in reflection and prayer, immersing himself in the serene surroundings of the ashram. The sounds of birdsong, the gentle rustling of leaves, and the rhythmic chanting of mantras created a symphony of peace around him. As he walked through the ashram grounds, he felt a deep connection to the land, to its people, and to the ancient spirit that permeated every tree, rock, and river.

Sanatani treaded through the dense foliage of Gupt Kashi, a secret forest that seemed to hum with an ancient energy. The air was thick with the scent of medicinal plants, and the occasional rustle of rare birds added a melody to his steps. This sacred land, veiled from the world, was a testament to nature's quiet majesty and the spiritual aura of Rishi Agastya, the legendary sage who had made it his abode.

Upon reaching the heart of the forest, Sanatani was greeted by Rishi Agastya and his wife, Lopamudra. The sage's serene countenance radiated wisdom, while Lopamudra's presence exuded grace and compassion. Sanatani bowed deeply, his journey-weary body finding solace in their tranquil presence.

The Gupt Kashi forest, with its unparalleled biodiversity, stood as a testament to Agastya's teachings. The Agastyaarkoodam, a revered peak in the biosphere reserve, became a pilgrimage site for devotees. The rare medicinal plants and vibrant bird species thrived under the sacred energy that permeated the land.

Gupt Kashi remained shrouded in mystery, its linga consecrated in pure kriya. The energy work initiated by Agastya and later strengthened by Sanatani's penance created an unbroken chain of spiritual power, transforming lives and dimensions purely through divine energy.

"Revered Sage," Sanatani began, his voice resonating with reverence, "I have fulfilled the mission entrusted to me by the Saptrishis. The ancient manuscripts have been safeguarded, and the knowledge preserved for generations to come. The Saraswati River is once again reflowing though her physical form wanes, lives eternally as a beacon of knowledge and culture. I come now seeking your counsel and permission to rest the remainder of my eternal life."

Rishi Agastya's gaze softened as he listened. "Sanatani, your journey is a testament to unwavering dedication and divine purpose. To relinquish the life granted to you by the Saptrishis is not a mere act but a profound transition. Let us consult the celestial energies and the Saptrishis before granting your request."

As twilight descended, the three gathered near a sacred fire. Agastya invoked the Saptrishis through ancient kriyas, and the air shimmered with their ethereal presence. Sanatani's request was conveyed, and the Saptrishis, in their infinite wisdom, blessed his wish. They entrusted his life to Rishi Agastya, symbolizing the seamless continuity of divine purpose.

"Sanatani," Agastya said, "You shall rest your soul in penance, yet your energy shall ripple across realms, inspiring those who seek the eternal truth. Go to Kanyakumari, where the land meets the ocean, and face the east. There, upon a rock from where I meditated at the dawn of Kali Yuga."

The sage's words resonated with Sanatani, who felt an overwhelming sense of peace. Before departing, he expressed his gratitude to Agastya and Lopamudra, bowing to their divine guidance.

As Sanatani journeyed to Kanyakumari, the August Star, also known as Canopus, illuminated his path. This celestial beacon, deeply connected to Sage Agastya, marked the changing monsoon winds and symbolized guidance and perseverance. The star seemed to bless Sanatani's resolve, aligning the heavens with his earthly journey.

Reaching Kanyakumari, Sanatani was awestruck by the confluence of the three oceans. The waves whispered secrets of eternity as he climbed a solitary rock overlooking the vast expanse. Facing the east, he began his penance, channeling his energy into the cosmos.

Sanatani's life transitioned into an eternal flame of inspiration, his penance becoming a guiding force for those who sought the truth. The August Star continued to rise and set, its celestial dance echoing the sage's journey and the cosmic order of life and spirituality. Thus, Sanatani's legacy merged with the divine essence of Gupt Kashi and Kanyakumari, a testament to his profound journey and the eternal wisdom of the Saptrishis.

At the southernmost sea point of India, near **Dhanushkodi,** a small yet profoundly sacred idol rests, carved from black stone and weathered by centuries of salt-laden winds and roaring waves. Known as **"The Eternal Flame of Dharma,"** the idol depicts a serene sage-like figure seated in meditation, a conch shell in one hand and a flowing river etched beneath his feet. Local lore reveres this idol as a representation of the spirit of the ancient sages who guided humanity through the timeless values of Sanatana Dharma. This sacred site marked the farthest reach of the ancient land. He felt the pull of destiny drawing him closer. He made his way to the towering statue by the sea, a colossal figure carved in striking resemblance to the revered sage. The statue stood tall against the sky, its face a reflection of wisdom and strength. Sanatani felt a wave of emotion wash over him as he gazed up at the figure.

He had always felt a deep affinity with Agastya, a sage known for his knowledge, humility, and spiritual power. It was Agastya who had crossed the Vindhyas and brought the sacred Vedic wisdom to the southern lands. Now, at the end of his journey, Sanatani found himself at the feet of this great Rishi, seeking his blessings for the final leg of his path. With calm determination, he walked to the foot of the towering statue. The sun rose behind him, casting a golden glow over the land and sea.

He performed *dandwat pranam* once more, laying himself flat on the ground in deep reverence before the idol. With a deep breath, Sanatani knelt down and performed a full prostration before the statue. As he lay on the ground, arms outstretched, he felt the earth beneath him hum with ancient energy.

He whispered a prayer, invoking the blessings of Agastya, and raised his hands to the sky, calling upon the divine to bless the land of Bharatavarsa, from its northern peaks to its southern shores. His voice filled with a fervent prayer that carried over the waves and into the wind.

Slowly, Sanatani rose to his feet and began walking towards the sea. Each step felt like a farewell to the world he had known, a world he had traversed with purpose and devotion. The gentle waves lapped at his feet, welcoming him like an old friend. As he moved deeper into the water, the sea seemed to embrace him, its vastness offering solace and peace. He felt no fear, no hesitation—only a profound sense of completion. In his final moments, as he immersed himself in the sea, Sanatani knew that his journey was not an end but a continuation of an eternal cycle. His life and actions had become a bridge between ancient wisdom and the ever-evolving present, a testament to the enduring spirit of Sanatan Dharma.

As the waters embraced him again, he found solace in the eternal ocean, the waves gently pulling him into their depths. Unbeknownst to him, a young Vlogger, present at the site, captured this poignant moment—the serene departure of a saint without knowing that this life had been a living testament to devotion, sacrifice, and eternal truth. Moved by the solemnity and serenity of the moment, the Vlogger captured Sanatani's steps into the sea, the soft waves engulfing his figure until he disappeared into the horizon. The next day, the video spread across social media like wildfire. The world watched in awe and reverence, captivated by the story of an unknown saint who had taken *Jal Samadhi* in the sea, a final offering of his life to the eternal waters.

As the video went viral, the legend of Sanatani spread across continents. People spoke of his journey with a mix of wonder and admiration. Here was a man who had dedicated his unique life to reviving the ancient river Saraswati, who had traveled from the Kalibangan, sacred banks of Adi Badri and to the ruins of Mohenjo-Daro, who had united people across borders, faiths, and generations. His journey was not just a path through geography, but a pilgrimage through time, a bridge between the ancient past and the present.

Sanatani had witnessed the rise and fall of civilizations, the ebb and flow of rivers, and the timeless legacy of his people. His actions had woven a thread between the past and present, creating a tapestry of faith, devotion, and endurance.

And so, the story of Sanatani, the guardian of ancient wisdom, came to a close. His life was a journey through the sacred land of Bharatvarsha, a journey that revived rivers, bridged divisions, and rekindled the spirit of a timeless tradition. His final act—disappearing into the eternal ocean—was not an end but a return to the source, a reminder of the cycle of life, death, and rebirth that defines the essence of Sanatan Dharma. His legacy of devotion, sacrifice, and eternal truth continued to inspire all who heard his tale, leaving behind a world forever touched by his spirit.

Legend connects the idol to **Sanatani**, the mythical guardian of ancient wisdom and protector of sacred traditions. It is said that Sanatani, during his eternal quest to revive and sustain the Saraswati River, journeyed to the very tip of the Indian subcontinent. Here, he meditated amidst the convergence of the oceans, where the waters of the Bay of Bengal, Indian Ocean, and Arabian Sea meet. In his meditative state, Sanatani is believed to have consecrated this sacred spot, leaving behind the idol as a symbol of harmony between the elements and the spiritual union of humanity with nature.

Local traditions claim that on auspicious nights, when the moonlight illuminates the sea, the idol exudes a faint, otherworldly glow, as though Sanatani's blessings continue to flow through it. Pilgrims visit the site not only to seek spiritual solace but also to reconnect with their ancestral heritage. Many offer prayers, whispering Rigvedic hymns, invoking the river Saraswati, and seeking the wisdom and blessings of Sanatani for their journeys ahead.

The people of Dhanushkodi believe that Sanatani's journey to this point was not an end but a culmination—a moment where the eternal flow of wisdom merged with the infinite ocean, symbolizing the unity of life and the timelessness of truth. The idol stands as a silent witness to his passage, inspiring countless seekers to walk the path of Dharma, guided by the eternal light of Sanatani's legacy.

209

CHAPTER THIRTY-FIVE

CHARACTERS

Dhananter -Spy-Silver- Sanatani.
Saptarishees: Seven rishis of Sanatan
Augusta: An ancient Rishi.
His Companion: Parmanand/Narendra
General Jaffar: NSA Pakistan
Abhimanyu Singh: NSA India
General Abdul Sattar: ISI Chief Head
Brigadier Abid Ali: Pak Army Brigadier
Colonel Salim Mirza: Pak Army Colonel
Behaviour analyst: Dr. Shama Ansari
Dandi Maharaj, a respected seer, head of seers
Mira- Resident on the bank of Saraswati
Mohd. Faz Husain: World-renowned Environmentalist.
The Mohano- An ancient Sanatan race who later embraced
Islam